MEN
in
UNIFORM

Courteous, courageous and commanding—
these heroes lay it all on the line for the
people they love in more than fifty stories about
loyalty, bravery and romance.
Don't miss a single one!

JEAN BRASHEAR

THE GOOD DAUGHTER

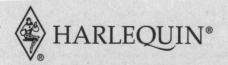

TORONTO • NEW YORK • LONDON
AMSTERDAM • PARIS • SYDNEY • HAMBURG
STOCKHOLM • ATHENS • TOKYO • MILAN • MADRID
PRAGUE • WARSAW • BUDAPEST • AUCKLAND

Recycling programs
for this product may
not exist in your area.

ISBN-13: 978-0-373-36291-2

THE GOOD DAUGHTER

Copyright © 2003 by Jean Brashear

www.eHarlequin.com

Printed in U.S.A.

JEAN BRASHEAR

is a three-time RITA® Award finalist, winner of an *RT Book Reviews* Series Storyteller of the Year Award and numerous other awards. Jean believes that love is the most powerful force in the universe and cherishes each opportunity she's given to share that belief with readers. She enjoys hearing from readers, either via her Web site, www.jeanbrashear.com, Harlequin's Web site, www.eHarlequin.com, or by mail, P.O. Box 3000 #79, Georgetown, TX 78627-3000.

To my editor, Beverley Sotolov,
who honors the heart of each story while
toning the muscles. Her challenge to excellence
is accompanied by such wit and grace that our writing
partnership has become one of my life's real pleasures.

ACKNOWLEDGMENTS

In researching this book, I've been fortunate to
have the help of some wonderful people within the
law-enforcement community of Travis and Williamson
counties. Sergeant Rory Clarke of the Austin
Police Department, Judge Evelyn Palfrey McKee and
former Assistant District Attorney Suzanne Brooks—
thank you for your time and wisdom.

Special thanks to Dr. Rick Bradstreet,
manager of Psychological Services for APD,
for his insights into Chloe's job and the mind of a cop,
and for his generosity in connecting me with others
in APD who helped me with research. And my
heartfelt gratitude to former FBI Special Agent now
Sheriff John Maspero of Williamson County, whose
agile mind has more than once raced to the rescue on
short notice to help me puzzle through fitting my story
elements into the real world of law enforcement.
John's devotion to duty and love of his profession
are in the best tradition of the many men and women
who daily put their lives at risk, for not nearly enough
pay or thanks, to serve and protect us all.

Any errors or liberties taken are my own.

CHAPTER ONE

Austin, Texas

BELL NOTES of Baccarat crystal…soft strains from the Steinway grand. Thick Persian rugs resting on gleaming teak floors, heavy damask drapes, priceless antiques… the silken swish of cocktail dresses as tastefully subdued as they were costly. Civilized, intelligent conversation devoid of any mention of sex, controversy or—God forbid—money.

Such was the scene in her parents' Tarrytown mansion, a gathering like so many others that had formed the backdrop of Chloe St. Claire's charmed life. A world of privilege taken wholly for granted, even, until the last eighteen months, by Chloe herself.

"You will help me with the Christmas auction, won't you?" said one of Chloe's mother's oldest friends.

"Of course," Chloe murmured, taking a sip of champagne to head off a burgeoning yawn.

"Bless you," the woman said, patting Chloe's arm. "You're such a good girl. Dolores and John have every reason to be proud." She glanced around the room and smiled. "And this is a wonderful show of support for Roger. You and he make a lovely couple."

"We're not—" Just then, Chloe's mother neared, and her protest went unheard as the two women exchanged air kisses.

"Darling," said Dolores St. Claire, resplendent in Valentino red. "Your father needs to introduce you to someone. You don't mind, do you, Helen?"

"Of course she must go. We'll talk soon, Chloe, dear."

Of course. Chloe saw her father with Roger and one of his banker friends. The political season was in full swing, and the prominent banker's support in Roger Barnes's upcoming race for district attorney could make a big difference. John St. Claire nodded at her, a clear invitation to join them and play out her role as Roger's political asset. She was halfway across the room—

When the pager inside her Judith Leiber purse buzzed against her hip. *Oh, dear.* The dispatcher wouldn't be paging her unless it was an emergency.

Chloe pressed one hand against a stomach suddenly tight with nerves. Whatever it was, she couldn't refuse— her supervisor had left her in charge for two weeks. Pasting on a smile and handing her glass to a nearby waiter, she prepared for the disapproval that would be silent but fierce from both her parents and Roger. Even after eighteen months, they were still assuming she'd come to her senses and leave a job they considered both unnecessary and sordid.

They were baffled at her decision to take the police-department psychologist job her graduate-school adviser had suggested, and she couldn't explain what she herself didn't understand. The world in which she worked was completely foreign and should be repellent. She was their good daughter, her life comfortable, her road already mapped out.

What she learned in this job and what she witnessed was at times raw, heartbreaking and horrifying. But despite her parents' hope that it was merely a minor detour, this unlikely rebellion had become fascinating and…important.

THIRTY MINUTES LATER, Chloe ducked under the stark yellow crime scene tape. Ahead, spotlights cracked the night into a scene she wondered if she'd ever see without feeling the impact.

In the brightly lit center would be a body and, likely, blood. Where light faded into darkness, too many people would be standing around while the forensics team did its work. A circus, with death as the star attraction.

Somewhere in the midst of it all would be an officer who'd killed a fellow human being, whether from noble motives or dark. That the motive was likely honorable wouldn't matter; few people, police included, escaped a psychic shock from the act of taking a life.

Her job was not to counsel at the crime scene, merely to debrief per police department regulations in the event of a "critical incident"—any situation in which the potential for post-traumatic stress syndrome was high. She'd have her chance to counsel later, but not to care now was hard; not to want to help was impossible. She knew all too well that by the time the officer visited for follow-up, the barriers would be back in place, the mask perfected. The cop who'd suffered, no matter how good his reason for shooting, would be less reachable. Less willing to admit the roller coaster his emotions were riding.

Detective Vince Coronado would be tougher than most, she already knew. He was a legend in the department, a cop's cop. He wouldn't come to her by choice—few of them did. They called it "being sent to the Arctic Circle," the deep freeze away from the action. Her office had power over when—and if—they returned. None of them liked it, and a lone wolf like Coronado would be worse.

"Excuse me," she said to the beefy uniformed officer in front of her, stepping around the last barrier between her and center stage. At the sight of the body, Chloe closed her eyes briefly, then opened them by sheer will. Coronado was around here somewhere, and she could not betray the slightest emotion. This was part of her job, no matter how little she thought she'd ever get used to the odd vulnerability death conferred, the reminder of just how fragile life is.

She felt a gaze upon her and looked up. Strong jaw clenched, Vince Coronado radiated power—and danger. He was dressed for his undercover role, jeans soft with age clinging to muscled thighs, broad shoulders encased in a loose Hawaiian shirt. Though his clothing might be casual, Chloe could see nothing soft on this man, nothing about his manner that didn't intimidate, until she glimpsed the dark curls on his neck glistening with sweat, making a lie out of his cold blue stare. He wasn't unmoved. He was human.

And his eyes weren't cold, she saw, drawing closer.

They were blanked out, a common reaction. The mind refused to accept the full impact of taking a life, however despicable.

That would come later.

It would rattle him—it rattled all of them, whether they admitted it or not. Cops either developed armor to keep the pathos and pain of their jobs at a distance or they didn't make it. But killing cracked those shields, and the man inside suffered, a cave creature forced into white-hot desert sunshine.

She noted Coronado's position. He was set apart, as though no one wanted to be contaminated. Shooting in the line of duty always triggered an Internal Affairs investigation and presentation to a grand jury. It meant time away from the job and being a pariah until the officer was cleared. That was one of the hardest parts of a fatal shooting for a cop: spending time on the other side, being a suspect. No longer automatically one of the good guys. She glanced at his empty holster; one of the first acts by a superior was to take a cop's gun away, rendering him not only suspect but feeling naked. The roller-coaster ride commenced.

"Detective, I'm Chloe St. Claire, department psychol—"

"I know who you are." Each word was a bullet. Coronado stared into the distance, hands tucked in the front pockets of his jeans, hard cop firmly in place. "Where's Bradley?"

"He's out of town." Senior staff psychologist Rick Bradley had left for a much-needed vacation, avowing confidence that Chloe could handle herself despite being relatively new on the job. Refusing to let him down, she tried again to return to her script. "Detective, our conversation is not part of the investigation into this incident. It is confidential and intended only to assist you in dealing with what has happened and with the days to come."

One curt nod. "I know the drill."

She'd heard that he'd been involved in a fatal shooting once before in his career and had been exonerated. Pretending it didn't affect him was the natural instinct for a cop, but the healing would only go harder. She suspected that this man felt things more deeply than he'd ever admit. No matter how much he'd wanted the person on the ground dead, he couldn't like what would happen from here.

Just as she was about to speak, a blond man, medium height, stepped up to his other side. "Hey, buddy. How's it going?"

Coronado jerked his head in her direction, and the second man noticed her for the first time. "Oh— Sorry, Doc."

"Hello, Mike. Good to see you."

Mike Flynn, Narcotics veteran and confirmed bachelor, had never been one of Chloe's clients, but his reputation for doing solid work while seemingly never having a serious thought was widespread in the department. He had helped her a few months back in an intervention with a troubled cop on his detail, and she'd been impressed with the brain behind the playboy facade.

Right now his eyes spoke of concern for a friend.

He nodded at her and squeezed Coronado's shoulder. "Catch you later, man. Bye, Doc."

"Goodbye, Mike. Detective?" She eased back from the bright circle and held her breath to see if Coronado would follow. He had no choice, really—debriefing after an incident was standard department policy—but she wouldn't underestimate this man. His walls were thick and very, very high. Perhaps he understood that she was trying to give him privacy, though, because he took the necessary steps to close the distance between them.

She kept her voice soft and calm. "I know you've been through this before, but I'd like to go over a few items for you to think about, then hear what you have to say."

He stood there like a solid block of granite, gaze stoic.

Chloe pressed on, remembering the cauldron of feelings she'd barely glimpsed before he'd slammed a lid on them. "It's human nature to second-guess yourself, particularly in reaction to extreme consequences. You may ask yourself what you could have done differently, how you could have prevented this. It's normal for emotions to be volatile, to range from anger to sadness to anxiety, because you know you're under scrutiny, no matter how convinced you are that this incident was unavoidable."

A flicker, so quick she might have imagined it, at the mention of scrutiny. For a man of action, as Vince Coronado certainly was, to be answering the phone, hearing complaints over traffic tickets would be torture.

This was a man who was used to chasing the bad guys, to street action, and plenty of it.

"You may feel guilty—"

"Not a chance," he interrupted. "Krueger deserved far worse. He murdered a child. Made his last moments hell."

"But that wasn't your fault."

His head whipped around. "No? Think again." If anything, his jaw clenched tighter. "I waited too long for proof, and now a boy is dead." His eyes were the blue of cold fury. "My only regret is that I didn't make this bastard suffer more."

"You feel responsible, protective of a child—"

"Don't try to crawl inside my head, Doc," he snapped. "You might not like what you see."

"Detective—" She placed a hand on his forearm, felt his muscles tense. The move was pure instinct to comfort, yet she knew it was a mistake the moment she did it. But because he'd feel like a pariah already, she wouldn't draw back.

That didn't mean he hadn't unnerved her. Chloe swallowed. "I'm not naive. I've heard a lot. Seen a lot." Yes, her life had been sheltered until she'd taken this job, but in these eighteen months, she'd learned more than she would have dreamed about the darker side of human nature.

Coronado scanned her attire, then pinned her with a stare as merciless as a laser. "You sure as hell don't look like you belong here, Doc."

Wishing that she'd had time to change from her

cocktail dress, she stepped back. "Appearances can be deceiving."

He leaned closer. "Can they?"

Chloe fought to stand her ground. "I'd like to see you again."

A second perusal of her body was slow and sure. Intentionally insulting. "Me, too."

He was itching for a fight, and he'd use whatever it took to make her back away. Very well, she'd done what was required tonight. The rest would have to wait.

"Tomorrow morning, in my office. Nine o'clock."

"Five o'clock, and we'll adjourn to this little place I know." A dimple flashed in a cocky smile sure to break hearts. The smile stopped short of his eyes.

Clearly her window of opportunity had vanished. There'd be no more revelations, and he wouldn't accept comfort. "Ten o'clock, Detective. It's my final offer."

"Offer?"

"I can make it an order if I have to. You said you understand the procedure." She exhaled. "I'll see you tomorrow."

He gave one curt nod, his gaze already shuttered, his shoulders braced against what was to come.

With an inner sigh, Chloe left. At the edge of the crowd, she glanced back. He stood alone in the darkness, an invisible circle keeping everyone at bay. Help might be available—

But this man was nowhere close to taking it.

"CORONADO."

Vince looked up at the sound of a voice full of bad

associations. "Newcombe." He crossed his arms over his chest.

"Should have expected you'd be in the middle of it." The Internal Affairs investigator pursed his lips. "You identified yourself as an officer?"

"Have the rules changed, or do you just break them for grins? I don't have to talk to you yet."

"You didn't tell him."

Vince ground his teeth. "He knew I was a cop."

"How?"

"Go to hell, Newcombe."

"Hey, I'm just doing my job." Newcombe smirked.

Vince bristled and took a step forward.

"Say, fellas, having a little chitchat?" Mike Flynn shouldered between them.

Vince tried to push past him. "Not now, Mike."

Mike didn't budge, gaze narrowed in warning, then swiveled back to Newcombe. "Nice night like this, sometimes a fella just wants to be friendly, shoot the breeze with his buddies."

"Beat it, Flynn."

"Get lost, Mike." Both men spoke in unison.

"Nope, I don't believe I'm going to do that, guys. See, I'm thinking that Vince doesn't need to hang around any longer, this not being the hearing or anything official."

Newcombe broke off his study of Vince to shoot Mike a heated glare. A tic in his jaw made the mole on his left cheek jump. "I'm going to enjoy this, Coronado."

Vince's hands clenched as he slowly and deliberately uncrossed his arms. "But you'll lose again. Go find somebody dirty, Newcombe. You're wasting your time here."

"We'll see, hotshot. I'm just warming up to the task."

"Don't screw with me—" Vince lunged.

Mike grabbed him by the arm and jerked. "Let's go, Vince."

Vince fought the grip for a moment, then cast Newcombe one more murderous scowl before shaking off Mike's hold.

Newcombe walked away, cocksure grin in place.

Vince started to follow. Mike grabbed him again. "Come on, man. Don't play into his hands. He already hates your guts for making him look like a fool seven years ago. Just sit back and let the department go through its paces."

"Over my dead body." Vince stared at the too-slick dresser who'd tried to ruin his career once. Newcombe's ambitions had only grown since then.

"Vince, pick your fights. This is not the time."

"Damn it." Vince exhaled in a gust. "I've got work to do. I don't need that jerk hanging me out to dry for months."

"Then leave him alone and quit antagonizing him, you thickheaded bastard."

Vince grimaced. "Pushed my buttons, didn't he?"

Mike grinned. "Like a pro. I have no idea why I'd want to buy a beer for someone so stupid, but first round's on me."

Vince smiled faintly. "Because no one else will let you drive."

Mike slugged him on the shoulder and laughed. "For that, the next two rounds are yours."

Vince shot a glance back at the crime scene. "Just a minute, Mike. I'm gonna check with the boss."

"Sure thing. I'll be in the car."

Vince approached his supervisor, Sergeant F. T. Woods. "Sarge." He nodded to the man who ran his detail with an iron fist but would go to the wall for his squad.

"Be careful with Newcombe, Vince," Woods said. "You know you're not on his Christmas-card list."

Vince met his gaze evenly. "He's not on mine, either."

Woods studied him. "You're taking too many chances lately. You should have waited for backup."

"The creep wasn't just a dealer and a pimp. He had this thing for kids—"

"No one's taking his side. My beef's with you. You're a good cop when your head's on straight. I'm wondering if you need to be using some of the vacation days you've got piled up. Go away somewhere."

Vince recoiled. "No." He shook his head hard. "Hell, no. Sarge, you can't—"

The older man's eyes didn't soften. "I'll do whatever's necessary to see that you don't burn out. Losing Quintanilla was rough, and you've had three difficult cases in a row. I say you need a change of scenery."

Vince stiffened at the mention of the cop who'd been like a father to him, shot down in cold blood nine months earlier. No one had paid for it, but someone would, if it was the last thing Vince did. He couldn't afford to leave town.

He sighed heavily, tired just thinking about the days ahead. Nodding toward the body, he spoke. "I'll get time off whether I want it or not."

"You know what they say, Vince."

Vince glanced up at the humor in his sergeant's voice.

"Hell's only a way station on the road to Internal Affairs."

Vince grinned in spite of the weariness creeping through his body now that the adrenaline was gone. "I always suspected Newcombe had a forked tail tucked down his pants."

Woods chuckled and leaned closer. "Plastic surgery to remove the horns was the story I heard." He clapped Vince on the shoulder. "Go on. Flynn's waiting. There's nothing left for you to do tonight. But get some sleep, hear?"

They both realized it wasn't likely. Bedtime was when the doubts crowded up on your chest and shoulders, whispering nasty thoughts in your ear and squeezing the breath out of you.

Nope, Vince knew he might as well go buy Mike a beer. Anything was better than being alone with his failures.

"Sure, Sarge." He waved and started off.

"And Vince?"

Vince turned back.

"Play it straight with the doc. Maybe she can figure out what the hell you think you're trying to prove."

Any trace of a smile vanished. "Just doing my job, boss."

Sergeant Woods nodded grimly. "Me, too."

CHLOE SLID into her car and reached toward the ignition, knowing she should return to the cocktail party.

Instead, she sank against the seat cushion. She didn't want to spend another hour—another minute—making chitchat. Her gaze cut back to the lights at the crime scene. Adrenaline surged again, and one knee jittered as she considered going back. Trying to talk to Coronado once more. Being a part of a world where important things happened, where men put their lives on the line instead of throwing around their influence and money—

She exhaled on a long, distressed sigh. Coronado was through talking for tonight. She'd only make things worse.

Her parents wouldn't like it, nor would Roger, but a cocktail party was out of the question now. She'd go home, get a good night's sleep and be ready to do her job tomorrow.

You sure as hell don't look like you belong here, Doc.

She put the key in the ignition.

She did. She would. She just had to prove him wrong.

VINCE SWORE SOFTLY in the moonlight as he fumbled his key in the lock and tried not to drop his mail. Pushing the front door open, he stepped into his living room, grasping for the light switch.

"Aiiyyowww!" A shrill cry split the air.

Vince stumbled and righted himself quickly, flipping the switch and flooding the room with lamplight. A streak of brown-and-white fur darted underneath the table behind the sofa.

"Damn it, cat, stay out from under my feet. You're the one who can see in the dark, not me," he grumbled. Dropping to his heels, he stared at the form blinking at him four feet away, one ragged ear flopping while the other flicked back and forth. A scroungy tail switched like a whip. Vince reached out and was rewarded with a hiss that dropped to a near growl. "Yep, that settles it. I'm definitely getting a dog. I hate cats."

Vince rose to his feet and stood, hands on his hips. "You heard me, didn't you?" He pointed toward the door. "Go on—I've been telling you for two weeks now, no cats allowed."

Golden eyes blinked. The tail settled. The cat lifted one front paw and began grooming himself.

"Yeah, sure. Like nonchalance is going to impress me. Man's best friend is definitely not a cat. I'll feed you tonight, but tomorrow, you're outta here." Vince threw his keys and the mail on the heavy oak table beneath an Amado Peña print of a pueblo done in vivid slashes of turquoise, black and terra-cotta, then headed toward the kitchen. He opened the pantry and pulled out a can from the tall stack of Feline Fancies. A brush of warm body against his ankles made him look down.

"Oh, yeah, now you care. I've got a long memory,

pal." After yanking the pull tab from the top, he set the can down on the scarred oak floor he'd found lurking under ancient linoleum, then filled an empty bowl with fresh water. His gaze wandered to the strips of yellowed wallpaper hanging from the shiplap wall across from the sink. Only one more wall to go in here. About time. This shotgun cottage in the once-grand South Austin neighborhood of Travis Heights had been his for a song. It hadn't stopped eating time—and money—since.

Still, it was his, the first real home he'd ever had. The work remaining might consume years, but that didn't matter. He'd spent thirty-two years rootless; he'd spend another thirty-two working on this place, if that was what it took.

He walked to the refrigerator and looked inside, taking stock. Leftover pizza, a six-pack of beer, a tomato with a beard. He spied a couple of eggs and smiled. Scrape away some of the blue shadows on that cheese, and he could have an omelette.

Not all that hungry yet, he wandered back in to peruse his mail first. Junk mail, junk mail, bill, junk mail— A postcard stayed his hand.

Tino's handwriting. Where had he gotten a postcard of the Bahamas? He was still in prison.

Vince squinted at the tiny scrawl. It took him a minute to sort out the coded phrases, then he cursed beneath his breath. Tino was getting out. Left the day after the postmark.

And he wanted to see his old friend Vince.

Hell.

Once he and Tino Garza had been as tight as brothers

in the way only surviving the streets together could make you. He'd happened upon a fight where Tino was trying to hang on to some food he'd stolen—and losing. At fifteen, Vince had been as big as most grown men and had had two years on the streets behind him. Tino, at nine, had been as naive as a babe.

They'd joined forces, and Vince had taught Tino to survive. Too well. Only the influence of one cop who cared enough to battle for him had kept Vince from winding up in prison just like his friend.

Then patrolman Carlos Quintanilla had cared about Tino, too, but hadn't been able to save him. Tino had disappeared into gang life, and Vince only barely escaped the same fate.

Carlos was dead now, and the loss of the man who'd been the closest thing he'd had to a father was a big black hole inside Vince. The crime was unsolved, and some nasty rumors about corruption circulated. Vince would never believe that Carlos had been on the take. He'd also bet money that Alfonso Moreno, head of a syndicate called Los Carnales, had ordered the kill, but Moreno had been jailed at the time, and there'd been nothing to tie him to it. Now Moreno walked free, while the best man Vince had ever known was lying six feet underground.

He had to get back on the job so he could keep looking for the evidence to nail Moreno. He couldn't afford any more distractions. What did Tino want with Vince after years with next to no communication?

He threw down the postcard and walked back to the kitchen, already knowing that he'd be wasting his time trying to sleep. The two beers he'd had would be no help, and he wasn't drinking any more just to dull the edges.

But as he'd told Dr. Cool and Elegant, he wasn't sorry Krueger was dead, only that he hadn't suffered.

She hadn't flinched when he'd said that, nor when he'd baited her. The only time she'd reacted was when he'd crowded her space.

He sneered. Probably afraid he'd sweat on her fancy dress.

He just wanted her to stay out of his head. He himself didn't even like looking in there. She'd be better off to leave him alone and let him get on with his job. Then he remembered the soft brown eyes and how they'd surprised him. High-class blondes were supposed to have icy blue eyes, maybe green, not warm, molasses-brown. Women like her weren't found at crime scenes, wading through the muck and blood.

A contradiction was Chloe St. Claire. Her clothes screamed money. She couldn't want to mess up her perfectly manicured nails or get a wrinkle in her silk gown. Why would a woman like that be digging into the brains of cops? All pearls and high society, she should be revolted by dealing with someone like him—rough, angry and a killer. Yet he couldn't forget the feel of that slim, pale hand on his arm or the sound of that low, calm voice. For a moment, Vince had felt himself relax a little, caught up in the oasis she'd created around her, untouched by the blood and violence.

It didn't matter. They came from two different worlds—the unwanted son of a whore and the cherished daughter of the elite. He had no choice but to see her tomorrow as part of the IAD drill, but he'd blow smoke at her until she was satisfied, then he'd be on his way, back on the job in a few days.

He drew the eggs from the refrigerator, cracked them into a bowl, then whipped them with quick, angry strokes as he thought about the sympathy he'd seen in her eyes. As if it wasn't just her job. As though she really cared.

Vince shook his head. *Don't waste time on me, Doc. Go soothe someone who needs it.*

CHAPTER TWO

THE NEXT MORNING, Chloe glanced up at the knock on her office door. "Come in, Wanda." But instead of her secretary, Don Newcombe stepped around the door, smiling. "Shrunk any good heads lately, Chloe?"

She couldn't help a grin in return. She and Don had become friends after a particularly grueling Internal Affairs case a year ago. He was a tough investigator, a little too cynical for her taste, but understandably in the context of what he faced day after day. Still, she'd always found him to be fair.

"Hi, Don. Long time no see." Suddenly, she realized that they might be working together again. Her smile faded. "Is this business or pleasure?"

"It's always pleasure when I get to see you." But there was no flirtation in his voice—another thing she respected about Don; he treated her like a sister or valued friend. He'd never made a move on her, never displayed a need to demonstrate his masculinity. In a department filled with macho, he was a welcome change. She took the compliment exactly as stated and smiled back. "Same to you, but you didn't answer my question."

His gaze grew solemn. "A little of both. I hear you're

on the Coronado case, and I wanted to warn you to be careful."

Chloe stiffened. "I'm always careful." She had far too much practice at it.

"Aw, Chloe, I didn't mean that you don't know your job. Just be wary of Coronado. He's not someone you want to trust. Did you get anything useful from him last night?"

Her unease grew. "My conversations with him are confidential."

"I'm only asking if he's cooperating with you."

She wanted to laugh but kept her face impassive. *Vince Coronado* and *cooperative* didn't belong in the same sentence. "We'll do fine."

"It won't be a cakewalk with him."

"Don," she warned, "I will not discuss him with you like this."

He threw up his hands. "Hey, not trying to trespass, but I want you to tell me if he does anything to alarm you."

She rounded her desk, her discomfort fading. He was a good friend. She stopped right in front of him in the doorway and smiled. "I'm a big girl. I appreciate your concern, though."

Movement behind him drew her glance. There stood Vince Coronado, eyes flashing anger. Chloe sighed inwardly. "I have to go now, Don, but I'm glad we'll be working together again."

"Me, too." He reached out and squeezed her shoulder. "Just remember—I'm here if you need me."

"Thanks."

When he turned and saw Coronado, his smile vanished. Chloe tensed as he headed straight for the detective, whose hands were clenched at his sides. Their brief exchange was too low to be heard, but agitation radiated from both men.

Chloe grimaced. This was really going to help her session.

As if he'd read her thoughts, Coronado shot her a black look that should have shriveled her right there. She understood his worries; she'd simply have to allay them.

Sighing once more, Chloe gestured to her door, then walked back inside.

WANDA GLANCED UP. "Hey, *cher,* how you been…" Her voice trailed off at his glower. "Go on in, Vince."

"What the hell was he doing—" His head swiveled back toward Chloe. "Never mind. I'll let Doc tell me what she and her buddy Newcombe were talking about." He still had a hard time believing what he'd seen when he'd entered the reception area. After all she'd said about wanting to help him, about confidentiality—

She was in bed with the enemy, for all he knew. That she was dating Assistant D.A. Roger Barnes was common knowledge around the department, and she and Newcombe had looked pretty cozy just now. Between the two zealots, her bed must be crowded. He stalked through the doorway.

"What do you think you just saw, Detective?"

Her icy tone took him by surprise. "I know what I saw."

"I ask you again, what do you *think* you just saw?"

"I *know* that I saw the woman who holds the keys to my future all but falling into the arms of a man out to ruin me."

She struggled visibly to stem a retort. He considered it a small victory that she was so rattled. "*Not* that it's any of your business, but I respect Detective Newcombe."

"You're even more naive than I thought. Newcombe is a liar and a cheat."

Her eyes widened. "I've worked with Don on several occasions, Detective. He's a tough man, but above all, he's fair. He plays by the book."

A long night and what was shaping up to be an even longer day ratcheted his temper beyond the breaking point. "Then you, Dr. St. Claire, are a fool. Worse, you're dangerously incompetent if you can't read the man better than that. You're too green, and I've got a career on the line—I'm wasting my time here." He whirled toward the door.

Before he could exit, she was in his path, one hand out to block him. "Stop right there—"

Vince blinked, amazed at how fast she'd moved.

Anger sparked in her eyes, but with visible effort, she banked it. "Detective, perhaps both of us should take a minute to calm down and sort this out."

"Why? It was a mistake to think I could put any stock in what you said last night."

"You're wrong. I meant it—I want to help you."

"You can't do that and be in league with Newcombe."

"I'm not in league with Don—Detective Newcombe."

When he snickered, she leaned forward. "I'm going to forget your insult that I would stoop to trading confidential information. I told you last night that everything we discuss is strictly between us. I've done nothing to earn your distrust."

Vince flexed his fingers, his jaw tightening. "He couldn't wait to hotfoot it down here to get to you first."

Her gaze remained steady. "I revealed nothing about you."

"But he asked, didn't he?"

"He only wanted to express concern."

"Yeah." Vince laughed harshly. "I'll bet. Did he try to tell you I'm a dirty cop?" She only wavered a tiny flicker, but he saw it. "I thought so. What else did he say? That you should be afraid of me?"

"It doesn't matter." Her chin rose. "I'm not afraid."

Vince closed the distance between them, crowding her space. Nerves sparked in her eyes. "Sure you're not."

She swallowed visibly. "I don't believe you would hurt me." Her eyes spoke of determination, if not faith.

He had to give her credit. A complex woman, this one.

"Detective—" One slender hand settled on his arm. The warmth somehow eased the ragged edges of this morning. "I will not lie to you. What we say is confidential from anyone and everyone. I'm willing to keep trying until you trust me. You've got so much to deal with now—please, let me help you."

She had that right. He was alone in the jungle with

threats all around, some visible, but more were only noises disturbing his peace of mind. He wanted to believe her, but—

"Give me a chance, Vince. We'll take it slowly. I don't mind having to earn your trust." Golden-brown eyes held his.

Hearing his first name from her shouldn't sway him, but he was too tired to think much more right now. He craved distance, time to sift through all that had happened. Maybe it wouldn't hurt to sit here and see what she did. She had an oddly soothing effect on him. That calm, quiet manner created a peace he sorely needed. He'd just have to be careful what he said.

Anyway, there was no getting around this meeting. If he wanted his job back, he had to walk through the procedure. No one said he had to tell her anything important. Vince stepped away, giving her room.

Chloe exhaled. "Thank you. You won't regret it."

"I'm not so sure about that," he muttered.

"You will be," she promised.

He questioned again what it was about her that made him want to believe her. So what if she was beautiful, he'd known plenty of good-looking women. Maybe that wider-than-normal, luscious-as-hell mouth gave him pause, but tight-ass wasn't his style. She shouldn't appeal to him at all.

Now, though, her features more mobile, her composure ruffled, he was surprised at the hints of passion he saw running beneath the surface. She might have perfected quite a facade, but in that moment, he couldn't help wondering…

He swore silently. He'd never find out, and it didn't matter. He only had to bluff his way through this procedure well enough to get her to cut him loose.

"I'll try to make your time in the Arctic Circle bearable," she said.

He couldn't help a quick grin of surprise.

"You thought we weren't aware of the term?" She gestured to two cozy chairs in the corner, a small table with a lush green plant breaking the sterility of police-department decor. "Please, have a seat. Would you care for coffee?"

"Let's not pretend we're going to be friends, Doc," he warned. "Trust me on this—we're not."

She merely gave him a calm stare. "We can sit wherever you prefer, Detective. I like those chairs because they're comfortable, but the choice is yours."

He stabbed a finger toward the more spartan desk and side chairs. "Forget comfort. Let's get this done."

Color rose beneath her skin, but she didn't rise to the bait. "I'd like to leave ourselves open to the possibility that this may be more productive than you think."

Touché, Doc, he thought. She might like calling the shots, but he had news for her: so did he. One eyebrow lifted, Vince settled into a chair, gesturing for her to begin.

But instead, she let the silence draw out.

He stifled a smile. This was starting to get interesting. She couldn't win this game, of course. He'd grilled a lot of suspects; he had one of the highest clearance rates in the department. Silence wouldn't work on him.

Neither broke the impasse for a long, long span.

Then she spoke. "Did the dead boy have a family to grieve for him, or are you the only person who cared?"

Vince jolted at the unexpected tangent. "His mother's a junkie. She's only sorry now because her meal ticket is dead."

"Why do you say that?"

"Kids get left to scramble for themselves all the time, Doc. A whole lot of kids never have June Cleaver for a mom."

"Is that what happened to you?"

Vince froze. "We were talking about the kid, not me."

She met his gaze evenly. "But the depth of your grief over him has roots farther back, doesn't it?"

"Doc, I told you to stay out of my head."

"It's common knowledge that you go hard on anyone who harms women or children."

Vince clenched his jaw. "So what?"

"So talk to me about why you feel this strongly."

"You don't mind people treating children like animals, maybe even mutilating and torturing them? You didn't see the kid—I did. The bastard used a razor to make tiny slices all over his body and let him bleed to death." He drew a savage satisfaction in seeing her eyes widen, her body recoiling.

For about ten seconds, then he felt as if he'd impaled a butterfly on a pin. All color had left her face. "You said nothing shocks you. Don't you know that adults do hellish things to children every day?"

She rose gracefully and walked to the console in the corner, where she poured a glass of water.

He saw her fingers tremble. And sighed. "Okay, Doc. Here it is. I'm sure my file shows that I never knew my father and my prostitute mother abandoned me at age four. It probably shows that I spent my childhood bouncing around from one foster home to another. Well, at one of those lovely homes, full of such goodness of nature that they took in stray kids, was a father who got off on making his son be his whore—"

Her glass struck the console.

"Still want to hear my story?"

She picked up another glass. "Would you care for some water, Detective?" Her voice was nearly inaudible.

When he didn't answer, she turned around, her face once again a perfect mask. "Detective? Water?"

He could almost have imagined her previous distress. Dr. Cool and Elegant had every hair back in place. "No. Thanks."

She crossed back to her chair and sat down, taking dainty sips. "Please continue." Her voice was too controlled.

"Forget it," he said. "It's not important."

Temper flashed in her eyes. "I'd like for you to finish your story."

"That's the last thing you want."

"You're wrong." Her gaze fixed on his. "I do want to hear what you have to say."

"How long have you had this job?"

"A year and a half." At his snort, she drew herself

up very straight. "Detective, simply because I've had a privileged upbringing doesn't mean I have no interest in making the world a better place. You don't have the market cornered on justice."

Whoa. Steel in that backbone. "I never thought I did."

"Very well." She accepted the apology he hadn't offered. "Please tell me how you feel about what happened to that boy."

He'd rather crawl through an ant bed with honey smeared on him. "No one thought it was important then, why should you?"

"You reported it? How old were you?"

She wasn't going to give up. He bit back an oath. "Not right then. I was eight. The boy's father threatened me, told me no one would believe me."

"What happened?"

"Two days later, I found myself in another foster home. The father was right. No one listened."

"What happened to that boy?"

"How would I know?"

"You didn't check? Later, when you were grown?"

He felt the same frustration that had choked him first as a kid, then as a cop who'd been ten years too late to save Peter. Staring out her window, he swallowed hard. "Peter killed himself when he was fifteen."

"I'm sorry."

He thought she probably meant it. "It doesn't help." He turned to face her. "Being sorry, I mean. I've been sorry for twenty-four years and Peter's still dead."

"So you've been trying to make up for it ever since."

He ground his teeth. "I'm no knight in shining armor."

"Some people would say you are."

"Not Newcombe."

"Tell me what happened between you."

No point in discussing it. She could read the file. Newcombe was a thorn in his side and would be until he got the better of Vince, which wasn't going to happen.

And he had to find Tino. "It doesn't matter. Are we through yet?"

She blinked. "Why?"

"I've got work to do."

"You're on restricted duty."

He shrugged one shoulder. "People to see, places to be."

"But what's the rush?"

He glanced at her. He wasn't going to tell her about Tino. Newcombe would have a field day knowing he would be meeting with an ex-con buddy. But he needed her goodwill to get back on the job. With a sigh, he forced himself to settle into the chair.

"You were going to tell me about you and Don," she prompted.

Vince shot her an amused grin. "You're damn persistent, aren't you?"

Her generous lips curved. "Be warned, Detective. You might as well give up all your secrets now and save yourself some trouble."

Vince found himself caught in that teasing smile,

despite how much he wanted out of here—*now*. "Not much to tell. He had an agenda. I made him look bad. He won't ever forget it."

"He investigated you?"

Vince nodded. "He was convinced I was taking kickbacks from a couple of pimps to leave their girls alone."

"Why would he think that?"

"Because he was new to the job and didn't check his facts well enough. He was ambitious and too eager. Hell, he watched *Serpico* too many times, for all I know. Bottom line is, he screwed up and lost his first big chance for glory. He knows it and I know it. Most of the department does, too. He may have done everything right since then, but he'll never be able to put that failure completely behind him as long as I'm around to remind him."

"He's done a thorough, careful job when I've worked with him."

Vince shrugged. "You can believe whatever you want."

She seemed troubled. "I can't imagine—"

"Your prerogative." Frustrated and oddly disappointed, he stood up, towering over her. "Doc, I really gotta go."

"We're not through, Detective. You can walk away now, but you'll just have to come back. Please make an appointment with Wanda for tomorrow."

He didn't have time for this. He planted his palms flat on her blotter, leaning much too close. "Can't wait to see me, Doc? How about instead I buy you a beer? That way we can really get to know each other."

Visibly steeling herself, she held his gaze. "I don't date clients, Detective."

Smiling, he pushed away from her desk. "Well now, that's good news, isn't it?" He walked toward the door, pausing before he opened it. "You just go ahead and write your report, then I won't have to be your client."

"Detective." Her tone commanded him to look at her.

When he did, he saw exasperation—and resolve. "I take pride in my work, just as you do, and we're not done. We can make this hard, or we can make this easy. It's your call." She followed him to the door.

He thought about the statement he still had to organize, about searching for Tino, about how he had to get Newcombe off his back. Leaning inches from her face, he pitched his voice low. "Stop pushing me, Doc. I don't have time for this."

"You don't have any choice, Detective."

He had to give it to her. Though he had a distinct size advantage over that delicate frame, she didn't back down an inch, some of that passion he'd seen earlier sparking in eyes gone wide and dark.

"It doesn't have to be this difficult," she said.

"Tell that to Newcombe." He stalked out the door.

VINCE STORMED past Wanda, swearing under his breath.

"Hey, *cher,* where you goin' in such a temper?"

Hearing her voice, he felt the anger drain right out

of him. Wanda Dupree had been a records clerk back when he was a rookie, and had saved his hide when he'd messed up on an affidavit that could have invalidated a search. He respected the tiny Cajun who never seemed to find a good man. Wanda was on the downside of fifty, yet something sensual smoldered in the air around her. She never lacked for companionship, but she tended to pick the worst of the litter with unerring accuracy.

He turned back with a grin, aware as he did it that there'd be a smart-aleck one on her face. "Me, Wanda? You know I'm even-tempered and mild."

Wanda snorted, then broke into a racking cough.

"Sugar, you got to ditch those coffin nails."

Sassy as ever, she retorted, "*Cher,* there's three things that make life worth living, and not a one of 'em good for you."

"You just haven't found the right man."

"That's 'cause you never asked me."

Vince shook his head. "I know when I'm out of my league. I'm just a poor country boy, not ready to run with the big dogs always sniffin' around after you."

She laughed, coughing slightly again. "Get out of here, you con man." Her gaze sobered. "She's a good person, Vince." Her head tipped toward Chloe's door. "Helps a lot of people."

His grin vanished. "I don't need a shrink. I'm fine."

"Of course you are, *cher,*" Wanda soothed. "But everybody needs a friend sometimes."

Vince knew that she truly cared. "I can get a dog if I need someone to talk to. They don't talk back."

Wanda giggled. "Go on, you. I'm writing you down for tomorrow at 10:00 a.m."

"Write all you want, sugar. I won't be here." He saluted as he walked away.

CHAPTER THREE

CHLOE CROSSED the grass blanketing the front yard of her little gray house, with its glossy black shutters. Something inside her, as always, eased at the mere sight of it. The smell of freshly mown grass wafted down the block.

Her parents still didn't understand why she lived in this eclectic Rosedale neighborhood filled with small, unremarkable houses. Trees lined the streets, sheltering an odd assortment of neighbors—families with small children, senior citizens who'd bought their homes new in the forties, single professionals like Chloe, gay couples. Its main virtue was proximity to the University of Texas and downtown; as a result, prices had risen but were still modest compared with old-money Tarrytown, where her parents lived. They might have understood if she'd bought a Northwest Hills condo, but a small two-bedroom whose oak floors she'd refinished herself? They still shook their heads over it.

But it was hers, purchased with her own money, decorated with no thought to a spread in *Southern Living*. She loved every inch of it.

Picking faded scarlet blossoms from the round white pots on her porch, Chloe inserted her key in the lock of her Chinese-red front door. She drank in the rich scent of her roses, the sharp spice of the geraniums. Rustling trees outside soothed her, the sound fading with the closing of the door. After shedding her high heels, Chloe padded across the faded green-and-rose Aubusson rug she'd picked up for a song at a secondhand store.

On the way to the refrigerator, Chloe cast a glance at the old rosewood clock on her mantel. She didn't have a lot of time; Roger was picking her up for dinner and *La Bohème* at six-thirty. She loved this particular opera, but her session with Detective Coronado had been only the beginning of a long and frustrating day. For a second, she studied the telephone and considered the flak she'd take if she canceled.

Roger didn't deal well with surprises.

Even if he did, it would be rude and thoughtless of her. Unacceptable behavior in a St. Claire.

Chloe sighed, then drank a quick glass of orange juice and headed for the shower.

Relaxing her stiff neck under the heated spray, she let her mind drift, mulling over the past several hours. One image stood out: the glint of anger in Vince Coronado's eyes. A fire burned deep in his belly to right old wrongs. Chloe suspected that he'd never forgotten what it was to be a child adrift in a system too often callous and ineffective. She marveled at his caring; he could so easily have turned his back on all that and run away as fast as the wind.

But he hadn't. Instead, he was eating himself alive over not saving a boy he barely knew. The boy had a mother, but it was Vince who was his champion.

Vince, who was rough and raw, and undeniably sexy. His outrageous invitation sprang to mind. Alone now, Chloe could afford to consider what an evening spent with Vince would be like—

She shook her head. It didn't matter. He was her client, no matter his wishes. Still, Chloe indulged herself in a slowly widening smile, pondering just how different it would no doubt be from an evening spent with Roger.

And what her parents and Roger would say if they knew how much, for a few insane moments, she'd been tempted to find out.

VINCE STRODE into the squad room to write up his statement for IAD. He planned to slip back out before somebody made him answer phones in the captain's office. He'd find some other way to pass his restricted-duty time.

"Vince," Woods called out from his doorway. "Come on into my office."

He noticed Sarge's frowning glance at something behind him. His gut clenched when he saw Barnes and Newcombe approaching. Newcombe smirked in triumph, his dark eyes hard with menace. "You heard your sergeant, Detective. Let's go."

"I didn't hear your invitation, Newcombe."

"I don't need one. Now, get in there, unless you want to discuss this with a crowd."

Vince glanced up at Barnes, noting the hostility radiating from the man cops called Mr. GQ for his always-perfect looks.

"Newcombe's right. You don't want everyone hearing this," Barnes said.

Vince's fingers flexed, clenching into a fist. He'd like to stand his ground and have it out here, but his instincts told him that whatever this was about, it was bad. With a brisk nod, he preceded them into the room, his mind racing.

Criminals had more rights than cops under investigation. He just had to be cool and see what was happening. He hadn't done anything wrong. It would all work out, he told himself.

So why didn't that reassure him?

Barnes closed the door quietly, while Newcombe walked around to the side of Sarge's desk, crossing his arms across his chest, a smug smile on his face. "I knew you were dirty, Coronado. You're finished and it's about time."

"What are you talking about?" Vince glanced over at Woods. Sarge wouldn't meet his eyes.

Barnes planted himself at Vince's right side, radiating hostility. "You lied to me, Coronado. You made me look bad in an election year. I don't need problems."

If only Vince knew what he meant. He decided to stay quiet and see who spoke first.

"Nothing to say for yourself?" Newcombe taunted. He shot a superior grin toward Barnes. "I told you he did it on purpose. The law means nothing to him."

Vince couldn't stand still for that. The law meant everything to him. Why else would he put up with this stinking system? "That's not true and you know it. It was a good shooting."

Newcombe smirked. "Not with a bad warrant."

Vince recoiled. "What do you mean?"

Barnes responded. "You gave false information in your affidavit to obtain the search warrant."

"The hell I did."

"There were no drugs at Krueger's, Coronado."

He already knew that much. Everyone on the scene last night was aware that the shipment hadn't arrived. It made things iffy for him, but they still had probable cause. "You got his ledgers."

"The so-called ledgers are garbage—they're nothing. We've heard from your source, and she says she never told you about the drug room you alleged to exist on the premises, nor did she ever tell you that Krueger kept his records there."

Vince was stunned. Gloria Morgan was his friend. He'd baby-sat her child, for heaven's sake. He'd bought the kid presents and taught him how to throw a football. Worse yet, he'd cared about both of them, tried to get her to leave the life, move out from under Krueger's thumb. What was going on?

"You got to her, didn't you?" he accused Newcombe. "You'd do anything to paint me the villain."

"Don't make this worse, Vince," Woods warned.

Vince whirled on him. "How could it get any worse? He wants me off the force any way he can get it."

Barnes intervened. "She never talked to Newcombe, Coronado. She spoke with me. I'm the one you've got to worry about. You told me it was a good bust."

"It was."

"We've got nothing to show for it but the dead body of a man everyone knew you wanted taken out."

"I had good information."

"Your source says not."

"I acted in good faith. She's given me tips before that led to arrests. That's allowed."

"She says she's only seen you in passing, swears she's never exchanged more than hellos with you."

Vince stared at Barnes. Newcombe smirked behind him. He wouldn't look away from the D.A., wouldn't back down. It had been a good bust. He wanted to look at Woods to see if his sergeant's confidence was slipping, but he would not give Newcombe the satisfaction—nor Barnes.

Barnes broke the impasse, checking his watch and frowning. "I'm going to be late for a dinner engagement."

Vince's jaw tightened. *With the woman who wants me to trust her?* Not hardly.

He itched to grind his fists into something, preferably Newcombe's face. He forced his fingers to uncurl. "This isn't over. You can't take me down this way, Newcombe."

"I won't have to. You're going to hang yourself. One less hot dog on the streets."

"Then they'll be a lot safer for your shiny behind, won't they? Get me off the force and make the world safer for slime like you, you pathetic—"

Barnes stepped in the path of Newcombe's charge. "Get out of here, Coronado. We'll deal with you soon enough."

"Yeah, got to tidy up the reputation before campaign season, right? Well, I've got news for you, Barnes. You're backing the wrong horse. It was a clean shooting, and people are lying to you. I'm not your problem."

But Barnes wasn't listening. He'd already pronounced sentence. Vince bit back a curse, knowing there was nothing else to say. It was up to him to figure out what Gloria was doing—and why.

Finally, he looked over at Woods, but the sergeant's face was impassive. Maybe he believed Vince, maybe not. Vince got the message. He was on his own. Without another word, he left the room.

"VINCE?"

Deep in thought, he almost didn't hear the soft voice behind him. He turned and saw a face filled with worry. "Sally."

"How are you?" Her head came barely past his shoulder, her long, dark hair braided neatly, completing the starkness of her black uniform. At her shoulder, the radio mike jiggled slightly when she moved.

"Me? Fine." *Just great.*

Solemn gray eyes scanned his face. A rookie under his training the last year he was in uniform, Sally had developed a crush on him. On the rebound from his divorce, he'd made one of his bigger mistakes. Only two nights, but he still didn't kid himself that it had been smart. He'd been relieved that she'd taken it well when he'd backed away. They still went out to grab a beer now and again, but he was careful to keep things light.

"Vince, if I can do anything…" Obviously, she'd heard about last night's events.

"It was a good shooting, Sally."

"But the warrant—"

Vince cursed under his breath. News did travel fast. "What have you heard?"

"Word is that Newcombe says he's got you cold."

"Newcombe's an idiot."

"A lot of people think he's solid."

"Not when it comes to me."

"Vince, you know I—" She stopped, then cleared her throat. Her eyes glistened as if with tears, but that couldn't be true. Sally was too much cop to be sentimental. "I want to help you. Promise me you'll tell me what I can do."

He smiled at her. "You're a good friend." A tiny flicker of pain sparked in her eyes. "I don't know where all this is headed. Newcombe has wanted my hide nailed to the barn door for a long time, but he's dead wrong on this one."

"I believe you. All you have to do is ask for help, anytime, anyplace, Vince. Even if it's just for company."

He was sorry that he hadn't been able, back then, to give her what she deserved. "Thanks, kiddo. I gotta be going now, but I'll catch you later, all right?"

Sally managed a tiny smile. "I'll hold you to that."

He nodded and gave her a thumbs-up before heading back to his desk. Sally was quickly forgotten, however, as thoughts of Barnes and Newcombe stalked him. *Dinner engagement.* With Chloe St. Claire.

Just give me a chance, Vince. I don't mind having to earn your trust.

Trust. Sure, he was going to trust her now.

Vince looked around the squad room, seeing it anew. Wondering how long it would be before he would be back at work, could belong again.

You're finished. Newcombe's confident sneer.

Rapping his knuckles twice on the scarred metal surface of his desk, Vince stifled a quick shiver.

Newcombe was wrong. He had to be.

"CHLOE?"

She roused herself from perusing the operagoers below them. Having box seats had always been a treat; Chloe enjoyed scanning the crowd between acts almost as much as the performances.

"You're lovely this evening," Roger said. One finger trailed along the side of her neck.

She faced him, easing away from his touch. "Thank you, Roger. You're quite dashing yourself." It was true. He was always impeccably turned out. Tailor-made, most of his clothes, including this charcoal-gray suit. His blond hair gleamed under the amber houselights.

He touched the knot of his burgundy tie as though it was a totem. "You're quiet tonight—rough day?"

She couldn't—and wouldn't—discuss Vince Coronado with him. "I have a headache. Probably just the heat."

Roger smiled, reaching for her hand. "Not long until ski season in Utah. How does a week in Park City sound?"

Chloe wondered why he'd never noticed that she hardly skied at all when they went. He loved it, so he assumed she did. Just like her parents, Roger concerned himself more with what Chloe should be doing than what she might want. "Cold weather would be welcome," she demurred.

He lifted her hand to his lips. "It's a date." A figure entering the next row caught his eye. "Excuse me, darling. I need to speak to Tom Griffin a moment."

Chloe nodded, turning back to her people-watching.

And found herself caught in the gaze of the man who'd been too much on her mind today.

She blinked. Vince Coronado—here? At the opera?

He touched his forehead in salute. She broke the contact, wishing for her opera glasses to be sure she wasn't seeing things, but Roger had them in his pocket.

As the houselights lowered, Chloe chanced one more glimpse. It was really Vince, and his eyes remained locked on hers long after she should have looked away. He didn't release her until Roger settled into the seat beside her.

Chloe tried to lose herself in the music; however, it was not so easily managed as in the past.

"CHLOE, will you come with me? I need to speak to Tom again."

She shook her head and smiled. "I'd rather wait here. My head is still pounding."

"Very well. I won't be a moment." Roger slipped into the crowd bunching at the exit.

Chloe struggled to understand the strength of her reaction to Vince Coronado. Unbridled emotions had been discouraged in her household; dignity was paramount. Beyond her upbringing, her profession had made her all too aware of the price of losing control in any manner. Roger had never pressed her on having sex, their relationship based on the sounder principles of common backgrounds and views. He'd never stirred her to want more.

She closed her eyes against the headache and sighed softly. Was she ready to make this her future? Lately, she felt as though she'd sleepwalked through her life.

Just then, a sense of being watched assailed her. She opened her eyes.

Vince Coronado stood perhaps twenty feet away. Around him shimmered that raw, rugged energy that emanated from him whether still or in movement. Having only seen him in jeans before, she was frankly astonished at how polished he appeared, yet how uniquely his own man. Black pleated slacks and soft, black band-collared shirt, a pearl-gray jacket draping his broad shoulders—he could have stepped off a runway in New York.

But the vivid blue eyes drew her back to his face. He made no move to approach her, yet somehow she felt as though he stood right beside her, whispering in her ear.

"Ready to go?" Roger's voice jolted her. She

glanced up at him; when she looked back, Vince had disappeared.

"What is it?"

"I thought—" She shook her head to clear it. "I could have sworn I saw Detective Coronado." There—she'd said his name. Maybe speaking it to Roger would rob Vince of the odd pull he exerted.

Roger laughed. "Coronado at the opera? Not likely. He's probably shooting pool and drinking beer tonight." His laughter turned harsh. "He's got nothing else to do. In fact, he should probably be considering a new career."

"I don't think he's—"

"Be careful, Chloe. You don't have enough experience to understand men like him. We can't allow rogue cops in this city." His tone hardened. "We're under enough heat for the recent crime wave. Someone like him only makes things worse."

Chloe started to retort, but decided not to waste her time trying to open Roger's closed mind. She was operating on instinct, anyway.

Instinct told her Roger was wrong. Vince wasn't a rogue cop. He might be unconventional—aggressive, even. He quite certainly carried baggage from a past she could hardly imagine.

But he'd defended a child when he was one himself. He cared, probably too much for his own welfare. None of that, however, was grounds for taking a good cop off the force.

One of the reasons she'd taken this job was that she'd seen a chance to really help in a way she'd never have been able to in a safe suburban practice. Cops were human and they made mistakes, but they were extraordinary, too. Every day they put themselves in harm's way for little money and few thanks.

Sometimes, however, they needed help, even the strongest of them. She might not have the makeup to strap on a gun and run toward danger, but she had her own contribution to make.

She smiled then. Even if certain recipients, like one Detective Coronado, fought like crazy to avoid taking it.

JUST SOUTH OF Town Lake, Vince sat on his back-porch steps in the darkness. Through the screen door, the 1958 Maria Callas recording of *Bohème* wafted. He almost hadn't used his ticket tonight, yet he was glad he had. His problems hadn't vanished, but the music had shifted his focus for a few hours.

Beside him, the old tomcat purred loudly, butting his head against the hands clasped between Vince's knees. Vince stirred, then looked down at the furry form weaving a figure eight around his feet. "I thought I told you to leave."

Another head butt.

"I'm not feeding you forever. I hate cats."

Fur brushed the side of one hand. He shook his head and scratched the cat's neck while he stared at the moon through the trees.

Chloe St. Claire unsettled him. He didn't like it.

Nonetheless, he couldn't help a grin at the memory of her shock tonight. He didn't go often, but no law said cops couldn't appreciate opera. Vince thought he liked having taken her off guard.

Then he recalled Barnes beside her and frowned. They looked like matching bookends: Ms. Cool and Elegant and Mr. GQ, Couple on the Rise. They'd have two golden children and a golden retriever to match. He'd drive a Lexus, and she a Mercedes. They'd live in Tarrytown, with a weekend place in the Hill Country, each one featured in *Southern Living* or maybe even *Architectural Digest.*

It was good to remind himself of who she really was. He couldn't believe he'd told her so much. He didn't like how easily she invited confidences. He couldn't afford to trust her; she worked for the same department that wanted to hang him. If he could get by with never seeing Chloe St. Claire again, he'd be better off.

He reached for the screen door. "Tomorrow, cat— you're outta here." Then he opened the door, stepping carefully as brown-and-white fur slipped between his feet.

CHAPTER FOUR

"CHLOE?" The raspy voice of her secretary rang out the next morning.

"Wanda, if you'd stop smoking, your allergies might improve." She smiled at the thought of the frown no doubt decorating the diminutive redhead's face.

"Don't start with me, *chère*. It's the end of the month."

Monthly reports. Chloe hated them, too. Her voice softened. "Are you all right?"

"I will be when Lester gets the hell out of my apartment."

"Want to come talk about it?"

Wanda's breath hitched, and Chloe could almost see her struggle. Passion made people foolish. Wanda refused to see the whole man; she'd never have taken up with Lester otherwise, or the last two Lesters, for that matter.

"Detective Coronado is here for his appointment."

Chloe tensed. "All right." Good. At least her voice sounded even. "Send him in." Then she stared at the doorway as he strode inside, still larger than life.

For one long span, neither moved.

"Doc." He nodded, voice clipped, blue eyes shuttered.

"Hello, Detective." Had she imagined the previous night? "Did you enjoy the opera?"

A cocky grin. "Surprised to see me there?"

"I shouldn't say yes."

"Not proper cop music?"

"Is there such a thing? I didn't know they taught music at the academy."

One dark eyebrow rose as he conceded the point. "Let me surprise you more. I even finished college. Night school while I worked patrol, but still… college. As a matter of fact, one of my professors introduced me to opera."

Female, she'd bet anything. But she wouldn't ask. Chloe turned away, gesturing to the corner seating. "Your choice, Detective."

"You've got dynamite legs, Doc. You should wear short skirts more often."

Chloe frowned past the spike of pleasure. "That's an inappropriate comment for this meeting."

"Barnes got the only claim?"

Chloe crossed her arms over her chest. "It's none of your business."

"It is when the woman who holds the key to my future is sleeping with a man who wants my head."

"I'm not—" She stopped. His raised eyebrows maddened her. "My personal life has nothing to do with your case. I've told you before and I'll repeat it. Everything you say in here—"

"Is confidential," he parroted. He stepped closer,

leaving less than a foot between them. "Is it, Doc? Can lovers ever keep anything totally secret from each other?"

Chloe forced her gaze up to his, wrapping her arms tighter.

He leaned forward, so near she could feel his warmth.

Her gaze flicked to his mouth. She swallowed with effort. "I'm very good at keeping secrets."

"I can't afford to assume that."

"You can take it to the bank."

"You sure?" He cocked his head. "You have to admit that you'd be uneasy in my place. You're buddies with Newcombe and sleeping with Barnes—"

"Don't say that again," she snapped.

"You're not buddies with Newcombe?" His eyes challenged.

"Detective, insulting me is not going to get you off my appointment list any sooner."

"What will?"

Surprised that his words stung, she locked her eyes on his. "Being honest with me will go a long way."

"I haven't lied to you."

"Perhaps not. But not lying and being honest are not necessarily the same thing. You're kidding yourself if you don't admit that the pressures on you right now are enormous. You may be a legend in the department, but that doesn't mean you're not human. Anyone would be having problems with all that's been thrown at you lately."

He stood very still, eyes searching hers. She thought

the real Vince might be peering over the barricades, just a little. "Anyone, Doc? Even you?"

Chloe froze. "We're not talking about me."

One eyebrow lifted. "Maybe we should. Why are you so nervous?"

"I'm not nervous."

He shot a pointed glance at the arms wrapped against her body. Immediately, she dropped them, but she knew she had to reciprocate with something or he'd never trust her. And whether or not he wanted to believe it, he needed someone to listen, somewhere to turn. Too much was bottled up inside him, and it was only going to get worse. "Of course my job impacts me, but I know how to handle what I hear, and I want to help you."

He studied her. "One of the guys said you really came through for him. Told me to give you a chance."

"Will you?" She was surprised at how much she cared.

"I don't know. You've heard about the warrant?"

"Yes." She understood what he was asking. "But I didn't hear it from Roger." She sighed. "Do you want to wait for Rick to come back from vacation? Perhaps that's better."

"Wait two more weeks? No way. I can't afford the time."

"Then give me a chance to prove you can trust me."

"It's not that easy, Doc."

"I know it's not. The shields you've built to survive your work don't come down without effort." She leaned forward, willing him to believe her. "I don't want to destroy them, Vince. I'm only asking you to come out and talk to me for a while. I realize that you need them, but this is a safe place."

Vivid blue eyes bored into her. Chloe was on trial. Never before had she felt so much the burden of that vow she made to every client, a pledge not to weaken him if he gave his trust. For this man, rebuilding his defenses would be a painful process if she, by failing him, destroyed their foundation.

"If I had any choice, I'd be out of here."

"I know."

Endless seconds passed, strung taut with challenge. Finally, he spoke, his voice strained. "I'll try, Doc. That's all I can promise." *Don't let me down,* his eyes demanded. But he turned away before she could answer. "I'll set an appointment with Wanda on my way out."

When the door closed, Chloe sagged into her chair.

THAT NIGHT, Vince pushed through the crowd at the bar, using his height to advantage in scanning for Tino. This was his next-to-last option of places Tino used to haunt. The Tejano music was deafening, the smoke thick, the smell of sweat and beer all too familiar. His job took him into too many dives like this, ones he'd once happily frequented himself. Now, more often than not, off-duty nights were spent sanding floors or stripping wallpaper. *Gettin' old, son,* he thought.

Just then, someone stumbled against him. Only quick steps on his part kept the beer from spilling on more than his shoes. Shouting erupted, and more shoving—

And at the center of the brewing fight was none

other than Tino Garza. For a moment, Vince examined the changes prison had wrought. Without the old scar across Tino's left temple, would Vince have recognized him? Even as he assessed the transformation, his heart sank.

Prison gang. The tattoos, the abundance of ripped musculature...Vince didn't have to see a distinct gang symbol to know it was true.

It shouldn't be a surprise—the greater shock would be for Tino to have come out of prison straight. He'd always been wild, always hotheaded. Vince knew the stats: prison-spawned gangs recruited from street gangs. They were syndicates, a well-oiled machine. Guys on the outside funded the lifestyle of those in the joint by whatever crimes were necessary—robberies, for sure; auto theft; drugs; gambling—whatever it took. You got caught, you took your sentence, knowing that you'd be well tended on the inside, that the obligation would hold for as long as the revolving door existed.

In the eyes of the members, honor bound them. Families were cared for, time served made less painful by plentiful funds, drugs, whatever an inmate wanted, as long as he knew the score. Once out, you hooked up with your area commander and got your assignments. Funnel the money into the system as expected, and you could live your life in relative peace. Get crosswise with it...you and anyone you cared about were history.

Organizational charts, disciplinary system...the adult gangs were half corporate, half military in their behavior, but a taste for violence lay at the heart of it.

That was the bottom line: a world more brutal than

any bleeding-heart liberal could imagine. Those exhorting prison as rehabilitation were kidding themselves. As long as blood and money were entwined, no one got out alive. Get along, play your part—you might live to be a little older. Fail, or worse, try to get out—you were dead. Period. End of story.

"Hey, buddy, how the hell are you?" Tino spotted him and abandoned the brewing fight to greet Vince.

Though Vince had gone to a certain amount of trouble to adopt a disguise he'd never used undercover, without making it impossible for Tino to recognize him, he had no desire to be the center of attention. He jerked his head toward the exit and left without checking to see if Tino followed.

He did. "Let me buy you a drink, man. For old times." Grabbing Vince around the neck, Tino hugged him and slapped his back. "Help me celebrate my independence." He clasped Vince's arm and tried to pull him back toward the door, but Vince resisted. "Hey, check you. Been workin' out, man?"

Vince stepped back into the shadows. Half a head shorter, Tino showed the effects of what had to be years of doing weights, no doubt with the addition of steroids. Vince kept his tone light. "Me? I just grew up. What happened to you? You decided against majoring in the arts?"

Tino laughed and clapped Vince's shoulder. "What can I say? I'm not a kid anymore, *carnal*."

Carnal. Brother. Once they had been that in all but blood. "So you came back to the old hometown, eh?" Vince asked.

Tino shrugged, his eyes glittering with God knows what chemical assistance. "Missed my buddy. How the hell you been doin', Vince?"

"Can't complain."

"I heard about you in the joint, you know. You got a rep, big brother. Fair number of guys wouldn't mind doin' a tap dance on your head."

"Popularity's a curse."

"Yeah, but you got a real fan club with the boss, *ése*." Eyes glittering, feet jittering…Tino was laying down a load of BS too deep for boots.

"What are you after?" Vince asked.

"I don't know what you mean. Me, I'm just here with my big bro—you ain't so much bigger than me now, are you?" Tino brandished his fists and danced around. "Want to go three rounds? Bet I can take you, not like when we were kids."

"Cut the crap. Tell me why you'd do something as stupid as sending me a postcard. To my house, man. What the hell were you thinking?" *And how did you know where to find me?*

Tino's feet stopped dancing. His arms dropped to his sides. "Hey, don't worry about that. That wasn't no prison thing. I found out from Leticia. You told her how to get in touch if she needed you."

Leticia. Tino's old girlfriend, mother of his child. Vince had checked in on her and Tino Junior periodically to make sure she was all right.

"Leticia wouldn't give you the time of day," Vince said.

"She does now. She still loves me, man." Tino scowled. "You been trying to move in on me, Vince?"

"You know better than that."

Tino's eyes still glittered too brightly. "Do I?" Menace trembled in the air, and Vince could feel how far away from their boyhood bond Tino had moved.

Then Tino laughed. "Yeah—" He socked Vince on the shoulder, harder than strictly affectionate. "You wouldn't poach. Leticia wants us to be a family now, her and me and little Tino Junior."

"That's good," Vince said. "Every boy needs a father."

"'Cept you and me, eh? We don't need those rotten sonsabitches who ran out on us. You had it best—yours left before you knew him. That way he wasn't knocking you around, you or your mama."

Their eyes met, and Vince knew Tino was thinking about the battered boy Vince had first met on the streets.

Tino's voice softened. "You were *mi padre, Vicente,* young as you were. You were the one who showed me how to make it on the streets."

Vince shook his head. "But I didn't save you from them."

Tino's juking and jiving stopped cold. "You could do that now, bro."

At last they were at the heart of why Tino had written.

"I didn't leave anything on that postcard that could tie it to me, so no one would make the connection. I was watchin' your back, Vince. Just like always."

Vince didn't argue, though he could have. Tino had been a skinny, scared kid who, more often than not, started the fights Vince had to finish to rescue him. "I appreciate that you were careful." He studied Tino, already a bad feeling in his gut. "So what is it you need now?"

"This ain't for me. It's for you. I got your dream operation, man. You'd be a hero for sure."

"Heroes are for comic books."

His friend leaned closer, the jittering under way again. "No, listen to me, man. This can work. See, I got my assignment from my area commander. The D.A.'s office is pushing the cop shop to turn up the heat on Los Carnales. Crackdowns are a pain in the ass and just make it harder to do business."

Los Carnales. Moreno's bunch. Tino's gang. Though his every nerve leaped to attention, Vince managed a simple shrug. "In case you haven't heard, I'm not on duty right now."

"Oh, I know that. The boss knows that. He's got a proposition for you."

A proposition from Moreno, the man he wanted to take down more than breath. Vince nodded for Tino to continue.

"See, the boss hears you're not getting much appreciation for the job you do. You put a lot of the boys in jail, but your own people ain't givin' you your propers for that. Word on the street is that your job is on the line. We can help you out."

The little prickle that always alerted Vince to danger zipped up the back of his neck. Adrenaline followed it whenever he neared the center of the action, and already his heart rate was speeding up. Vince battled back the urge to let any of it show on his face. "I won't be out of the game long. Just routine procedure."

Tino shifted on his feet. "Not what the boss is hearing. IAD's after you, *compadre*. That's why this is a great thing for you. Hear me out, man."

"I'm not promising anything, but go ahead." For a moment he wished that he hadn't met Tino in public. If word of this meeting got out to Newcombe…

"The boss, he can make it worth your while if you help out now and again. Nothin' big, just keep your ear to the ground and let him know if somethin's coming down."

Vince's fingers curled into a fist. "You want me to be a freaking snitch—am I hearing you right, Tino? You lost your mind?" He took a step forward. "What the hell are you doing even asking me a question like that?"

Tino held up one hand. "Hey, listen to me, man. Shut up and let me finish."

Vince turned on his heel. "I've heard enough."

Tino grabbed Vince's arm. "That's what he told me to ask, bro, but that's not what I'm asking."

"It better not be."

Tino's eyes had sobered, but they still darted all around. "I can't talk here. Let's go somewhere else."

If he had a brain in his skull, Vince would walk away now, but the weight of their history and the pleading in Tino's eyes stayed him. His gut was greasy with an instinct that what he was about to hear would only make a complicated situation worse.

"All right. Head down the alley. I'll pick you up at the other end." Without waiting to see if Tino did it, Vince left.

But after he got in his car and drove around to the end of the alley, Tino never showed. Vince parked down the street and doubled back, but his friend was nowhere in sight. He edged back toward the bar through the shadows.

There he saw Tino in a heated argument with a guy whose every move screamed syndicate. The part of Vince that had known a scared nine-year-old boy wanted to rush to Tino's defense—

But the experienced cop knew that to do so would sign Tino's death warrant. Vince's only choice was to leave and try again later to discover exactly what the devil was going on.

And hope Tino was still alive when he found him.

THE TELEPHONE RANG while Chloe picked at her solitary salad. "Hello?"

"How are you, darling?" The soft, Southern tones of her mother's Georgia upbringing slid easily through the line.

"Mother—" Chloe glanced at the clock. "Are you all right? I thought you and Daddy were going to a fundraiser."

"Oh, well, we were, but your father's been working very hard lately, and we decided a night in might be the thing. Am I interrupting?"

"Only my dinner."

"This late? Chloe, that job requires too much of you. Why, your father and I—"

Before the usual lecture could begin, Chloe interrupted. "It wasn't work, Mother." Not that her mother would like what she'd been doing any better.

"Oh. Well then, I hope it was something fun. Shopping with a friend or drinks with Roger, perhaps."

"Just a little volunteering." Though her mother would hardly consider the Women's Shelter any less sordid than her job.

"That's wonderful, dear. Junior League or your sorority?"

Her mother had too many sources in both for Chloe to lie. "I'm providing free counseling at the Women's Shelter."

"Oh, Chloe…" Silence hung in the air between them.

But instead of the long-suffering sigh Chloe expected, she heard what almost sounded like a sniff. "Mother? What's wrong?"

"Nothing," Dolores St. Claire breezed on. "I called because I'm planning a little dinner party to introduce Roger to more important backers for his campaign. As Roger's fiancée, you'll be a hostess."

"We're not engaged."

"It's only a matter of time. You haven't gone out with anyone else in ages, and you two are a perfect match. You're one of his biggest assets in the race."

It sounded so cold, especially coming from her own mother. She didn't want to be anyone's asset. She wanted to be…more. No longer the good little Chloe who always did the right thing. A woman who, for once in her life, took a chance or two. Danced closer to the edge instead of always staying behind secure fencing. Except she didn't know what edge.

And then she thought of one with blue eyes and a go-to-hell grin. "Maybe I want to go out with someone else."

A shocked silence bled through the line. "You're not serious."

Chloe took a mental step back from the cliff crumbling at her feet. "I don't know. But please stop making assumptions about Roger and me. I'm involved in my career right now."

"Chloe." Her mother spoke carefully and slowly. "I'd be the first to say that you've accomplished far more than your father and I ever envisioned. You've made us very proud—"

Chloe could hear the *but* coming.

"But, darling, don't you want more from life? A family? Children to cherish? Your father and I so hoped—" Her mother's voice cracked.

Chloe closed her eyes and bit back a retort, reminding herself that her mother meant well. Her parents had always held her to a high standard, but she had never doubted her importance to them. She'd been showered with every advantage since birth. She owed them more than this growing impatience, but being their first—and in her mother's case, only—priority sometimes smothered her.

Still, she felt selfish for even thinking that way. "Mother, I don't want to disappoint you. Yes, I'd like to have all those things, but—" *With someone like Roger?*

"Darling, you can't wait forever." Her mother's voice held an odd urgency.

"What are you saying?"

"Nothing." There was the sound of her mother's nose softly blown.

"What is it? What's wrong?" A cold fist grabbed her heart. "Is it—are you ill, Mother?"

"No." But tears were clearly present.

Oh, no. Not— "What's wrong with Daddy?" He'd looked tired lately, but he'd ascribed it to overwork. "Mother, talk to me. Tell me what's going on."

"He doesn't want to worry you, and neither do I."

"I'm not a child. I haven't been one for a long time. I don't need you to protect me from life."

"We've only tried to keep you safe because you're everything to us, sweetheart."

The burden of that sometimes pressed Chloe beyond bearing, but right now she couldn't concern herself with how much she wanted out from under the suffocating blanket of that love. "Mother." She used her most soothing voice. "Talk to me. We both love Daddy. Let me help." Once again, she thought she heard a stifled sob. "Do you want me to come over there?"

"No—no, honey, not tonight. It would only upset your father if he knew—"

"Knew what?"

Finally, her ever-dignified mother's voice broke. "He hasn't been feeling well for some time, but he wouldn't go to his doctor. Your father always has to be in control. Always on top of his game."

"Ever the strong one," Chloe supplied.

"Yes." Her mother paused. "Men don't take aging well, darling. They don't like feeling vulnerable. Women have to cope with drastic changes in their bodies all their lives, once a month or through pregnancy. But barring serious illness, for much of their existence, men never have the experience of their bodies betraying them. Your father hates growing older because it's a force that his will can't completely overcome. Still, he was managing, but now—" Her mother fell silent.

A multitude of horrors cascaded through Chloe's mind. She seized on one. "Daddy's…dying? Is it cancer or—" She tried to think what could be responsible for her mother's fear.

"It's leukemia. He was recently diagnosed."

"What can be done about it? Don't they perform bone-marrow transplants? I can donate. I'll call his doctor tomorrow—"

"No."

Chloe was already spinning plans, and her mother's flat refusal took a minute to sink in. "No?" she echoed.

"You can't do that."

She frowned at an odd note in her mother's voice. "Of course I can. I'm Daddy's only living blood relative, and I want to do it. He gave me life, and now I can give it back."

"I can't talk about this now." Her mother's voice was so faint, Chloe could barely hear her.

"I understand that you're upset, but surely you see that there's an easy solution."

Strain invaded her tone. "Chloe, I have to go. Promise me you won't take any steps yet."

"What? How can you possibly rationalize waiting? How can you jeopardize Daddy's health?"

"I should never have mentioned this. Your father will be furious."

"Mother—"

"If you love me, you will not say one word about this to your father or anyone else until I have time to think."

"Think about what?" It was so unlike Mother to be irrational. "What can you possibly need to consider?"

"I can't discuss this anymore with you tonight, darling. Please." Weariness and sorrow coated every syllable.

Pity stirred in Chloe. "I don't want Daddy to die."

"A few days won't hurt anything, but he'll be upset if—please, Chloe, promise me you'll wait."

Chloe had never heard her sound so defeated, had never heard her plead. Dolores St. Claire was always in control, always composed.

Her parents were not demonstrative with each other, their relationship restrained but cordial. As a little girl, she'd assumed every couple was like that. In junior high, she'd secretly yearned for passion and grand sweeping gestures but had always known better than to voice those longings. St. Claires did not air their dirty laundry, she knew that, and the base emotions were not allowed rein.

A lack of disturbing passions was part of who they were. Who she was supposed to be.

But sometimes…she wondered. Only once had she seen that restraint breached, when she was in junior high. She'd overheard an argument between them that had opened her eyes when she learned that her mother had been wealthy, while her father had struggled his way up from a poverty he had loathed. As she grew older, she'd had inklings of a subtle competition between them, a delicate balance of power.

If they weren't affectionate with each other, however, each had lavished Chloe with attention. Their love was accompanied by high expectations, yes, but Chloe had no reason to doubt that her parents cared for her. Her mother had built her whole life around the only child she would have.

Still, she knew her father did not receive the same devotion. "You are absolutely certain that you're not endangering Daddy's health by asking me to wait?"

Her mother's response was quick and cutting. "Do not *ever* doubt my loyalty to your father, Chloe."

Shame rose. "I'm sorry." She might wish for a different relationship for herself, but marriages came in all shapes and sizes. She held out an olive branch. "Of course you want what's best for Daddy. It's just that this—" Tears burned her eyes. "He's always been so strong," she whispered.

"I understand," her mother said. "He's seeing the best doctors, and you can be certain money won't be an object."

"But I don't understand why you don't want me to—"

Her mother cut in. "Please, darling. Your father could never accept any risk to your health, and there would be risk."

"I don't care."

"But he does." Her mother's voice held firm. "And so do I. I'll talk to him, but I want your promise that you won't speak to him about this yet." Then her mother's voice quavered again. "I don't want anything to happen to him, either, Chloe."

Chloe could not deny the real concern in her mother's voice and chided herself for all her doubts about their marriage. "All right, Mother. But I'm going to worry every minute."

"I understand, darling. Now—" her mother hesitated for a second "—I do need your help with this dinner party."

Love warred with the urge to scream that dinner parties didn't matter, that nothing mattered but her father's return to health. But Chloe stifled the words straining to emerge from her lips. All Chloe's life, her mother had made it clear that one didn't falter in one's duties, regardless of feelings or needs. One carried on.

Maybe this dinner party was a welcome distraction for her parents. So Chloe carried on, good daughter that she was. "Perhaps we can talk about it tomorrow."

A long silence, then her mother's voice held more warmth than usual. "Tomorrow will be just fine. Good night, my darling girl."

Fury battled with love, and Chloe thought she might

choke on both. Dragging herself into her role, Chloe said in a voice whose calm no doubt made her mother proud, "Good night, Mother." With shaking hands, she slowly hung up.

CHAPTER FIVE

THE PHONE RANG just as Chloe was slipping into her heels while fastening an earring. She glanced at the clock on her nightstand. Drat. If she took this call, she couldn't get to the office far enough ahead of her first appointment to telephone her father's doctor.

But it might be her mother. Knowing how sick her father was, Chloe could not blithely let the recorder catch it. "Hello?"

"Oh, good, I caught you." Not her mother but Helen Masters.

"Hello, Helen. I'm sorry, I have to get in to work early. Could I call you later?"

"This won't take but a moment, dear. I'd like to schedule a meeting for this week to discuss the Christmas auction. What about ten o'clock on Thursday?"

The middle of work. Chloe stifled her impatience that Helen assumed she should be free. "Would it be possible to schedule for lunch sometime, instead? Most days I have appointments straight through."

Helen paused. "Oh, dear. Jane Ann has tennis on Thursdays, Mamie has bridge on Wednesdays and my hairdresser appointment on Friday can't be canceled short of nuclear war—Freddie gets very testy, you know."

Chloe remembered. Freddie had done her mother's hair for years. His clientele planned their lives around his schedule. "What about next week, then?" Glancing at the clock, she winced.

"Oh, Jane Ann will be on a cruise all next week, didn't you hear? That Harvey—he's trying to make up for—"

"Helen, I'm sorry," Chloe interrupted. "My calendar is at the office," she lied, trying not to scream. Her father might be dying, and Helen wanted to gossip. "I need to call you back."

Helen's voice chilled noticeably. "Chloe, this auction is a big responsibility."

So is my job, Chloe wanted to say but didn't. Helen had as little respect for it as her parents had.

"It's a worthy cause, Helen, and I'll do my part." She looked at the time again and prayed for patience.

"I'll be leaving for my mah-jongg game at two, dear. Make sure you reach me before then, please."

Chloe scribbled herself a note and tore the paper off the pad. "I promise. Goodbye, Helen." She didn't wait for the older woman's goodbye before disconnecting.

Twenty minutes later, she all but ran up the two flights of outside stairs to her building, racing down the hallway and into Wanda's office.

Wanda was busy taking a message and grimaced as she met Chloe's gaze.

Chloe picked up her messages and turned toward her office just as Wanda hung up.

"Hold it. Another one here. Your *maman* wants you to call her your guest list today."

Chloe's shoulders sank. "Good grief."

"For Roger's dinner party for the fat cats," Wanda added, her opinion plain in her tone. "Not, of course, that she would put it that way."

"Of course not." Chloe's mouth quirked.

"Don't your *maman* know more fat cats than you do, *chère?*"

"Wanda—"

Wanda shrugged. "Just askin'. It's not like you ain't got better things to do." Her eyes sparkled. "Not as if you got an important job or anything. Sure not as important as your fiancé's campaign to rule the world."

"He's not my—"

"You ever gonna clue that man in, girl? Or your folks? He don't stir your blood. Bores the hell out of you, in fact, so what are you waiting for?"

"Wanda, I can't—" Chloe glanced at her watch. She had ten minutes before her first appointment. "I know you mean well. And I've tried to make them understand that I'm not ready—"

"You'd be ready if the right man came along, I promise you that. How come a woman who can see into other people's heads can't see what she's doing to herself? You're more than they think, Chloe. You deserve better than some Ken doll."

The restlessness that had been boiling higher and higher within her for months rattled the lid she'd slammed on it. "I'm trying to be fair to all of them, Wanda. This will be a tough campaign, and I don't want to make things harder on Roger." *And I can't upset my parents right now.* "I have to make a call before this first appointment."

Wanda held up a hand. "All right. I've said my piece, *chère*. But I just want you to think about why you turn yourself inside out for everyone, trying to be two different people when you know you don't like one of them."

"Thank you, Dr. Wanda," Chloe said stiffly.

With a cheerful grin, Wanda waved her on. "Don't think you're insulting me with that. Some folks don't need a Ph.D. to see what's right."

Chloe relented. "I thank you for caring. I just—"

Wanda's hand fluttered. "Go on and make your call. You'll do what you'll do—and I'll be here, regardless."

Chloe found a smile. "And I'm glad for it—sometimes." She closed the door as Wanda's husky laughter filled the room.

VINCE HAD LOST TRACK of how many times he'd paged Gloria in between answering stupid phone calls in the chief's office. He already knew it was useless; she wasn't going to answer.

What he didn't understand was why.

Could Krueger have suspected him and used her to set him up? Had Gloria just lost her nerve about leaving Krueger and warned him? But the raid hadn't had the feel of a setup; he'd developed a sixth sense for that long ago.

And how had Barnes and Newcombe even found

Gloria to obtain her denial? She'd have had to approach them because he'd never broadcast her name. Confidential informants came and went, but Gloria had been his CI for a long time. She had kept her head about drugs better than most prostitutes. She'd never touched the deadly addictive high of crack, though he was aware that she'd sold it. Within her was a woman who wanted badly to be a good mother to Jason—that desire had probably saved her.

He'd tried to convince her to go straight, to return to school, to apply for assistance with her son. She'd only shaken her head sadly as though he were demented. Her mother had been on welfare—she knew the score. "You never get out of that system, Vince. I'm making the most money I can this way. Minimum wage won't take care of my boy."

Vince shook off his sense of futility. He'd keep looking for Gloria, but at the moment he had to figure out what was going on by some other route. He'd have to dig up information fast. He couldn't put himself at the mercy of IAD's investigation, especially not with Newcombe on the case.

He didn't trouble himself with worry that he was going against the regs, that if he were found investigating on the sly, he'd be off the force in the blink of an eye. Department legend said he had the best nose for sniffing out undercurrents others couldn't find. Well, now he'd use it on his own behalf. If he took the rap on this case, it wouldn't matter—he'd lose his job anyway. He couldn't just sit on his hands and wait.

Then Vince remembered Gloria's mentioning a

friend of hers who'd left an abusive boyfriend a couple
of weeks ago. Her friend was staying at the Women's
Shelter, Gloria had told him. Maybe he'd get lucky and
find out where Gloria was. He needed some answers.
Bad.

CHLOE SAT VERY STILL, willing herself to be calm, to
keep her mind clear. The woman in the chair across
from her stared at the Women's Shelter's frayed blue
carpet, eyes unblinking. Chloe knew scenes of horror
played on the carpet as if on a movie screen; Danielle
was so very close to opening up. Chloe felt like holding her breath, all too conscious of how important this
stage was.

Danielle was a prostitute who'd sought refuge at the
shelter from her pimp. As with many prostitutes, she'd
likely been sexually abused as a child. When Danielle let
loose the protection denial afforded her, the pain would
be brutal. It had to happen, but both she and Danielle
would have to go through hell to get to the other side,
where healing was possible. It was the hardest part but
the most essential.

"Who hurt you, Danielle?" She saw the woman recoil
as if struck by an unseen blow.

Danielle's head shook violently. "No one hurt me."

"Who touched you?"

Danielle's body shrank away from the memories
Chloe could see crowding in on her. "Nobod—" She
choked on the word. A tear leaked from her right eye.

Chloe reached out, sliding her hands under Danielle's,
holding lightly. "He can't hurt you now. I'm here with

you. You can't shock me. I won't be disgusted." Pressing her advantage, she continued. "I understand."

Danielle's head snapped up. "You bitch—" She jerked away, but Chloe wouldn't release her. "Someone like you can't know what it was like, having them touch me, having their hands, their—" A sob broke free.

Then her hands tightened, squeezing Chloe's fingers in a vise. Chloe ignored the pain, concentrating on the woman before her.

Danielle began to rock, moaning softly. A keening erupted into a near scream. "I hate him." Her eyes flashed pure venom. "I want to kill him for what he did to me—it hurt, it hurt so bad—" Anguish shattered her frame. She dropped Chloe's hands and bent double, burying her head against her legs, hands gripping white knuckled at the back of her neck.

Chloe could barely hear her muffled voice. She slipped to her knees in front of Danielle and rubbed her hands over Danielle's back in long, soothing strokes, cradling the woman's head against her chest. "Tell me," she urged. "Release it."

Danielle uttered words of such horror, a child's sobs of terror, lost in a world gone evil and frightening. Chloe's heart ached, her gorge rose. She thought she could have killed the man herself if he'd been in the room.

But it wasn't her revenge to take. She drew in a deep, steadying breath. The body beneath her hands was wire tight and shivering.

"It wasn't your fault."

The woman shuddered. Her voice barely came

through. "He said I was too sexy, that he couldn't help himself."

"He was lying. He was an adult. You were a child. You did nothing wrong."

Danielle jerked upward, her body shaking, eyes crazed with pain. "Then why did it happen?" She went on, voice rising in anger. "Why me? Why didn't anyone stop him? How could he say it was my fault if it wasn't?"

She glanced toward the floor, and Chloe's relief at escaping those eyes shamed her.

"I wanted to be grown up," Danielle whispered. "I always did, even when I was very little. I couldn't wait to be big." Her gaze rose to Chloe's, eyes shifting rapidly, side to side. "If I'd stayed a little girl, he would have left me alone."

"No." Chloe's voice strengthened. She grasped Danielle's shoulders. "He didn't want a woman. He wanted a little girl."

"He's sick," Danielle shouted.

Chloe wanted to close her eyes in relief, but she didn't. "Yes." She nodded. "He is. *He* is, Danielle—not you. You did nothing to bring it on. He's the one who's to blame. You couldn't have stopped him." Seeing the woman's doubts, Chloe persisted. "There was nothing you could do to prevent it. Nothing."

Danielle wavered on the brink of trusting. Finally, she swallowed deeply and spoke. "Are you so sure?"

Chloe placed one hand on Danielle's hair, sliding the other arm around her shoulders, knowing that a safe touch was something prostitutes craved yet seldom received. It was the best way to let Danielle feel that she wasn't disgusting, wasn't subhuman. "Yes." Chloe pressed Danielle's head against her shoulder. "I'm absolutely sure."

Danielle's body collapsed, huge, shattering sobs shaking her frame. Chloe tightened her arm and stroked the woman's hair, murmuring sounds of comfort. "Let it go, Danielle. Let it go." Her own eyes burned with unshed tears.

CHLOE WALKED OUT of the shelter, holding herself erect, fighting against the urge to scream, to pound at the earth, to raise her fists to the sky and curse God.

So much pain. What kind of world subjected children to such destruction? Sheer will propelled her to her car. She'd go home and shower and try to scrub away all that she'd absorbed from Danielle. Counselors needed walls, too, but if the walls were too strong, the counselor lost the ability to feel. Drained by Danielle's emotion, she had to fight to remember that she was separate from that woman, that her body had a boundary those stories shouldn't cross if she was to help.

A boundary regained at great cost. Right now every nerve was rubbed raw from bone-deep anger at adults who victimized children and set up cycles that passed down through generations. The world was full of Danielles who never got help breaking out of that self-hatred.

Despair swamped Chloe; the minuscule difference she could make felt so futile. Almost to her car, she suddenly knew she couldn't drive. Not yet. She headed for a nearby cluster of oaks, seeking shelter in their shade while she pulled herself together. She was so tired she could barely put one foot in front of the other.

"Doc, what are you doing here?"

She jerked around to stare at Vince Coronado, his hands filled with bags from a toy store. For a second, his appearance seemed fated. He would understand Danielle's pain and would have defended her. A part of Chloe craved his strength and his anger.

But yielding was unthinkable. "I could ask you the same," she challenged, glancing at the bags.

Color rose on his cheeks. He shrugged. "I'm visiting someone—" He shifted on his feet, then took a good look at her. "You okay?"

Compassion. Concern. Both crept beneath her meager defenses. Chloe focused on the trees. "I'm fine."

"I don't think so."

Refusing to give in to weakness, she pointed at his bundles. "For the children at the shelter?"

"Yeah." But he wouldn't be deterred. His voice turned gentle and coaxing. "Tell me what's wrong."

His kindness undid her. "Nothing," she insisted. Then it all caved in on her. *Only that my father is desperately ill and the world is an ugly place and—* "Excuse me, please. I just—"

She headed blindly for the shade. Darting behind the huge trunk of a very old oak, she crossed her arms over her chest, hands gripping her shoulders. Lips pressed together, she squeezed her eyes shut as though she were a child who believed that would make her disappear.

Vince dropped the bags on the lone scarred picnic

table and followed. He wanted to shake her out of the obvious lie, yet she appeared so fragile and distraught that he obeyed a different impulse. "Come here," he said, laying a comforting hand on her shoulder.

At first she held herself erect. Then her shoulders sagged toward him. Awkwardly, Vince slid an arm around her, feeling her delicate frame tremble. Wanting to shield her from whatever had upset her so badly, he began to draw her against him.

Instantly, she went rigid, stepping back, arms tight around herself once more. "I apologize, Detective." The soft, vulnerable woman straightened into military rigor, rapidly disappearing inside the icy woman who'd sat across the desk from Vince only the day before. "That was unprofessional. Absolutely inexcusable."

The transformation was so complete he could have almost convinced himself he'd imagined her earlier distress, except that his body retained the feel of her curves against him. But that woman was gone, and the one standing in her place was a cold, closed stranger.

It pissed him off. "Screw that." He moved toward her. "Chloe, I can help. You can talk to me."

"Thank you, but I don't need your help." Princess to peasant. "Please excuse me. I have to go now." Turning, no monarch ever made a more regal departure.

But her eyes gave her away. She wasn't tough enough for this world, and he couldn't afford to care. Vince quelled the urge to go after her, cursing roundly. He had to stay focused on his priorities, none of which had to do with a golden girl who could be unraveled by the world in which he was at home.

To find Gloria, to bring down Moreno, to save Tino meant he couldn't afford any distractions. All he required from Chloe St. Claire was his ticket back on duty, nothing else.

But still he watched her go, unable to escape the feeling that maybe even a princess might need a friend.

VINCE'S LONG STRIDES took the stairs at headquarters two at a time. He didn't want to chance crossing paths with the brass in the elevator; he was one of a handful of cops who liked using the stairs, anyway. He considered it simply part of his workout, along with lifting weights in the police gym.

But tonight he was also in a hurry. He hadn't found out anything from Gloria's friend, so he was switching gears for now. He wanted the file he'd assembled on Los Carnales. He might not get another chance to come up here until he was cleared. He'd only managed one day of dealing with complaints about traffic tickets and rerouting wrong calls to other city departments before his temper had gotten the best of him. Rather than do his career more damage, he'd grabbed a rookie who'd wandered in and convinced him it would enhance his record to volunteer free time to help out. Not that Vince was required to do the light duty. He had plenty of personal leave coming, but they'd expect him to be away from the premises if he wasn't going to finish his stint in the chief's office.

Sarge wouldn't be happy, but Sarge should be gone by now. Family life had settled well on him; he was religious about being home on time whenever possible.

"Hey, Vince, how's the Arctic Circle?" Fellow detective Jerry Akers looked up, probably loving Vince's predicament.

Vince zinged him back. "Screw you, too, Akers. Still in love with that drag queen?"

Akers flushed and made a crude gesture. Undercover cops could generally sniff out a female impersonator, but one had gotten past Akers last month, and no one would let him forget the guy's tongue in his ear on a buy-walk.

"A buy-walk means you pay but cancel, remember, Akers? You don't get to sample the merchandise."

"You know I didn't—" He raked his fingers through rapidly thinning hair. "That he-she just moved too fast."

"So you say, Akers. So you say." Vince winked and strolled past, hearing Akers muttering behind him. They barely tolerated each other. Vince couldn't stand cops who cut corners, and Akers was one who took the easy way out too often. Akers wouldn't have let Vince off the hook if the tables had been turned.

But it could have happened to any of them. Some of those guys could teach Cindy Crawford about being drop-dead gorgeous. Most of them were just ugly men with two pounds of makeup on their faces, but Vince had seen some himself that had caused him to do a double take.

Whistling softly, he sat down at his desk, dogged by the same strangeness that required a while to rub off after the few vacations he'd taken. That odd feeling where things don't quite fit anymore. *You* don't quite fit anymore.

He shrugged. Everything would be fine once he was cleared. All the more reason to dig in and find out where things had gone wrong. He withdrew his key ring, fingers coming to rest on the small key to the lateral file behind his desk. After swiveling in his chair, he unlocked the cabinet, his fingers going to the brown unmarked envelope folder mixed in with dead files in the back. If Woods caught him removing files while he was under IAD investigation, there'd be hell to pay. Never mind that this was his own and not related to his current assignments with the Eastside Gangsters. Vince was doubly glad he'd written all his notes in his oddball shorthand.

Quickly, he removed several sheets of paper from his Moreno file, folded them and stuffed them in the waist of his jeans, then loosened his shirttail and let it hang out.

Vince locked the file cabinet, then glanced around for something to take with him to explain why he'd been here. He seized upon a paperback thriller he'd left behind. No one had to know he'd already read it. Picking up the book, he rose from his chair and made for the door.

Sarge walked in at that moment. His eyebrows lifted slightly, then he nodded toward his office. "Got a minute?"

Oh, hell. Sarge was supposed to be gone by now. Vince gripped the paperback and followed him.

The door safely closed, Woods turned. "Thought you were in the chief's office."

Vince struggled to look unconcerned. "I, uh—oh, hell, Sarge, you know what that's like. If one more jerk called to ask why cops were writing tickets instead of putting criminals in jail—"

Woods chuckled. "Yeah, I do. So you're taking personal time, instead?"

Vince nodded. "Just forgot a book I've meant to read."

The piercing gaze told him Woods wasn't fooled. "I see. You wouldn't be up here trying to do a little work, would you?"

Sarge would never buy an outright denial. "Would you let me?"

"Vince, I don't like it any better than you, but we have to let the system play out. I understand that it's grinding at you not to be on duty, but don't do anything stupid."

The papers at his waist burned like a brand. Vince seized on a distraction. "How's Carol?"

Woods narrowed his gaze. "She's fine."

"Got any baby pictures?" Vince hoped to trade on Sarge's devotion to his family. Carol Woods had polished his rough edges and given Sarge a family life most cops could only dream of.

"Got a whole stack of 'em." But his gaze said he wasn't buying. "How's it going with St. Claire?"

"It's going." Vince forced himself to meet Sarge's eyes. He shrugged. "She's not so bad."

"Good, good." A ponderous silence fell between

them. "Vince, you know I wish I could—" Words he shouldn't voice spoke from his eyes.

"Yeah." All his men understood Sarge's loyalty to them. "Nothing to do but wait it out. I'll be all right. Newcombe can't nail me."

Both men shifted uneasily, the knowledge that Newcombe could hurt him anyway hanging in the air between them. An IAD officer with an ax to grind looked to support his theory, not acquit the cop.

"Listen, I'll keep my ear to the ground. You just concentrate on putting the doc's mind at rest. I need you back and not taking stupid chances."

A tightness in his throat, Vince nodded quickly. "Thanks, Sarge."

Woods straightened and clapped him on the shoulder. "Now scram, Coronado. Go get some rest—you're gonna wish you had when you're back on the job."

Vince shot him a brief smile and left, hoping to God that Sarge was right. He needed back in the game. Soon.

THE NEXT MORNING, Chloe was well aware that she was being a coward, but she could not face Vince Coronado yet. She was still too embarrassed by how she'd lost her composure with him. Besides, he hadn't wanted these sessions, anyway. He'd be relieved. "Wanda, please call Detective Coronado and cancel our appointment for today."

Red curls bounced as Wanda glanced up. "Something wrong?"

"No, I just have a conflict."

"You have an opening late this afternoon."

"I can't—" Seeing Wanda's curious glance, Chloe straightened, trying for the cool expression her mother used to such effect. One eyebrow arched; her voice was neutral. "Detective Coronado will be glad for the break."

She didn't think Wanda was convinced, but the woman didn't argue. "When shall I reschedule?"

"I'll get back to you on that." Chloe walked to her office before Wanda could ask another question she wasn't ready to answer. He *would* be glad. He didn't want to talk to her. Chloe pushed away the memory of the promise she'd made that he could trust her. She wouldn't let him down. She only sought a little time, a little distance. It was for his own good.

Sure it was. Chloe's mouth twisted at the attempt to delude herself. Over the course of a restless night, she'd thought about him too often. Unnerved by how he made her feel.

For one treacherous moment, his simple compassion had undone her. She'd wanted to lean into that awkward hug and let his strength surround her. It was absurd. Unthinkable. She simply needed to regroup, then the cool professional would invite Vince Coronado back and finish his evaluation.

After that she'd send him on his way, never to cross paths again, God willing.

VINCE DRANK his coffee, staring into the soft green shadows that would all too soon give way to blistering heat.

A loud purring broke his concentration. "If you'd catch that mouse that's been into the birdseed, there's another week's food in it for you."

Yellow eyes blinked at him with disinterest. Licking one paw, the tomcat swiped at his fur.

"Tell you what—you work on the mouse thing until tomorrow, then we'll renegotiate. My final offer—take it or leave it."

His pager beeped. He checked it, punched in numbers on the phone, then pulled at dangling strips of old paper. "Coronado."

"It's Wanda, Vince. Chloe, uh, Chloe has a conflict with your appointment this afternoon. She'll have to reschedule."

He frowned. Conflicts happened, but he didn't like the odd note in Wanda's voice. "Okay. When?"

"She said she'd let me know."

Suddenly, what Vince would have done anything to avoid days ago he now wanted. He didn't have time to waste. It had nothing to do with worry about her, not really, except that all night he'd thought about—

"Vince?"

He shook himself. "Yeah?"

"Something happen between you two?"

Vince narrowed his gaze. "Why would you ask that?"

"She seems…I don't know. A little shaky today. I've never seen her like this. I suppose it might be the King of Hair Spray, but Chloe's never cared that much. When she mentioned you, though, she—" Wanda sighed. "Just wondered."

The King of Hair Spray. Vince didn't want to feel the small tug of satisfaction that he unsettled her and Barnes didn't. The only thing worse than trusting Chloe St. Claire would be falling for her. "Sure. No sweat. Tell her I'll try to make time whenever she's ready, but no promises."

"Vince—"

"Goodbye, Wanda." He could still hear her protesting as he hung up the phone.

"Son," he said to the fur-laden muncher, "my best advice to you—stay away from women altogether."

CHAPTER SIX

VINCE STARTED in the bars along East Eleventh, looking for Tino. If he didn't find him there, he'd continue
onward to the topless joints favored by Los Carnales. If
it took all night and the next week running, he'd track
Tino down and figure out exactly what was happening
with his friend.

His foul mood had the bar patrons giving him wide
berth. He didn't have time for her to hold him up, damn
it. Whatever was going on with Chloe St. Claire, she
didn't have the right to string him along.

At the fourth bar, he found Tino shooting craps in
the back room.

"Hey, *carnal*," Tino greeted. "Whassup?"

Had Vince been in a better mood, he'd grin about how
Latino gangs had adopted black lingo. But he wasn't.
With a jerk of his head, he stalked outside.

Tino took his time about it, but he followed.
"What's with you, man? Why you dis me in front of
my friends?"

Vince rounded on him. "Where the hell have you
been?"

Pride stuck out all around Tino like thorns on a
cactus. He walked away, shooting Vince the finger.

Vince exhaled. "Okay, wait up. I'm sorry."

Tino stopped but didn't turn back.

"Look, I've got a boatload of crap to deal with right now, and…" He paused. "I was worried about you."

"Me?" Tino turned. "Why?"

"Because you were a stupid little kid and I got in the habit, all right?"

Tino rolled his eyes, but his shoulders relaxed. "I ain't been a little kid in a long time, *pendejo*." The epithet was uttered with reluctant fondness.

Vince grinned. "But I can still take you."

"Bet me—" Tino feinted and managed to clip Vince on the arm. "You and me. Anytime, anywhere—"

Vince slugged him on the shoulder. "I'm a lover nowadays, not a fighter."

Tino laughed. "Yeah, right." Then he sobered. "You give it any thought, what I said the other night?"

"I did." Vince cocked his head. "The answer's no."

"Listen to me, man—" Tino looked desperate. "I need your help. What I meant was—" he glanced over his shoulder "—I want out, Vince."

That got Vince's attention. "Why?"

Tino's gaze danced around, scanning the shadows, dusting the ground. "It's Leticia and Tino Junior. I don't want my boy caught in a drive-by someday." When his eyes lifted, Vince saw truth and more than a little fear.

"You really want out?" Vince asked. "All the way out?"

Something dark flared in Tino's eyes. "Yeah, but I'm

not stupid. I know it ain't gonna work. But if I could get Leticia and Tino Junior someplace safe—"

"I can make it happen for all of you," Vince interrupted. Tino was right, no one resigned from gang life. You were in or you were dead. But an idea was forming, and he thought rapidly.

Prison had removed every last trace of the naive kid in Tino. "I don't think so."

His idea was a long shot, but to save Tino and get Moreno, too… "I know a way," Vince said.

"Digame." Tell me.

"You help me take Moreno down," Vince said. "And I'll get all three of you into the Witness Protection Program."

"You lost your mind?"

"He murdered Carlos."

"He was in prison. And he don't do his own dirty work," Tino sneered.

"You know that and I know that, but he ordered the hit and I'm going to prove it." Vince leaned closer. "No matter what else happened, Carlos was good to you, Tino. He cared about you and me the way no one else did."

Tino's eyes shifted. "He's dead, Vince. He ain't comin' back, no matter what you do."

Vince's jaw tightened. "I can't let this go. If it takes the rest of my life, Moreno's going to pay."

"You are one *loco hombre.* You got a death wish? Moreno could have you killed just like that—" He snapped his fingers, and the sound echoed in the darkness. "Forget him, man. It won't change anything."

"So you didn't mean it when you said you wanted out for Tino Junior and Leticia."

"Hell, yes, I—" Tino cursed long and loud. "Vince, man, you can't do this by yourself."

"I will if I have to," Vince said. "But I could use your help." He played the card he'd never before played. "And you owe me. You know you do."

For endless moments, they studied each other. In Tino's eyes, Vince could see doubt and fear and a hint of hope.

Finally, Tino spoke. "Maybe that's true, but you can't collect if you're dead. Give it up, bro. It's crazy."

"Are you in or out?" Vince refused to let him look away.

After a long, tense pause, Tino's shoulders sagged. "You really think you can get us protection?" He frowned. "We'd have to leave everyone behind."

"That's right."

"Feds don't take small-timers."

"This won't be small-time. I'm going for federal charges. *Day for day.*" It was a code phrase veteran cons used to signify a sentence with no parole. "You help me make this case, they'll take you."

Cynicism slowly gave way to a trust that had once filled a young boy's eyes every time he'd looked at Vince. "What do I have to do?"

Worry swamped Vince almost as quickly as gratitude. He'd meant it when he said he'd do it alone, but Tino was closer to the inside and everything would go much faster with his help. But Tino would be in danger. "I'm not asking you to stick your neck out big. Just let me register you as my informant on the Eastside Gangsters—"

"What? You crazy, man? Eastsiders are part of the L.A. Bandidos. They're sworn enemies of Los Carnales."

Vince held up a hand. "It's a smoke screen. It won't draw attention to you if anyone bothers to check. I'm not supposed to be working Los Carnales, but with you registered as my snitch for Eastside, we can get together anytime and no one on the force knows that I'm gathering information on Moreno."

"Where you plan to get that information?"

"You, of course. But you'll be meeting me in Eastside territory, so Moreno won't know."

"*Cristo,* Vince, you don't want much, do you? I get caught on Eastside turf and I'm dead anyway."

"We'll be careful." Vince hardened his tone. "And I mean that, Tino. You watch your back."

"You're playing a dangerous game yourself, eh, *carnal?* I already heard that Quintanilla is a cold case and nobody's working it."

"I'm working it."

"But not with permission."

Vince eyed Tino and shook his head. "No. But I'm going to get Moreno anyhow."

Tino's eyes shifted uneasily. "You gotta promise me that if anything happens to me or you, Leticia and Tino Junior will be okay or I'm outta here, you got that?"

Vince nodded. "Yeah. I have a friend who'll take care of it. I'll talk to him right away."

Tino shook his head. "You are one crazy mother. When this is finished, I don't owe you nothin'."

"Agreed. Okay, listen up. Here's how we'll work the meets." With a few short instructions, he set out his plan.

Now all he had to do was smoke the good doctor out of hiding and convince her to put him back on active duty.

She didn't have a chance.

IN THE HEAT of late afternoon, Chloe inserted her key in the car door.

"I never took you for a coward, Doc."

Chloe fumbled the keys, whirling and clasping one hand to her chest. "Vince—Detective," she gasped. "What—what are you doing here?"

He stood there, tall and dark and entirely too disturbing. "Why'd you cancel?"

"Surely Wanda told you I had a schedule conflict."

"So she said. But you didn't offer an alternative." Vivid blue eyes called her bluff, those firm lips quirking at one corner, revealing the dimple that so contradicted his raw power. "I'm ready to reschedule."

"I—I don't keep my appointments calendar with me. Call Wanda tomorrow."

"And will she find an opening?"

Chloe glanced away. "I'm sure she will."

"Positive, Doc?"

Flight seemed the best recourse, yet his gaze dared her to concede to her fear. She reached behind her for the car's door handle, fingers fidgeting against the chrome. "Yes."

He glanced the length of her vehicle, one dark eyebrow lifting. "I thought a Tarrytown lady had to drive a luxury SUV or some sporty coupe, Doc." He grinned and stuck his hands in his back jeans pockets, weight cocked on one hip. The dark blue T-shirt stretched tight across his muscled chest. A more compelling man Chloe had never met.

"My mother's the Tarrytown lady. *Consumer Reports* ranks this economy car one of the best." She sniffed, pulling her gaze away. "It's quite safe and reliable."

Vince tilted his head slightly, examining her in minute detail. Softly, he challenged, "Do you always choose safety, Chloe?" His eyes warred with his mocking tone.

Suddenly, Chloe almost wished she didn't.

He straightened, pulling his hands from the pockets. His expression was all seriousness now. "Come with me. Let me buy you a drink."

She shouldn't want to go with him, but she did. "You're my client. I can't."

"You abandoned me. I'm not your client now."

Chloe gasped in outrage. "I did not. I would never—"

He chuckled. "But you did chicken out on me—admit it."

What could she say? He was too perceptive by far.

Vince saved her the answer. "Come on, Chloe, give me a chance. It's just a drink. Who knows? You might even get me drunk and make me spill my guts. I'm safe—I swear it." He drew a cross over his heart, holding up the other palm in a pledge.

She'd never met a man less safe. But by-the-book didn't always work. She'd assured him she wouldn't let him down, but she'd been very close to doing exactly that, out of fear that she couldn't control a man with such potent appeal.

She wanted to laugh at her own foolishness. One didn't control a man like Vince Coronado; she was foolish to try. Finally, she did smile. "There's absolutely nothing safe about you, Vince."

Even knowing that she was walking straight into the den of the lion, she couldn't recall the last time she'd felt so alive. Maybe this was the opportunity she needed to win his trust. It could be simply another session in a different setting, not personal at all. Sometimes you learned more on a client's turf.

"All right, you win."

The slash of even white teeth against his olive skin was her reward. He gestured the way with a sweep of one arm, the other hand grasping her elbow lightly. "This way, my lady. Your chariot awaits."

He led her between rows of cars, his manner solicitous and every inch the gentleman. When the space narrowed too much for them to walk side by side, he let go of her elbow and grasped her hand in his, leading the way.

The feel of his large warm hand around hers distracted Chloe; she bumped into his back when he stopped to reach for his keys. He leaned to unlock the door and swung it wide, but Chloe couldn't get in just yet.

First, she had to gawk at the gleaming black convertible. "A T-bird?"

"Sixty-four." He grinned.

"Vince, it's beautiful. Do you drive it all the time?"

He lifted one shoulder. "I'm not into museum pieces. If you can't use it, what's the good of having it?"

"But aren't you afraid of—" Chloe stopped herself. "I guess you don't choose safety, do you?"

Blue eyes speared her. "Never."

Wishes and needs tumbled together. In that moment, she remembered how safe she'd felt for those few seconds under the oaks. A long gaze passed between them.

Chloe broke the link, stepping toward the car and sliding into the roomy, plush seat. Movement behind him caught her attention. A young female patrol officer with a long, dark braid shot her a look of pure venom.

Vince followed the direction of her glance. "Hey, Sal, what's up? Doc, this is Sally Davis. Sally, this is Chloe St. Claire."

The young woman barely nodded at Chloe, her eyes riveted on Vince. The soft plea Chloe witnessed spoke volumes. She wondered if Vince knew Officer Davis was in love with him.

And how much of that love he returned.

He excused himself and stepped away with the younger woman, participating in an intense conversation. His demeanor gave nothing away; he was all business.

But what business? None of hers, she reminded herself.

They finished quickly. The young woman turned to go.

"Nice to meet you, Officer Davis," Chloe called out.

Murmured politeness warred with the woman's fierce expression.

Vince climbed into the driver's seat and started the engine. "You want the top down or up?"

"Either's fine," Chloe said. "She's in love with you."

"No, she's not. She just—" He got out, busying himself with the ragtop. His forehead creased. "I was her training officer and I hadn't been divorced long. I—I didn't handle things well for a little while there."

"She fell in love with you, but you were on the rebound." An old story.

His jaw clenched. "She's not in love with me, Doc. Stop playing shrink. I made a mistake, all right? It's been corrected. It was a long time ago." He finished fastening the top down and got back inside, then shifted the car into gear and pulled away.

Chloe didn't know why she persisted. "She's not over you, Vince. Don't kid yourself."

Tapping the brakes, he faced her, pain in his gaze. "Look, Doc, I screwed up. I knew better—she was just a kid. I don't encourage her, and she accepts that this is the way it has to be." Staring out the windshield, he seemed to contemplate elaborating. Then, shaking his head, he sighed. "I'm not proud of what I did, and I've tried to set things right."

"I'm sorry, it's none of my business."

He exhaled, and tense shoulders settled. "It's okay. I shouldn't be so touchy about it."

"Divorce is never easy, and each person deals with the pain in a different way." Chloe was surprised at how much she wanted to know about the woman who'd been married to Vince Coronado and had lost him.

He gave the car gas. "No—" his voice tightened "—it's not easy. A cop's wife has a bad lot. She never knows each morning when he leaves if she'll ever see him again. The knowledge eats up a lot of women. A family makes a cop vulnerable, too—if he can't focus, he'll blow it. Single is the best state for us."

"But a family can give love and support."

His harsh laughter chilled her. "I wouldn't know about that."

She glanced over at his stony profile. "Have you met any of your relatives?"

"Nope. Don't care to, either."

"Have you ever tried to find out who your father was?"

The white grip of his knuckles would have alerted her, even if the set of his jaw hadn't. "Yeah, once, when I was still married. I thought maybe my kids should meet their grandparents."

Her heart sank. "You have kids?"

"No." His curt tone warned her off. "We're not in the office, Doc. I said *maybe* I'd spill my guts, all right?

Cut me some slack. It's just a damn drink." He stared straight ahead, his jaw flexing.

Coming had been a mistake. "Perhaps you should take me back."

Vince's head jerked around, his gaze fiery. He stared at her for a long moment, then twisted to watch the traffic. With ease, he slid the T-bird into a parking spot. "Forget it, we're here. You can tough it out."

"Vince, I—" Too late. He was already rounding the hood. Drawing a deep breath, she stepped from the car, moving away from him quickly. "Fine. I'll call a cab."

"Oh, hell—" His hand shot out and snagged her elbow, turning her toward him with gentle but irrevocable force. "I'm sorry, Chloe. You don't deserve my anger. I just—" He glanced away, then back. "I've got a lot on my mind, and I'm not too good with women anyway. I've never figured out how to handle them right." His eyes crinkled with his grin. "No big news there, huh?"

Chloe thought of his kindness under the oaks, of the gentle way he'd spoken to Sally. "No, I'm the one who owes the apology. Curiosity about people is a part of my makeup, but I went too far. The difficulty of drawing the line is why I don't mix business and pleasure."

His hand slid down to hers, warm fingers clasping, his thumb stroking across the back of her hand. His smile almost boyish, he glanced at her, dimple deep and disarming. "But you're already here. Let's call a truce, okay? Start all over?" With his free hand, he traced another cross over his heart. "I'll add not being touchy to the list of promises."

He was wrong about his effect on women. That smile alone was a killer. "All right." She nodded. "A new start."

VINCE HAD NEVER expected Chloe to be funny. Beneath that cool elegance lay a shyness that surprised him, along with a wicked sense of humor. Maybe the drink had relaxed her, but she'd only had one glass of wine. He'd like to think that perhaps their truce had helped. The first few minutes had been awkward, but they'd finally found something in common when he'd discovered that she loved playing darts. At last she appeared more comfortable around him.

He sure felt easy with her. This was what he'd needed: a respite from the gnawing in his gut, the sense of impotence when he had so much to accomplish.

Standing behind her, he scanned her from the honey-gold hair over a figure with more curves than he would have first guessed, all the way down long, long legs to trim ankles. She'd doffed her suit jacket, leaving her arms bare; she'd kicked her heels off under the table, and the tight French twist had strands escaping everywhere. Just now, her concentration was focused on only one thing—the dartboard in front of her.

Vince smiled. A fierce competitor, too—that had surprised him. She'd always seemed as if nothing really ruffled her, except that evening at the shelter. He was realizing that he'd bought into the facade, but beneath the patrician appearance lay someone altogether different, someone fascinating and elusive. Vince found himself wanting to uncover all her secrets.

You've got plenty else to investigate, Vince. Leave her alone. But the Vince who dared much cast sense to the winds and moved closer behind Chloe. "You're going to bite off that tongue if you don't stop sticking it out before you throw," he murmured beside her ear.

She stiffened slightly but tossed a smirk in his direction. "Out of my way, Detective. You're just hoping to throw me off."

"And your point is…?"

She merely arched one slender eyebrow.

Damn, he wanted to touch her. He put up his hands in surrender but only backed up about six inches.

He could still feel the heat of her all along the front of him, and his body responded. Instead of grabbing her waist with both hands the way he'd prefer, he settled for one escaping lock of her hair, sliding it through his fingers.

Chloe went still. But she didn't move away.

He exhaled, stirring the wisps at her nape.

A shiver rippled through her. From his height, he could see her nipples peak beneath the thin silk of her blouse. The hand that held the dart trembled, but she didn't turn around.

This was insane. Swallowing hard, he moved aside, striving to lighten things. "You know, you've got one hell of an aim."

"Thanks." Her gaze darted toward him and quickly back.

"For a girl, that is." He grinned.

Her chin rose. "Those are fighting words, Detective." Squaring her shoulders, she studied the board.

Vince looked down for a brief second, aware that he'd just dodged a bullet. He had to be crazy to even consider letting this go any further.

Chloe did a little skip-dance and clapped, eyes sparkling as she pointed out the dart sitting squarely in the center.

Well, hell. Everybody knew he had a taste for danger.

THE RIDE BACK to her car passed in silence. He wanted, more than was wise, to shoot past the right exit and take her home with him, but even if he thought she'd let him, he didn't dare. Tino was supposed to make contact tonight.

Chloe sat, legs curled beneath her, head leaning against one hand, elbow propped against the door frame. Light shifted over her as they passed each street lamp, tendrils of hair escaping her tight French twist, flying in the breeze swooping over the windshield. He kept waiting for her to ask him to put the top up, but she seemed not to mind the whip of the wind.

"Home Warehouse," she murmured. "I've spent a bundle in that place."

Vince did a double take at the superstore that carried everything from lumber to faucets to nails. "You go there?"

She turned toward him. "You, too?"

It was hard to tell who was more surprised. "Oh, yeah. I bought this fixer-upper in Travis Heights that should have come with a warning tag—Lifetime Project."

Chloe laughed. "Mine could have the same. What's your least favorite thing?"

He was still trying to imagine her doing any type of home repair at all. "That's easy. Plumbing."

"I leave that to the experts." Her smile grew. "But there's something rewarding about refinishing wood floors."

Vince glanced down at those slim, perfect hands. "You refinished your own floors?"

"Careful, Detective. Your snobbery is showing."

"I'm no snob. It's just that—"

She began to laugh. "The look on your face is priceless. My mother gets that same expression of horror that her perfect little girl likes to get dirt on her hands."

Vince studied her, marveling at the thought. "You're not kidding, right? You really did your own wood floors?"

"Every last one. Also stripped and stained all the trim in my house."

"I'll be damned."

Chloe chuckled. "You don't exactly look like the Bob Vila type yourself, Vince."

He shot her an appreciative grin. "Surprised the hell out of me, too, but there's something about—" He glanced over. "Don't suppose you like to wallpaper?"

That wide, lush mouth curved at the corners. "I had to redo the first room three times to get it right, but I could practically teach a wallpapering class now."

"Good," he said, forgetting all the reasons why it could never work. "A demo, then, this Saturday. My kitchen."

"You think I'm going to volunteer to wallpaper when I don't have to?"

"It would be a service to mankind."

She giggled. Dr. Cool and Elegant…giggling. "To one man, you mean. Chicken. Learn the hard way, as I did."

"I'll feed you like a queen. Fix breakfast, lunch and take you to dinner when we're through," he wheedled.

"You hate wallpapering that badly?"

"I stink at wallpapering. Have mercy, Chloe. My house deserves the best."

She stared at him. "You love it, don't you?"

He nodded. "I never had a place of my own before."

When sympathy swamped her eyes, he shook it off. "Don't start feeling sorry for me. Where's your house, Tarrytown?"

"Rosedale."

He knew his surprise showed. "Is that allowed for society ladies?"

"You really are a prisoner of your prejudices, aren't you? My mother and you would get along well."

"Somehow I don't think that's a compliment."

"It's not. My mother can't stand that I'm straying from the preordained path. She and my father—" Her voice caught, and she fell silent.

"You okay?" When she didn't answer, he found a place to pull over. "What's wrong?"

"It's nothing." But the stiff set of her shoulders made a lie of her words.

Vince knew the smart thing was to let it go. He had

plenty on his plate—more than enough. But he remembered her valiant insistence on refusing comfort under
the trees. Thought about how hard she tried not to recoil
at the sordidness she encountered through this job when,
best he could tell, she'd led a sheltered life.

And he realized something else about Chloe St.
Claire. She was a giver, when most of the people he'd
ever met were takers, including him. He wondered again
what motivated someone like her who could have any
luxury, who could avoid contact forever with the seami-
ness of the real world, to tackle the job she had.

She might have been raised a princess, but she didn't
expect to be treated as one.

He was the least likely prospect, but a part of him
wished he could be the shining knight she deserved.
Lacking that, he could at least be a friend. "You're a lot
better at giving out help than you are at accepting it,
aren't you, Doc? You ever think that's a damn selfish
attitude?"

Her head whipped around. Frost invaded her voice.
"I don't believe I deserve that, Detective."

She was right. And she probably had a boatload of
friends to comfort her, but they weren't here. "Princess
to peasant, eh?" he goaded.

"What?" Icicles melted against fury. "You have no
right—"

He shrugged. "That's true. But something's bother-
ing you, and I'm here with time on my hands, thanks to
Newcombe. So just pretend I'm a wall and talk to me
about what's got you worried."

For long seconds, she was silent. Vince was almost

ready to give up, when she spoke. "My parents have sheltered me all my life as though I were fine crystal that would break at the slightest touch." Her voice trembled again, but when he looked at her, he realized that anger was causing it.

"Overprotective?"

One corner of her mouth quirked. "To put it mildly." Then sorrow darkened those golden-brown eyes again. "I just discovered that they've been hiding from me that my father has been diagnosed with leukemia and may need a bone-marrow transplant." Sad eyes sparked. "And they refuse to let me be tested as a donor—" Her gaze whipped to his. "I'm twenty-seven years old, and they're treating me like a child."

He'd never been a child. "So what's holding you back? Go get tested anyway."

Mutiny tightened her lips. "I made the appointment today."

"Good for you."

"But they'll be so furious. Mother says I'll make Daddy worse if I admit that I know. He's sure he'll solve this himself and that his little girl doesn't need to worry her pretty little head over it."

Vince had to laugh. "He really doesn't understand you, does he?"

She looked startled. "Why do you say that?"

"If I ever met a more stubborn woman in my life, I can't recall it. Oh, you look like some sort of arm candy, all right, but I knew that first night that I might as well give up and let you do whatever it was you were determined to do."

"Really?" He heard pride and wonder in her voice. Then she shot him a sideways glance. "You did not. You bring new meaning to the word *stubborn*."

He threw his hands wide. "I promise. Gave up right then."

Her somber gaze eased. "You are such a liar." Her lips curved.

At that moment, he wanted to grab her and drag her off somewhere private, away from investigations and gangs and—

Moreno. Tino. He had a better chance now to prove that Moreno murdered Carlos, and he couldn't let any momentary attraction, however tempting, deter him from justice.

And she had Roger Barnes, who wanted to nail him. As well as a life that could never include someone like him, no matter this momentary rebellion at its restrictions.

"Doc, I need back on duty."

All trace of animation drained from her face. He watched as Dr. Cool and Elegant took over the body that had housed the laughing, cutthroat darts player. She stared out of the windshield of the car, as still as stone.

Vince cursed beneath his breath. "I'm sorry." But that changed nothing. "I didn't mean—"

She cut him off, hands folded carefully in her lap. "If you'd take me to my car or let me off so I can call a cab—"

"Chloe." He clasped her arm. "I'm sorry. I wish I could make you understand, but—"

"I understand perfectly. You took me out to soften me up so I would see things your way."

"Damn it, listen to me." But if he explained his urgency, it would only feed into Sarge's concern that he'd lost balance, that he was pushing too hard on a case that wasn't his. He ground his teeth. "It wasn't that way. I had a great time."

"I should never have gone with you." Her tone was so neutral he might as well have been a bug on the sidewalk. "It won't happen again."

"It will."

"It can't," she insisted.

Vince called himself every foul name he could think of. He'd probably set his cause back by weeks. In a vile mood, he started the car and took off, tires squealing.

"Let me out," she demanded. "I'll get a cab."

"Don't push me," he growled. "I said I'd take you back, and I will."

The rest of the trip played out in a silence that grated on his nerves. Tension throbbed in the air until he could barely breathe. As he drove through the department parking garage, he wondered how in the hell to salvage the mess he'd made.

He was still pondering what to say when he found her car.

She reached for her purse and grasped the door handle. He reached past her and jammed down the lock.

"If you try to stop me from leaving, Detective, I'll be forced to report you." Beneath her brave words, her voice quivered with nerves.

"You can do that," he admitted. "But I don't imagine you want to be revealing where you were this evening."

If anything, her frame stiffened more.

Vince dropped his head for a second and struggled to contain the temper that had always been his Waterloo. "Look, Chloe—"

"I don't think first names are appropriate."

"You really don't want to be called a pampered princess, I suggest you take that snotty tone out of your voice."

Her head whipped around and he saw not icy control but blazing fury.

And the glistening sheen of tears held back by the barest margin.

It leached the anger right out of him. "I'm sorry, Doc." He exhaled loudly. "My damn temper will be the death of me. And my big mouth." He held her gaze, willing her to listen. "Look, I had a great time with you back there."

"It doesn't matter," she said softly. "You're my client. We can't do this."

Then cut me loose, he wanted to say. *I've got to get back to work.* But he reined in his disastrous way with words. "How much longer do I need to be your client? You don't really believe I have a death wish, do you? Sarge worries too much."

He thought he saw a trace of amusement before she turned her head away and discreetly wiped at her eyes. "No," she admitted. Then her gaze met his. "But

I do think that there's a lot more going on than you're admitting. We should discuss that."

Vince wanted to groan. Wanted to howl. "The bad guys don't stop working just because I'm on leave, Chloe."

"I know." Her voice was whisper quiet. "Call Wanda in the morning and work out a time, even if I have to stay late."

His head whipped around and he stared at her. "You're going to cut me loose."

Sorrow and wisdom and rue swirled in her gaze. "Maybe. But first we have to talk."

He resisted the urge to roll his eyes. She held the cards. "Tomorrow, then."

She grasped the handle. "Good night, Detective." With a whisk of hosiery across the seat cushions, she was gone.

"Good night, Doc." Despite the urge to burn rubber on the concrete, he forced himself to drive away slowly. He would prove to her that he was fit for duty if it killed him.

And it very well might.

FOR THE FIRST TIME she could ever remember, Chloe didn't want to go home. Didn't want to be alone. Maybe she would go back to her office. Catch up on paperwork.

Doc, I need back on duty.

None of it had been real; that was what hurt. Not the laughter or the teasing. Not the way he stood so close to her, nearly touching…the heat of his big strong body…

I had a great time.

For most of the evening, those words had appeared to be true. He'd shed the tension that hadn't left his frame since that first night at the crime scene. The intensity that was his trademark had been banked; for long moments, he'd seemed younger, more carefree, the way he might have been had life granted him a normal childhood. He was a fierce competitor, yes, and she appreciated it that he hadn't let her win. She'd had to battle for every point.

He even fought dirty. Chloe smiled. No one in her perfect, ordered life had ever done that to her.

At the memory of his hand lifting one lock of her hair from her neck…the feel of his breath upon her nape and how shockingly much she'd wanted him to press his lips just there—

Headlights entered the parking lot. Footsteps sounded, coming up the stairwell.

Chloe shook her head. None of that mattered. She had no reason to feel hurt. Vince Coronado was simply acting in his own self-interest, trying whatever methods would allow him to get back to the work at which he was so good. If he didn't care so much about being a cop, he wouldn't be so effective.

She was the one who'd studied the human psyche in such detail; none of what had happened should be a surprise.

Turning the key in the ignition, Chloe reminded herself that she had a job to do, and that was all that was important. She'd gambled that she could make inroads on understanding Vince by accompanying him into his world.

She wasn't a gambler by nature, and this only reminded her of why.

If you didn't risk, you didn't lose. She left the parking lot and headed home to resume her normal routine. To bed at a sensible hour so she'd be fresh for the next day's demands.

Even though one of them would be seeing Vince Coronado again.

VINCE ENTERED the Crystal Pistol, loud country music and cigarette smoke assaulting his senses. The cavernous interior would be tough to search if Mike didn't insist on claiming his own particular table every time. Vince veered to the right side of the room, spotting Mike's blond head easily.

The redhead on his friend's lap made it even simpler.

Vince watched as Mike pulled her head down for a long kiss, and wondered how many other women he'd charmed in the dark corners of this place. Dark corners, hell—Mike seduced them on the dance floor, at the bar, probably in the parking lot, too. A fair number he took home. Vince had had his share of women, but he preferred them one at a time. Mike went for quantity; he loved women easily, at the drop of a hat, the wink of an eye.

The redhead pulled back from Mike slowly, her expression dazed. Her squirming glance at Vince grabbed his buddy's attention, and Mike turned.

"Hey, man, decided to have a little fun for a change?" Mike's easy grin showed no embarrassment. The redhead tried to stand up, but Mike held her still with one arm across her thighs. "Come on, take a load off. Let's get you a beer."

His head already pounding from the noise, Vince shook his head. "Can I talk to you outside?"

Mike's gaze grew immediately serious. He spoke to the redhead. "Will you excuse me for a minute, Joanie darlin'?"

"Jo Nell," she corrected.

"Ah, but sugar, you look just like that cute Joanie from *Happy Days*."

She pouted prettily. "Joanie had dark hair."

"I mean those dimples of yours, sweet darlin'." He set her on her feet and stood. "And these luscious lips." Leaning down, he planted one more slow kiss. "You won't let any ol' shitkicker wander off with you while I'm gone, will you?"

Shoulders moving in a coquette's shrug, she showed some mettle. "Maybe...if you take too much time."

"Oh, my buddy here knows how to get to the point, don't you, Vince?"

Her gaze moved to him. Vince nodded. "I won't keep him long, Jo Nell."

Her smile revealed the deep dimples. "Thanks, Vince. Then you two come back—I've got a friend."

Mike slung an arm around Vince's neck. "Oh, sugar,

that's the pity of it. Vince here suffered a war wound, and he can't—"

Vince's elbow connected with Mike's midsection, and air expelled in a sharp gust. "Maybe another time, Jo Nell. But thank you."

Eyes soft with sympathy, the redhead smiled. "It didn't affect your dancing, did it, Vince?"

Mike guffawed.

"Go to hell, Mike," Vince muttered, stifling the urge to laugh himself. "My dancing's all right, thank goodness," he answered Jo Nell. "If you'll excuse us…" He all but dragged Mike to the door. Outside, the music still carried, but at least he could hear.

"What's up, buddy?" Mike wiped tears of amusement from his eyes.

Vince shot him a glare. "Real funny, man. She's too sweet for you."

"Yeah, but she hasn't figured it out yet." Mike sobered. "How are you?"

"More than ready to get back in the hunt."

"So what's the word? Doc signed off on you yet?"

Vince uttered one quick curse. "No."

"Don't tell me, you're being your usual sunny self."

"Bite me," Vince replied. "But that's not why I came."

Mike merely nodded for him to continue.

"I've got a new snitch, but he's nervous about his girlfriend and son taking heat if things go south. I told him I'd take care of them, but he's worried about what if something happens to me."

"What could happen—" Mike stopped in midsentence.

"He's heard about your threats to Moreno. But that was months ago."

Vince hesitated. He wasn't prepared to saddle Mike with the knowledge that he was still actively working to build a case against Moreno. If things went bad, he didn't want Mike taking any heat for being his friend. He shrugged. "He worries too much—not the hero type. He'll be a good source on the Eastsiders if I can get him to loosen up, but I had to promise him that someone else would help if there came a time when I couldn't."

"Sure, man, whatever," Mike said. "What's his name?"

"Tino Garza."

"Got it." Mike paused. "Any news on your other informant, the one who turned around on you?"

Vince grimaced. "Not yet."

"You know I'll do whatever I can."

"Yeah. I do." Vince clapped him on the shoulder and forced a grin. "Get on back in there with that little honey."

"You sure?" Mike's forehead wrinkled. "We could go grab a beer or something."

"Nah, been a long day. I'm headed for the sack."

"Okay, man. Call me if you need me."

"I will. You still owe me for that war-wound remark."

Laughing, Mike waved goodbye over his shoulder.

STARING OUT into the darkness, heat still rising off ground baked to a crisp, Vince rolled the brown beer bottle across his forehead, beads of cool moisture transferring to his skin. Stripped to shorts and sandals, he'd cleaned the last paper off the kitchen walls, hoping that physical labor would help as it had in the past, letting his mind sift through details to come up with an answer.

But nothing was clearer. He'd spent hours chasing down snitches, searching through bits and pieces of garbage, trying to find one piece of solid information. Junkies and hookers were the most unreliable people on earth. He'd learned long ago that out of the information he gathered, he'd have to winnow through bushels of chaff to get to one useful grain.

Only chaff today. No one seemed to know what had happened to Gloria. She'd apparently vanished as though she'd never existed.

His gate creaked, and Vince tensed. His off-duty weapon was in the house. He peered through the darkness.

"Vince? Are you out here? I knocked on the front door, but I guess—" Sally announced herself before she rounded the porch. She knew better than to sneak up on a fellow cop, especially one who operated undercover.

He leaned back on the porch rail. "Yeah, I'm here. Come have a seat." He could use some distraction from his thoughts.

Light from the kitchen window spilled across her form. She wore shorts and a tank top, her dark hair still braided. What he could see of her eyes looked pretty serious.

"Want a beer?"

"Yeah." She nodded. "But I can get it." She moved

past him, the screen door shutting softly behind her.
One of these days he'd install central heat and air, but
for now, window units bore the brunt of the duty. He'd
left them off while working, not wanting to feel closed
in by his house tonight.

Sally settled on the step just below him and to his
right. He studied the long braid bisecting her back, remembering a cascading, dark waterfall, and mentally
kicked himself for nearly ruining a friendship.

"Just get off duty?" He kept his voice light.

Sally nodded, then took a long swallow.

"Tough night?" The tension in her frame already said
yes.

She shrugged. "It's over."

Fur brushed past his leg and slipped next to her. Sally
jerked in surprise, then reached out to pet the animal.
Her head swiveled, eyebrows lifted. "A cat, Vince?"

He took a sip. "He's not staying."

She felt the cat's round belly, grinning. "You sure he
knows that?"

"We've had discussions."

Sally laughed, and Vince found himself suddenly
glad for the company. A loner by nature, to his ex-wife's
dismay, he hadn't realized until now just how much he'd
miss the job.

Something of his thoughts must have shown on his
face.

"Are you going crazy, being on leave?"

She'd opened the subject; now was the ideal time to
ask for her help, yet Vince was reluctant to involve her.
His gut told him he was in trouble this time, though,

maybe more than he could escape on his own. "I'm working on the house."

"That's not what I asked."

"I don't like sitting around, waiting for Newcombe to hand me my head on a platter."

"I never assumed you were idle." She turned toward him, and her eyes were warm and soft. "I told you I wanted to help, Vince. What can I do?"

Here was his chance, yet guilt over their past involvement kept him quiet. He could have screwed up her career back then with his poor judgment. The kid deserved better.

"Come on, hard case. I've already got my ears open, hoping to pick up something around headquarters."

"Sal, I—" He stopped.

"Look, Vince, every day I use skills you taught me, ways you showed me to be the best, when other guys just sat around, hoping I'd wash out. I—" She placed one hand on his thigh and squeezed. "All you have to do is ask." Her fingers spread across his skin. "Even if it's just comfort for the night."

If those fingers had been another set, slim, pale and elegant... Disturbed that he'd carried the thought of Chloe that far, he shoved it away ruthlessly.

He grasped her hand and removed it gently. "Sunshine, you deserve better than providing comfort to someone who—" *Can't love you,* he started to say.

Her hand tightened around her beer bottle. He thought for a moment he saw a flash of anger. Good. She *did* deserve better, and if it took getting mad at him to drive her away, well, that was the price he paid. "You're a hell of a woman and a damn fine cop. Don't settle for someone like me."

Staring out into the darkness, Sally didn't answer.

They sat quietly for a few minutes, the cat's purring twining with the sounds of the night. Vince wished to hell he knew what to do, what to say. He'd be lucky to have a woman of Sally's goodness to love him, but he'd learned from one bad marriage that he wasn't good husband material. Too solitary. It was better, anyway, in his line of work, not to be distracted by matters of the heart.

He told himself that, even as his mind filled with the image of Chloe's anguished brown eyes. Vince hung his head, raking fingers through his hair.

"Tell me what I can do to help out." Sally turned back toward him, all cop now. "Don't be a dope, Vince. You can't fight Newcombe alone."

He wanted to say that he was grateful she understood it wouldn't work between them, but her eyes dared him to bring the topic up. So he concentrated on peeling the label off his bottle. "I need to see my old case files, but I can't get into the department computer right now."

"I can do that for you."

"You can't access my files without using my password, and I don't want alarms sounding when it appears."

"Then I'll go to storage and dig out the paper files. What am I checking for?"

"Sal, I can't let you—"

Anger flashed in her eyes. "Damn you, Vince, don't shove me away on this, too."

Guilt made him relent. "Okay, but don't try to get

into the report files yet. You can examine the evidence rosters without my password. Look through them and tell me what's logged in from the bust."

"What are you after?"

"I'm not sure yet. I just need to see what they found."

Sally nodded. "I'll go up there now."

"No, do it on your normal schedule. You on duty tomorrow?" She nodded. "Combine it with something else. Don't take chances on this, Sally. I'm not bringing you down with me."

"You won't go down, Vince. What Newcombe is saying is wrong. You're not a rogue cop."

Frustration rolled over him. "Krueger shot first, damn it. And the drugs should have been there."

Her touch was light and quickly withdrawn this time. "I believe you." She rose to her feet, handing him her empty bottle. "You can do the cleanup. I'm headed home."

"Sally, I—"

She stiffened. "Don't say it, Vince. You're being shortsighted, but you'll change your mind. I can be patient."

He wanted to protest that he'd never change his mind. Even if Chloe St. Claire wasn't taking up far too much of his attention, he wouldn't be coming back to Sally.

He held his tongue. She was acting from hurt pride right now, but she'd get over it.

"I'll let you know what I find out." At the gate, she

turned and saluted. Vince watched her leave. Then, empty bottles clinking together, he went inside, ignoring the fur that brushed past his feet.

CHAPTER SEVEN

CHLOE GLANCED at her watch for the third time in the last five minutes. Vince was due soon, and despite getting to bed on time, she'd spent a restless night. She still had no idea how to handle him in light of what had happened yesterday.

Her knowing he'd manipulated her didn't seem to help. She'd never felt that kind of temptation to cross the boundaries of a proper therapist-client relationship. No, Vince hadn't sought her out, as would be the case in private practice, but there should be a certain distance. Her decision to accompany him to that bar might have been sound if they'd stuck to talking; some people did open up better outside the office.

But the physical awareness that had gotten stronger every minute they were together had nearly boiled over last night. Chloe had never reacted to a man the way she did to Vince Coronado. If she couldn't rein in that response, she'd have to remove herself from his case, and that would only set him back in his quest to return to work. Despite what had happened, she didn't want to keep him from his job if, as she suspected, he'd done nothing wrong.

His sergeant had asked her to do an informal

assessment because he thought Vince was taking too many chances lately. This morning Chloe had dug deeper into the files on Vince and had discovered what close friends he'd been with the murdered officer, Carlos Quintanilla. More than anything else she knew about Vince, this could explain what worried Sergeant Woods. Vince had a strong protective streak. Since Quintanilla's case had never been solved and his reputation had been tainted, grief and guilt could be at the root of Vince's behavior.

But she also recognized that Vince wouldn't be a legend in the department if he wasn't willing to take risks. All cops had that element to a certain degree—a disregard for personal safety in service to others was part of their makeup.

Vince was needed. The world was full of bad guys, and Austin couldn't afford to have a good cop out of action. She believed that Don was wrong; Vince probably pushed the limits of the law from time to time, but it was in an effort to take down criminals, not from any sort of corruption. His zeal for justice was both a strength and a detriment if not restrained.

Her phone buzzed. "Yes?"

"Your mother's on line one," Wanda said with that tone of Mama Bear she took. "And Vince is here."

"Tell my mother—no, on second thought, I'll talk to her." She'd dodged initiating a long discussion with her mother until she could get past her appointment for testing because she was a lousy liar, but what if something had happened to her father? "Ask Detective Coronado if he could give me a minute." She heard Wanda's voice and the low rumble of Vince's answer.

"He's okay with it."

"Tell him thank-you." She punched the button. "Mother, is everything all right?"

"Nothing has changed, Chloe."

Chloe settled against the back of her chair. "I can't help worrying. Mother, I wish—"

Her mother didn't let her finish, probably just as well. "I called to invite you to dinner tonight. Your father would like to see you." Beneath the flatness of her mother's tone, Chloe heard tension.

"You're sure he's not worse?"

"I'm certain. Don't—" Her mother sighed. "Please, darling, just come tonight."

"All right." Chloe frowned at the entreaty. "What time?"

"Seven, if that will work."

"Perfect."

"Good. Chloe—" A strained silence ensued.

"Mother, what's wrong?"

"Never mind." Brisk now. "I'll see you tonight." With that, her mother was gone.

Chloe held the receiver in her hand, wondering if she should call back and inquire more deeply. Something was going on that disturbed her mother.

But if she'd learned one thing in her life, it was that Dolores St. Claire could not be budged on what she believed was the proper way to do things. Chloe would pay close attention at dinner, but for now, calling back would only make things worse. She sighed and pushed the intercom button. "Ask Detective Coronado to come in, please, Wanda." After replacing the receiver, she carefully folded her hands on the desktop to still the sudden attack of nerves as the door opened.

Then there he was. Looking far too good.

His gaze locked on hers. Blue eyes spoke volumes in a voice she couldn't afford to hear...but reverberated deep inside her.

Chloe couldn't tear her gaze away.

"Chloe—"

She stirred. Blinked. "Detective." She nodded carefully.

For a second, something in him seemed almost... vulnerable. An answering softness rose in her; ruthlessly she quelled it.

He searched her face, and disappointment flickered. Then the hard cop took over. He seated himself in front of her desk.

Chloe tried to remember what she'd thought they could talk about. Opening the file in front of her, she grasped at a topic. "About your family—"

"Don't—" His dark tone wounded her. "Just let me go, all right? Cut me loose."

She gripped her fingers together until the knuckles went white. "My terms were clear. I have a job to do."

He slapped both hands on his thighs, then rose to pace, jamming his hands in the front pockets of his jeans. Jaw flexing, he faced her windows, his powerful frame tense.

Chloe waited, trying to give him room. She'd been kidding herself that this wouldn't be hard.

Suddenly, Vince whirled, strode across the room and pulled her to her feet. Before she could react, his lips claimed hers.

Shock stilled her, then she tumbled in the onslaught of too many sensations—his body hard against hers, the tantalizing taste of his kiss. She grabbed his shirt for an anchor, wanting—

More.

When he felt her press closer, Vince groaned. "Chloe—" Against every instinct he possessed, he knew he had to pull back. *Now.*

But he only wanted to get closer.

With great effort, Vince disentangled his mouth from hers, placing a gentle kiss to the corner, then dragging himself away from the pulse point of her neck.

"Fire me," he said, his voice hoarse.

"What?" Confusion swirled in her eyes.

"I can't be your client. You're driving me crazy."

Chloe stared at him, mourning his distance even as returning reason told her it had to happen. Her fingers tingled with the texture of his shirt, of his warm, muscled torso. Her body hummed with the longings he elicited with little effort. She'd never felt like this, never even imagined it.

If she'd ever doubted it, she was certain now that Roger's time was at an end, but there could be nothing between her and Vince until his troubles were over. If she cared about him at all, she had to help him, and that meant not letting anyone know that he was becoming important to her. If Roger found out, he'd crucify Vince out of damaged pride, if nothing else.

Sobered by the realization that she could do Vince great harm, she escaped toward her credenza and poured a glass of water for her suddenly parched throat. Drawing upon reserves she'd never realized she had, Chloe asked, in her mother's best hostess tone, "Would you care for a glass of water?"

"No." Jaw tight, stance rigid, he looked at the trees. "Thank you."

She desperately wanted to talk about what had just happened; instead, Chloe retreated into a professional mode. "Tell me how you're feeling about being on leave."

"Damn you." Immediately, she looked stricken, and Vince cursed himself. His undercover experience made him as much actor as cop; he could handle this. All he had to do was to forget about her as Chloe. Pretend she was a target. A means to an end.

All he had to do was not remember tendrils of hair curling on her neck. Forget her laughter, blank out her softness…

Hell. "You know this is our last session," he said.

To his surprise, she didn't immediately refuse.

"I have a responsibility to the department, as well as to you, to be sure you're fit for duty."

He stiffened. "Do you honestly doubt it?"

"At this moment, I doubt everything about my judgment."

The uncertainty in her eyes dampened his building fury. "What would it take for you to trust yourself again?"

Her lips curved with wry amusement. "I have no idea."

Vince dropped his head. "I'm sorry, Doc. I never meant for this to happen." He looked up, grin crooked, dimple winking. "You're not my type, you know."

"Vince—"

"You don't have to tell me," he said, holding up a hand. "You don't date mongrels."

Honest surprise slid over her features. "You're not a mongrel."

"Get real. You're a registered purebred, and I'm a mutt straight from the alleys."

A flicker of humor united them for one brief instant.

Abruptly, Chloe sobered. "We can't have this discussion right now. I have a report to turn in, and despite how I've botched things so far, I can't live with myself if I release you before I've made my best effort at completing the requirements to render a sound opinion."

"Do you believe them, is that it? Newcombe and Barnes?"

She appeared startled. "No."

"Then what will it take for you to let me go?"

"Vince, a positive report from me isn't going to cure the problem with that warrant."

"I know, but it's one barrier removed."

Chloe rubbed at a spot between her eyebrows. Exhaling in a long, heartfelt sigh, she stared at the top of her desk. Finally, she looked at him again. "You're already here. There are questions I must ask, and I need your honest answers. If you can quit playing games with me, maybe I can obtain the information to be able to issue my recommendation, but if you persist in dodging them, the only course available to me is to wait until Rick returns from vacation and turn you over to him."

"Playing hardball, huh, Doc?"

Determination glittered, cheek by jowl with a plea. "I don't want to, but I couldn't bear it if I released you and something happened."

Her honesty knocked the pins from beneath him. He tried to figure out any other solution, but he could see none that wouldn't either delay him—

Or hurt her. With effort, he assumed the role. "Okay. You win." He glanced toward the glass she'd proffered. "Yes, I could use a drink of water." Then he grinned. "Maybe you could just pour the pitcher on my head."

Her surprised smile helped them both.

Taking the glass from her, he resumed staring out the window. He'd never pull this off if he had to gaze into eyes he'd seen alight with mischief or confused by desire. "The answer to your question is—being on leave sucks. Want to talk about the weather next?"

Chloe's laughter was shaky and faint, but the sound of it warmed his heart.

AS SHE DROVE TOWARD her parents' house that evening, Chloe thought about her session with Vince. It had gone better than expected, and though she was certain that there were still depths in him she hadn't plumbed, she'd been able to honestly render a report to Internal Affairs that she didn't believe the shooting had held any premeditation. Not being sorry that Krueger had died didn't equate to intending to kill him.

She'd also spoken with Sergeant Woods about his unofficial concerns and eased his mind that Vince wasn't acting on an urge to self-destruct, though he was definitely dogged by a type of survivor's guilt over the unsolved murder of a man who had been the only father figure in his life. Sergeant Woods had promised to stay in contact with her, and vice versa.

And Vince had even agreed to seek out Rick Bradley, the senior staff psychologist, if he felt a need for his services. Chloe was almost certain he'd said it only to comfort her and not from any belief that such a need would ever arise, but she would count on her arrangement with Woods being a fail-safe.

So somehow they'd survived the session, carefully keeping her desk between them. She almost could have imagined that kiss, except for its indelible imprint on both her lips and her heart.

But when her next appointment had arrived and the session was over, Vince had stood, rapped his knuckles on her desk and told her he'd be by first thing in the morning to pick her up for their wallpapering date.

And while she was trying to dredge up a response, he'd escaped. The man certainly had no dearth of sheer nerve. Despite her concern over this meeting with her parents, she had to fight an urge to chuckle.

Parking her car in the circle drive in front of her parents' Niles Road mansion, Chloe touched her stomach lightly, willing it to settle. Once at the front door, she rang the bell. Their houseman answered. As she followed him across the soaring marble-floored entry into the formal living room, she glanced around at the splendor that had so impressed her childhood friends. They'd oohed and aahed about descending that curved mahogany staircase in a bridal gown; Chloe knew her mother had cast Roger in the role of groom.

"There you are, dear," her mother said. "You look lovely, as always."

Chloe noticed that despite her mother's usual ramrod-straight posture, there was something defeated in her frame. "Are you all right, Mother?"

Completely out of character, her mother clasped Chloe's hand and drew her close, wrapping her arms around her daughter. "You know I love you, darling, don't you?"

The desperation Chloe heard alarmed her. "Where's Daddy?"

Her mother clasped Chloe's cheeks. "He's in the library. And no, he's not any worse."

"Then why—"

"Where's my girl?" her father's voice boomed.

"I'll be right there, Daddy." Chloe's nerves skittered. "Mother, what—"

Her mother shook her head. "We'd better go in. Just remember that everything we've ever done has been because we love you."

"Mother, you're frightening me."

But her mother had already moved ahead to open the library door.

Seeing John St. Claire for the first time since hearing about his illness, Chloe wondered how in the world she hadn't realized that his health had turned for the worse. His skin was pale, and he'd lost weight. Tenderness swept her. She'd always viewed her father with a certain amount of awe. He was larger than life, a commanding presence who'd been the foundation of her world. She'd always felt that nothing bad would happen to her as long as John St. Claire watched over her, and nothing ever had. Chloe struggled past this girl who'd always known that in the shelter of her father, she'd be safe.

He was the one who needed shelter now. Ignoring her resolve, she blurted out her intention. "Daddy, I'm going to get tested for bone-marrow compatibility. I want to help you."

Chloe wasn't sure what she'd expected—anger that she'd disobeyed, gratitude that she would help him? She saw neither. Instead, her father looked, if possible, even older. A glance at her mother revealed the same thing.

"Chloe, come sit by me. We have to talk." In her father's tone was not his usual order but, rather, a plea.

"Why?" A visceral dread settled inside her.

"Please." He held out the big hand that had, for so many years, steadied her in a hundred different ways.

She took it, surprised to feel a tremor in him. "What is it?" She halted, almost sure now that she didn't want to hear whatever was making both of them behave so oddly.

"Sit down, darling," her mother said softly. "Your father tires easily these days."

So Chloe did, gripping her father's hand while

wishing she could turn back time and feel reassured instead of threatened.

"You aren't necessarily a viable bone-marrow donor, Chloe."

"What?" She frowned. "Why not? I'm your only living blood relative."

His eyes were sad and old. "Please…don't blame your mother for this. She was trying to protect me."

"By not telling me that you're sick?"

"No." His shoulders sagged. "By not telling you that you're adopted."

His words echoed around her, but she couldn't make sense of them at first. Then the air in the room splintered into crystals. Icy needles of shock rained down so thick she was blinded.

"What?" She hadn't heard right. Couldn't have. "What did you say?"

"It doesn't mean anything, sweetheart. Nothing has changed—"

"But you—" She blinked. "No—" A crushing weight squeezed her chest.

"I'm sorry. We never wanted you to find out this way."

She saw his mouth move. Saw her mother step toward her, but she couldn't hear a word they were saying for the cacophony of her own shattered thoughts.

"I can't be—why would you—" But even as she denied it, something in her knew. A whole life fell into place, all the reasons that fitting into this world had sometimes been so hard. Why the expectations of her had been so stringent.

Not because she was theirs—

But because she wasn't.

She tugged away, but her father's hand tightened. "Chloe, we love you so much—"

"How can you say that?" Chloe leaped to her feet, swiveling her gaze between them. "You lied to me." She couldn't breathe as the enormity of the fact sank in. "All my life…everything about me…is a lie."

"It's not, darling. Our love for you has never been false. You've been the sun and the moon to us—"

But Chloe couldn't hear past a horrible thought beginning to dawn on her. "You were ashamed of me. That's why you never told anyone. Why—what was wrong with my past?"

Her mother's head shook in denial, but guilt swept over her father's face.

"You were," she insisted, her heart breaking. "But I tried so hard—" Chloe turned to run—only, she didn't know where to go.

"It wasn't like that," her father protested. "We were never ashamed of who you were, Chloe. You can't believe that."

"Darling—" Her mother's hand clasped her arm.

Chloe jerked away. "What's my name? My real name?"

Her mother looked stricken. "You're Chloe St. Claire. Don't ever doubt that."

Shock gave way to fury. "I doubt everything right now." She tore her gaze from her mother and pinned her father. "What's my name? What happened to my real family?"

All the remaining color fled from his face, and Chloe knew an instant's shame. He was a very ill man. "Tell me," she insisted. "Then I'll leave you alone. I don't want to hurt you—" Her voice broke on a sob. She didn't want to harm either of them, but she felt as though they'd gutted her.

"Chloe—" He started to rise.

"Don't," she ordered. She looked down and fought for composure. "Please. Don't get up, Daddy. Despite what you've done, I don't want anything bad to happen to you."

"Sit down, darling," her mother said. "Let us explain."

But Chloe knew she'd fly apart if she lingered. Start screaming or, worse, devastate them the way they were killing her. "Give me the truth," she demanded in a voice she didn't recognize.

Her father—but he wasn't her father, was he? The magnitude of the betrayal rolled over Chloe in a pounding, punishing wave. It was all she could do to stand there, fingernails digging into her palms.

"We didn't change anything but your last name. You were almost four years old, and we didn't want to confuse you."

One thing about her wasn't a lie. She wanted to sink to the floor, but she had to hold on. "What was it?"

His jaw worked. "Malone. Chloe Elizabeth Malone."

She'd try to think later if the name fit better somehow. "What do you know about my family?"

He settled heavily on the sofa. "Your birth parents are dead, but—"

Even as her stomach clenched at the loss of people she couldn't remember, she seized on the last. "But what? Who else is there?" And how could she not remember, if she'd been four years old? She was so busy trying to figure out the youngest age she could remember that she almost missed his next words.

"You had two sisters."

Sisters. She'd prayed at night for a sister. "Had?"

"They were much older. Teenagers."

"Why was I separated from them?"

"They were too young, darling." Her mother's voice wavered, then gained strength. "They couldn't have taken care of you."

"How did my parents die?" She had to know, even though she was terrified of what she'd find.

"Your mother apparently died of natural causes. Your father had abandoned all of you years before, then died, as well."

Abandoned. He hadn't loved them, then. But maybe her mother had. Maybe her sisters— "Didn't they want me?" If they'd cared, why wouldn't they have stayed in touch?

Then she knew. "You bought me, didn't you? Somehow you used your money to make them go away."

Neither would look at her at first. Then her father raised tormented eyes to hers. "Your adoption was private, and the records were sealed. We didn't want anyone to know you weren't ours. We moved to Austin and started over." His voice turned fierce. "You were ours, Chloe. You still are."

"No—" Desperation and rage and heartache kept her strong even when she wanted to fold. "I want everything you have on this. I'm going to find them." Chloe held her father's gaze, daring him to deny her. Beside her, her mother sobbed.

Some of her father's old steel returned. "Chloe, no one could love you more than we have."

Even as she recognized that there was truth in his words, bitterness for all the times she'd felt so alone and out of place shoved that truth away. "We'll never know, will we?"

His shoulders slumped. Her mother gripped her arm again. "Chloe—"

She couldn't stand here one more minute. She had to have some time to absorb everything. Time to figure out—

"I have to go." She jerked her arm from her mother's grasp. On shaky legs, she crossed the floor, trying to imagine the little girl she'd been, the sisters she'd lost...

"Darling—"

She held up one hand without turning. Gasping for one solid breath, she managed to speak. "Not now. I'll—I promise I'll come back when I can—" Her voice cracked. "I have to go."

She ran out the door.

CHAPTER EIGHT

SATURDAY MORNING traffic wasn't half-bad, Vince thought as he drove north on Lamar Boulevard. Usually, he would have been out late on Friday night, trailing his suspects through an endless selection of dingy bars or topless joints. Soon, he'd be back at it; he was almost certain.

He stopped to pick up cinnamon rolls and coffee, having to guess at how she liked hers. There was a lot he didn't know about Chloe St. Claire yet, but he would find out. After that kiss, nothing else would do.

They had unfinished business between them. Lots of it.

Didn't matter that they were opposites in breeding and experiences and much more—she was a hell of a darts player and she loved old houses. She'd finished her own wood floors, though imagining it was still a stretch.

They'd start with wallpapering and work up to another kiss. He'd take it slow if it killed him.

It probably would. But you only won the game if you got out on the field. He'd had a taste of her, and he wanted more. She wanted more, too; he'd bet everything he owned on that.

Who the hell was he kidding? He was the son of a whore. Her father would probably put out a contract on him before he'd allow Vince's hands on his lily-white daughter.

Roger Barnes already wanted to take away his job.

Vince caught the name on the street sign ahead and realized he had only two blocks to change his mind.

Just as he was about to whip a U-turn and get the hell back on his side of the river, he remembered caramel-brown eyes full of mischief as Chloe pointed out a bull's-eye shot. Thought about a woman who'd trembled in his arms under the oaks.

Recalled the whipsaw of craving when her mouth softened under his.

Saw again the loneliness she worked so hard to hide.

Vince smiled and shook his head. Of course it made sense to turn around before he escalated foolishness to downright stupidity. But as Chloe had so accurately pointed out—

He didn't choose safety.

Just then he noticed the fire-engine-red door on the otherwise sedate and traditional house. Maybe there was a risk taker inside the good doctor, too. With a grin, he emerged from his T-bird and strode up her walk.

Two minutes later, he'd rung the bell, knocked and rung again. Her car was there—he saw it through the side window of the one-car garage. Didn't mean she was around, though. She might have spent the night with Barnes, her claim that they weren't sleeping together notwithstanding.

Disappointment rode him harder than it should have. Sure, he'd tossed off a promise to pick her up this morning, but she hadn't actually said yes, had she? He was about to leave, when the door opened.

"Vince? What are you—"

He got one glimpse of her and grasped the edge of the door to open it wider. "What's wrong?"

"Nothing." She averted her face.

He was having none of it. "You look like hell."

"I don't— Go away, Vince." She shoved the door toward him.

He blocked it with his shoulder. "Not until I know what happened to you."

"Please." Her voice was barely a whisper, her eyes downcast, her hair a snarled mess. She had on a thick robe far too warm for this weather, but her body shook as though gripped by fever. "Just leave. I can't—"

Her grasp faltered, and he pressed through the opening. She backed away, still not meeting his gaze.

Vince closed the door and crossed to her. "Are you sick? Have you called a doctor?"

She shook her head. "I don't need a doctor." But she looked as though she'd collapse in the faintest breeze.

"You should lie down." He clasped her arm, almost afraid that touching her would shatter her. He felt her tremble. "Chloe, talk to me. Do you have a fever?" With his other hand, he checked her forehead, but it was cool to the touch.

He smoothed her tangled hair away from her face; with a sob, she sagged against him. "Tell me what's wrong," he urged as he folded her into his embrace.

She came undone then. Heartrending sobs shook her whole frame. Hot tears soaked into his T-shirt. Her legs gave way.

Vince swept her up into his arms and moved to a wicker rocking chair filled with plump cushions. He sat down with her across his lap and, feeling absolutely helpless, didn't know what to do but hold her close while she cried.

As the woman he'd once thought too controlled sobbed against his chest, Vince rocked her and stroked her hair, awkward with words of comfort, since he had no idea what was going on. But even baffled as he was, something about this felt…right. As if a key had turned in a lock and opened a new place inside Vince with a smooth, well-oiled click.

There were only about a million reasons he should be scared half to death or on his feet running, but instead, Vince Coronado, the hard-ass who needed action and lots of it, who'd rather take a bullet than see a woman's tears, felt peace settle over him like the welcome weight of a blanket on a cold night.

He didn't know why she was crying or when she would stop, but somehow it didn't matter. He would stay with her, and her tears would eventually cease. When she was ready to talk, he'd listen and try to help. But in the meantime, he'd relish the feel of her against him and welcome the trust she'd placed by settling into his arms. He, who'd been careful never to let himself be vulnerable again, had other priorities, other ideas about how his life would play out.

But somewhere along the way, a not-so-cool brown-eyed blonde had blown the hell out of his plans.

CHLOE AWOKE with a raging thirst and a curious lightness.

And heard the strong, slow thump of a heart against her ear just as warm, firm flesh registered. Along with a definite bulge beneath her right hip. Oh, God. She wanted to look, but she was terrified of what she'd see.

"You can open your eyes, Doc," a deep voice rumbled with amusement. "I can't help how my body reacts, but I'm not one to take advantage of a woman who's cried her heart out in my arms."

She peered through her lashes and saw exactly what she'd feared: Vince Coronado's electric-blue gaze. But it wasn't laughing at her; instead, his look held a tenderness that would, if she wasn't careful, undo her again. She squeezed her eyes shut and tried to figure out how to disappear.

A chuckle shook his chest. "Come on, Chloe. I won't bite. And my leg's fallen asleep."

Mortified, she scrambled from his lap and would have wound up on the floor if he hadn't caught her. "What are you doing here?" Her voice sounded as if she'd swallowed sandpaper.

"Hey, easy…" Vince steadied her.

She couldn't stand the pity in his eyes. Then everything came crashing back in.

She couldn't think about it just yet. If she didn't get

a drink of water, she'd die. Turning too fast toward the kitchen, she tripped on the hem of her robe.

"Whoa," Vince said, grasping her by the elbow. "Wait a minute until you get your balance."

Chloe ducked her head, but he put one finger beneath her chin and forced it upward.

"I'm not the enemy, Chloe," he said softly. Then something oddly shy filled his eyes. "I never thought I'd say this to a woman, but I'm glad to be the one who held you while you cried."

And she, who thought she'd been drained of every last tear, felt a new rush of them stinging. "I—" Again her throat refused to work.

"Why don't I get you a glass of water." His voice was so gentle. "Sit down, and I'll bring it in here."

Nature made its needs known, though she'd have sworn not an ounce of fluid remained inside her whole body. "I have to—" She fell silent.

Vince smiled. "Want me to walk you down the hall?"

Chloe stifled a yelp. Shaking her head, she escaped, knocking one knee against a table and careening off the adjacent wall as she stumbled her way out of the room.

She expected to hear him laugh, but instead, his voice came to her, comforting and low. "Don't assume you're going to hide in the bathroom. I'm not leaving until we talk."

She closed the door and sank against it, eyes darting wildly as she tried to figure out some way to sneak out of the tiny window in her oldest robe.

Then she remembered all that had happened in the space of one night and knew embarrassment was the least of her problems.

Chloe braced her hands on the edge of the pedestal sink and stared at her face in the mirror. No wonder she'd never been able to find a resemblance to her parents.

Parents. The mother and father she'd always believed were hers. Now she didn't know what to believe. They'd given her so much. Demanded so much. Been there for every important event of her life, always in the front row, always…there. Maybe not demonstrative, maybe not the mother who baked cookies or the dad who gave piggyback rides, but…

There. Steady and dependable. She recalled the anguish on their faces before she'd run out of the house she'd taken for granted as home. How could they have been so deceitful?

Her bitterness wavered. How could she have been so cruel?

They'd lied, yes, but she hadn't heard a word of whatever explanations they'd offered. All she could think, all she could see, was that she was a fraud. An illusion.

Who am I? she wondered as she studied a face she'd glimpsed at thousands of times but never really seen.

Do I resemble my mother or father? My sisters?

What were their names? How could there be two people walking the earth who were part of her, shared her blood and bone, and she didn't even know their *names?*

Once again, anger rose, swift and fierce. Her parents had no right—Dolores and John, that was. She didn't know what to call them now, no matter that, deep within, she understood it was wrong to give short shrift to the years they'd spent caring for her, protecting her, guarding her from…what?

Her own nature? *Who was she?* Everything came back to that, a clawing, aching need to *know*. Like waking up with the sun shining and birds singing and stepping out of bed—

And falling into a huge black hole.

She had another life. Another family. A past, however brief, that was who she really was. Yes, barely four was very young, but how could she not remember any of it?

And the prospect of finding out who that Chloe was scared her to death, every bit as much as it lured her the way an oasis lures the weary traveler.

But sometimes an oasis turned out to be a mirage.

I have to know. I have to find them.

She stared at the blond hair and brown eyes and wondered if there were, somewhere on the planet, two women who shared them. She traced her cheekbones and eyebrows. Pressed long fingers against her mouth…

Uncertain if she was brave enough to find out.

"Chloe?" Vince's voice came through the door. "You okay?"

Chloe looked at her reflection and wondered if she'd ever be able to answer that question honestly again.

The doorknob rattled, and she knew she had to answer him with something. Quickly, she ran the water in the sink and grabbed her toothbrush. "I'm fine. I'll be out in a minute."

The face in the mirror that had suddenly become a stranger's stared back at Chloe, watching her every move.

FOR A MAN ACCUSTOMED to action, seldom at a loss to decide where he was going next, Vince found himself hesitating in the hallway of Chloe's jewel box of a house, having no idea if he should stay or go. Everything about this situation was foreign to him. He didn't do tears. Didn't do relationships. Didn't get involved with personal stuff.

Yet he was about to do all three, if he didn't find some excuse to get the hell out of here—now. Somehow, though, the litany of reasons that he should be anywhere but with this woman didn't seem to be penetrating his admittedly thick skull. She got to him, this daughter of privilege, this blueblood who would never consent to getting tangled up with him.

He was not, by the remotest stretch of the imagination, a long-term kind of guy, anyway. Maybe he should see a shrink. He had to be crazy to be here at all.

The bathroom door opened, and Chloe, head downcast, walked out, seeming as though a puff of wind would blow her over.

And Vince forgot everything but the need to make her back into the society girl who'd never take a second glance at him.

"Hey," he said, and was about to start asking questions, when she looked up, and he saw how close to the edge she was. Didn't matter that he had no idea what the edge was called or who had pushed her to it. Vince, whose instincts had saved him more than once, let his gut tell him the next move.

Give it a rest. Give her time to recover.

So Vince grinned past his worry. "I make a pretty mean omelette, if I do say so myself. Want one?"

He could see the refusal forming on her lips. The urge to coddle her all but overwhelmed him, but somehow he knew it was the worst thing he could do. He steered her toward her bedroom. "You go dress, and I'll get started. Coffee's brewing."

She hesitated. "Vince, I can't—"

"Reneging on me, Doc?" Though he wanted to tuck her into bed and stand guard over her, he thought that being idle might be the worst thing for her right now. "We had a date to wallpaper, and I'm holding you to it."

When her shoulders sagged, he was on the verge of giving in, never mind his instincts.

But just then, the shadow of Dr. Cool and Elegant made an appearance. Her head rose, and her body straightened. "If you could—" She turned her head halfway, and the anguish he saw in that pure profile was hard to bear.

"Never mind—"

"I'd like a shower," she interrupted. "But I won't—" Her voice faltered, and he watched as she grasped at the strands of her former composure. "I won't be long."

"Take all the time you need, Doc," he said, clenching his hands against the need to touch her. Hold her. Keep her safe.

"Thank you," she whispered, lifting a gaze so

vulnerable it was painful to see. "And thank you for—" she cleared a throat gone husky "—everything."

He held on to his resolve by a thread, reminding himself that he was in no position to be her knight in shining armor, even if he'd been the type. And forced himself to think of the thousand and one reasons getting any closer to her was a huge mistake—for both of them.

Drawing upon every ounce of acting skills he'd ever learned, Vince kept his hands to himself and shrugged. "I was just here at the right time." He made himself walk away before he fell headfirst and fathoms deep into those soulful brown eyes. "Breakfast will be ready when you are."

After a moment, he heard her footsteps moving down the hall.

In the kitchen, he stared unseeing out the window for a very long time.

CHAPTER NINE

CHLOE GLANCED AROUND at Vince's neighborhood, an eclectic mix of houses older than those where she lived. Shotgun cottages stood cheek by jowl with big, rambling two-story Victorians. Travis Heights had gone to seed, but nowadays, young couples were remodeling and restoring the neighborhood to a new vitality. She hadn't been here in a long time; South Austin and North Austin might as well straddle the Mason-Dixon Line, separate worlds divided by the river that flowed between them.

She would have pegged Vince Coronado as the type to live in some singles-only apartment complex, never a neighborhood as cozy as this. His house was one of the smaller ones on a street still half in, half out of decay, but she knew living here was a smart investment on his part. This northernmost neighborhood of South Austin had values skyrocketing simply because of its proximity to downtown. As Austin's traffic had worsened, formerly modest neighborhoods like this one and her own had become coveted real estate regardless of the condition of the housing.

She wasn't surprised that he'd made a smart investment; he was a very bright man, she'd come to realize.

Maybe he'd come from a deprived background, but the intelligence that crackled in the air around him could not be denied.

But that his house would feel so much like a home did surprise her. She could see the new roof, the trees he'd trimmed, the flower gardens weeded. New paint in a subtle but striking mix of cream and bronze and sable made this house stand out from its neighbors to either side and lifted the entire block a notch.

"I like it," she said. Just then, something brushed against her leg, and she jolted before spying the cat. "Is it yours?" Chloe sank to her knees and stroked the fur.

Vince recoiled. "No way." But the cat abandoned Chloe to wind around his ankles.

"Does he know that?"

"Not my fault he's hard-of-hearing. I've told him to scram."

Chloe grinned as the cat's purring increased. "I see how he's terrified of you."

Vince squirmed under her appraisal. "It's only a temporary arrangement. I don't have time for pets." But he'd already crouched beside her, absently stroking the animal.

She smothered a laugh. "It might be too late." She glanced at the cat, who'd rolled over onto his back in bliss. She couldn't take her eyes off Vince's strong, lean fingers.

He saw her laughter and jerked his hand back as if burned, then quickly stood. "Want something cold to drink?"

"Sure." She followed him inside and stopped in the living room in amazement. This room was finished, oak floors gleaming with what had to be hand-rubbed waxing. His furnishings were simple and clean of line—a long leather sofa saved from starkness by two overstuffed chairs, with ottomans, that looked like the perfect place to curl up and read. Bookcases lined the walls, crammed full; she itched to peruse the titles. His coffee table was burled wood, low and massive, and bore its own stacks of books. She saw no television, though there was a state-of-the-art sound system in place.

He'd turned back when she halted and noticed her absorption. "Sorry for the mess. I need more bookshelves," he said. "Or maybe I need to quit buying books."

"I love to read, too. My idea of a great vacation would be an all-expenses-paid four-star hotel with room service and an endless gift certificate at the bookstore next door."

"I never read much as a kid, never was in school that often. Carlos taught me that even a poor kid could travel the world in the pages of a book. He took me to get my first library card."

Sorrow cast a shadow across him. She marveled at how he'd triumphed over his background and knew she'd been right to think that Carlos Quintanilla's death still affected him. "I'm so sorry I never knew him," she said. "He must have been a wonderful man."

Vince's face shuttered. "He was."

A strained silence ensued, and she sought to relieve it. "This room is beautiful, Vince."

His smile was grateful. "Thanks. It's one of two

rooms that are complete. Well, three if you count the master bath I made out of a bedroom."

Chloe's eyes widened. "A whole bedroom?"

"Want to see?" His blue eyes held both challenge and temptation.

Did she want to see his bedroom? She'd never wanted to see a man's bedroom before, but…

"Yes."

Vince grinned. "Let me get you that drink, and then we'll take the nickel tour."

And they did, Chloe exclaiming over the whirlpool tub and separate shower, trying not to focus too hard on the enormous bed that dominated the bedroom, all the while intensely aware of a subtle hum of attraction that made her both breathless and wary. As they moved through the house, Vince's hand would rest on the small of her back or their bodies would brush in passing, and the voltage would increase until Chloe's nerves danced with a mingle of anticipation and fear.

In the doorway to his room, he paused to let her by but crowded her slightly, his gaze never leaving hers, tangible and dangerous. She tried to ease past him without touching.

But oh, how she wanted—

She could hear him breathing, registered the warmth of him on her skin. Inhaled the scent that was new and tantalizing and…all man. Chloe stared at his chest only inches away and wondered what he'd do if she closed the distance and pressed her lips to the cotton stretched over that expanse of hard muscle—

"Chloe." Her name on his lips was both entreaty and command.

Slowly, she dragged her gaze upward, preternaturally aware of the moisture gathering between her breasts, the softening of her body under the spell of power crackling around a man who'd stormed into her predictable life, sweeping away everything she thought she'd understood about herself.

It was too much. Chloe gasped and slipped past him, knowing herself for a thorough coward after all.

Yes, he tempted her unbearably, but she had only the slimmest grasp upon the reins of her life at this moment. Her head dropped. "I'm sorry," she whispered, bracing herself for an explosion of fury he would be justified in feeling.

But she heard only silence.

Finally, she dared a glance at him.

Vince still stood in the opening to his bedroom, arms braced against the frame as he stared down.

"I—I can call a cab," she ventured.

His head rose swiftly. "No." He closed his eyes and frowned. "No." He walked toward her with that slow masculine stride, and halted in front of her a careful distance away. "Talk to me, Chloe." Though raspy, his voice held no trace of anger. "Something happened last night, and I think I've earned the right to an explanation."

He was such a complex mix of cowboy and warrior and gentleman, all in the guise of an unredeemed rake. When he held out his hand, she slipped hers into his warm and reassuring grasp. Her whole world had shifted on its axis, and she had no idea how to regain her equilibrium.

Vince took one look at the pale, tender skin revealed in the part of her hair, the defeat in her body, and knew he would stand here forever if necessary. "Tell me what's wrong."

She was silent so long that he was about to give up, but then she spoke, her voice hushed, her eyes fixed on something past his shoulder. "I found out last night…" She paused and cleared her throat. "That I'm adopted."

Prepared for anything from violence to terminal illness, Vince realized his first impulse was to say, *That's all?* But something in the way she held herself so stiffly made it clear that she didn't consider herself lucky to have been adopted into such privilege, that she hurt badly. "You didn't suspect?"

Her head shook slowly. "It explains a lot now, but—" She lifted her gaze to his. "They lied to me, Vince. My whole life is a fraud."

A hundred questions popped into his mind, but he was no counselor. He was out of his depth to deal with something like this. Then he remembered one of Chloe's favorite questions in her sessions. "How do you feel about it?"

"I— A million things. I don't know what to think." Hugging her arms to herself, she began to pace. "At first I was stunned. I couldn't believe I was really hearing it. I wanted to deny it, but the truth was there in their faces, the guilt and the pain and—" She swallowed hard.

"Then I got outraged. I've never been that angry in my life. I felt so betrayed, and then I knew…"

"What?"

She paused. "Why they always pushed me so hard to be perfect."

"Which was?"

"Because there was something wrong, something shameful, in my past, and they were trying to discipline it out of me. They had to be on guard so I wouldn't turn out to be—"

"Be what?"

Fury sparked. "Who I really am. My father abandoned us before my mother died. What kind of father—" Her voice dropped. "I'm sorry. I didn't mean—"

"Forget it. Who your parents are—or aren't—doesn't matter. All that's important is who you've made yourself."

She looked stricken. "But that's it, don't you see? I didn't make anything. I'm product of parents who were too ashamed to admit that I wasn't this lily-pure blueblood, that I was a castoff whose parents didn't— Oh, God, Vince, I'm sorry— You know I don't mean—"

"Chloe, I'm no hothouse flower. My mother was a whore who had no idea which man fathered me. It's old news. It has no bearing on who I am."

"But how can I know who I am when one family didn't care enough to keep me and the other spent my whole life making me into a china doll?"

He cracked a smile at that. "You're tougher than china, babe, trust me."

In her eyes swirled hurt and hope. "I am?"

"China dolls are creampuffs compared with you. They sure don't refinish their own floors."

A faint smile curved that lush, wide mouth. "I bet they're not much at darts, either."

"There you go."

She paused. "How is it you make me believe that this news isn't the end of the world?"

He lifted one eyebrow. "It's not, is it?"

"I don't know. I feel so lost." She stared off in the distance. "But at the same time, I feel almost…relieved. Free, as if I don't have to keep trying to be perfect."

"You're too hardheaded to be considered perfect. I could have told you that the first time I met you."

Her eyes held gratitude. "You're determined to make me laugh about this, aren't you?"

He tapped her nose with one finger. "Did crying fix it?"

"No," she said. "But crying in your arms—" She glanced away. "I don't know how to thank you for that."

"I don't suppose getting naked is an option." When her gaze flew to his, he grinned. Beyond the panic, he saw again the temptation that had burned so hot a few moments ago.

Then her forehead wrinkled. "Vince, I don't…" She hesitated.

Years had passed since he'd last felt humiliated. "Never mind. Of course you don't." Keeping his tone neutral, he started to move away. "I'll take you home."

Chloe grasped his arm and stopped him. "It's not

what you think. I—" She drew a deep breath as if for courage. "I never really wanted to before. My parents aren't—they don't—" She looked puzzled. "I thought that it was in my blood, that I simply lacked the ability to feel passion, but—"

Vince swiveled to face her. "What are you saying?"

"Just that I—" She scrubbed both hands up and down her thighs, averting her eyes. "I've never—"

Understanding hit him like a ton of bricks. "Chloe, you're not telling me you've never—"

Brown eyes lifted defiantly to his. "Yes."

Holy— He was both terrified and unbearably aroused. "Why?" he croaked. "How could the men you've dated not—"

Frost crackled in her tone. "It was my decision, not theirs. Sex should be a matter of mutual consent between mature, thinking adults, not—"

Vince laughed and advanced on her. "Making love," he warned, "should be hot and sweaty and rip your heart right out of your throat."

If her eyes widened any farther, her eyeballs would pop out like a cartoon character's. She swallowed visibly. "I wouldn't know about that."

"Christ, Doc, are you trying to drive me crazy or are you just that damn innocent?"

"I'm not innocent," she said. "I understand all about the physical and psychological aspects of intercourse—"

Vince seized her then, barely keeping the beast inside him at bay, easing her against him with so much care he thought he just might die, and brushed his lips against hers, teasing hers open with his tongue.

But then this egghead society girl who understood the cerebral aspect of sex—

Moaned. And let him inside, her unpracticed moves so unabashedly carnal that Vince was sliding fast past the point of no return.

If his pager hadn't gone off at that moment, Chloe might not have remained a virgin past the next five minutes.

Fighting his way out of a need so huge that he was going under for the third time, Vince groaned from somewhere in his gut while he cursed whoever the hell considered anything important enough to interrupt this.

As Chloe stiffened in his arms, Vince reached to stop the damn pager and struggled to get one good breath. One solid thought not swimming in lust. He kept his eyes closed and rested his forehead against hers, muttering dark imprecations against whoever—

"Don't you need to check who it is?" she asked. The quiver in her voice puffed his ego as much as it savaged his control.

"Am I supposed to care after that kiss?" He opened his eyes. Drank in the color in her cheeks, the sparkle in her eyes. "Damn, Chloe, don't look at me like that."

"Don't you look at *me* like that."

"How?" He couldn't resist teasing her.

A blush rose up her throat. "As if you want me."

"I've never wanted anyone more in my life." He didn't grin. It was too much the truth. Too foolish for a lot of reasons he refused to think about yet. "But your first time should be special," he said. "It should matter."

"This doesn't?" she asked in a small voice.

It mattered too much. "Chloe—"

His pager went off again.

Vince swore and checked the number. Then swore again. "Tino," he muttered.

"Who's Tino?"

And at least half of those reasons came rushing back. Moreno. Tino. The danger she'd be in if any of them realized that she was rapidly becoming too important to him.

With superhuman effort, Vince resurrected the hard cop he'd been until this morning. Until he'd held this woman in his arms and felt her tears wet his shirt.

He had to protect her. Had to break away. "An informant on an important case. He's called twice, so I can't ignore it."

Her arms hugged her waist. "I understand."

No, you don't. You have no idea what I have to do to keep you safe. The prospect of hurting her again, after what she'd been through last night, tore out his guts.

Even though she'd thank him for it later.

Right now, the best he could summon was something close to neutrality. "I'd better call him." Before he could weaken, he forced himself to walk to the phone.

Cursing himself every step of the way for opening Pandora's box when he should have known better.

CHAPTER TEN

CHLOE WATCHED the river as they crossed the bridge heading north a few minutes later, feeling the unaccustomed freedom of letting wind whip her hair without worrying how she looked. She caught herself wishing she could rewind the clock and erase the page he'd received. For a few moments there, she'd had a glimpse of a world she wanted to enter—so much it surprised her.

She'd thought passion was not her lot. Vince Coronado had shown her that she merely hadn't met the right man. Now, like a child standing outside a candy store whose sign had just been turned to Closed, she wanted inside. Was eager to learn what else about herself she hadn't known.

"I'm going to look for my sisters," she said.

"I think you should. I have a former partner who's a private investigator now. I could give you his number."

She regarded him. "You really think it's a good idea?"

He frowned. "Don't you?"

Chloe stared ahead. "It will cause problems. I don't know what my parents will think."

"Is their reaction important?"

She worried at her lower lip. "Yes." After a moment, she continued. "Maybe it shouldn't be—" She shook her head. "No, that's wrong. I don't understand why they did it, and I'm scared of what I might learn about my birth family, but whatever my parents' reasons, they care about me. You can't fake that."

Vince snorted. "People fake things all the time. Affection is one of the easiest."

In that instant, she was reminded of the chasm of difference in their experiences. The therapist in her wanted to pursue the discussion; the woman whose body still hummed from his touch had no interest in what she might discover about his motives. Besides, he was obviously distracted by the call he'd made. "Is this case important?" she asked.

His head whipped around, but quickly, all expression was shuttered. He shrugged. "Just another case."

"Why did you become a cop, Vince?"

He hesitated. She saw the muscle in his jaw leap. Suddenly, they were back to earlier days, when she'd only been able to see his mile-high walls. Disappointment stepped hard on the heels of a loneliness more acute for its brief absence.

But some remnant of what he called her stubbornness refused to yield. "I'm not asking in my professional capacity. I simply want to know you better."

The muscle jumped again. Resolutely, he stared ahead. "The less you know about me, Doc, the better off you'll be."

Swift and sharp, the refusal sliced deep. Chloe

gripped her hands as she grasped for the protective shell he'd breached with so little effort.

Vince cursed. "Look, I'm sorry. I've got a lot on my mind."

Chloe shook her head. "Forget it." It shouldn't matter. After her parents' bombshell, she had no business getting involved with anyone.

Vince reached for her hand and just as quickly retreated. "It's not you." But every word was uttered with reluctance. He drove his fingers through his hair. "Chloe, I—"

"You don't have to explain," she said stiffly.

"Goddamn it, don't you understand anything? I'm a cop and the bastard son of a junkie whore. You're silk and satin and money. We're all wrong for each other."

"Please," she said. "Just take me home. You don't have to say anything else."

He slammed one hand against the steering wheel, but he didn't say another word until they reached her driveway.

Chloe bolted out her side and raced, head down, toward her front door.

Vince caught her on the first step. Even standing below her, he was still overpowering. Still compelling.

"This isn't about you," he insisted. "The problem is with me. The timing is all wrong."

She hid her face before the tears burning her eyes could escape. She fumbled her key in the lock.

"Chloe—" His voice was both plea and warning. "You deserve better."

She dropped her key on the porch.

Vince picked it up. Slipping beside her, he slid the key into the lock but hesitated before turning it. "I'm not sorry you cried on me," he said in a low voice. Then he unlocked the door and left.

Chloe stood there, head bowed over the door handle, and listened to the sound of Vince departing.

Knowing somehow that he wouldn't be back.

VINCE WRENCHED his thoughts from the woman he'd left behind. Tino had phoned from jail, the idiot, and wanted Vince to spring him. The worst thing Vince could do was show up at Central Booking and call in favors. He didn't need the visibility, not now when Newcombe hadn't backed off yet. With a deep sigh, he punched in Mike's number on his cell phone.

"Yo, what's up, Vince?" Mike said, obviously having glanced at the caller ID.

"I need a favor, buddy."

"Shoot."

"That snitch I told you about?"

"The one with the girlfriend and the kid?"

"Yeah. He got himself popped."

"Dumbass," Mike said. "What for?"

"Possession. Pot."

Mike chuckled. "Never overestimate the intelligence of the average snitch."

"Tell me about it."

"So, you want me to spring him?"

Vince sighed. "I wish I could do it, but—"

"Wouldn't be your smoothest move right now. Don't sweat it. Tino Garza, right?"

"Yeah."

"Any messages for him?"

"Only that I'm going to clean his clock if he does something that stupid again."

Mike snickered. "It may be an hour or so before I can wrap up, but I'll get down there as quick as I can."

"Let him stew," Vince said. "Maybe he's forgotten too much already about what the joint was like." Vince paused. "I'd say I owe you, but there's still that war-wound remark…"

Mike laughed. "Okay, so we're even on this one."

But Vince knew they weren't. Nothing grated on him more than owing. He hated to be dependent on anyone for any reason. Even Mike. "Thanks, buddy."

"You think Doc's going to clear you anytime soon?"

Vince tried to keep everything that had happened between them out of his voice. "She says she already wrote the report."

"So now you have to deal with Newcombe and the grand jury."

"Yeah."

"We need you back, Vince. The mean streets haven't gotten any sweeter while you've been out."

"Hot weather does that. Tempers rise with the thermometer."

Mike grunted in agreement. "Listen, buddy, I gotta run. I'll let this guy suffer awhile, but I'll have him out later today."

"Thanks again."

"Check you later, man." Then Mike was gone.

Vince stared out his windshield and wondered what to do with himself now. He had twenty-four rolls of wallpaper that needed hanging, but he wasn't sure he wanted to see his place just yet, not while memories of Chloe there were still so vivid.

He wasn't back on duty, but that didn't mean he couldn't do some checking. He could prowl the bars where his Eastsiders hung out and see what they'd been doing.

Or he could travel into Los Carnales territory and make his presence known to serve notice on Moreno that he hadn't been forgotten. The move would be a little reckless, but ever since leaving Chloe, Vince had been on edge. What he really wanted to do was turn around and head back to her place.

If he hadn't found out that she was a virgin, maybe he could have done it. Just the thought of being the one to initiate her into the delights of lovemaking had the power to render him rock-hard in seconds. Somehow she'd burrowed under his skin when he wasn't looking, but that didn't change the facts.

Whether she was born a blueblood or merely reared as one wasn't important. No matter how much satisfaction Vince might draw from knowing that Roger Barnes hadn't been able to tempt Chloe and he had, the fact remained that someone like Barnes was who she'd been raised to marry. There might be a little mischief inside Dr. Cool and Elegant—a damn sight more of it than he would have expected—but in the end, though she might want to experiment with a mutt like him, she would return to her pristine world when she'd had her fill.

Vince had been aware from a very early age that there was safety in solitude, no matter how lonely it might be at first. His disastrous marriage had reinforced the lesson the one time he'd forgotten.

The pleasures of the good doctor's flesh would have to be foresworn, no matter how his fingers itched to touch it, to taste it…to make her body weep with need.

Better for Chloe to think him a bastard now than to convince her of it when everything went south.

As it inevitably would.

CHLOE STRUGGLED up from the grip of a restless sleep, her body still desperate for rest but her mind traveling an endless maze of conflicting images. Staring at the gauzy canopy over her bed, she clasped a pillow to her chest as she attempted to sort them out.

Her parents' shocking revelation had opened a new vista for her, but there were no clear reference points, no signposts to lead her. They said she'd been barely four years old, but shouldn't something have remained, some image, some memory, of the life she'd once led? As she'd tried to do last night, she searched for her earliest recollection.

Prowling through remembrance, Chloe pondered what she'd learned about the science of memory and how it worked. As she sorted out stories she'd been told so often from actual memories of her own, she realized that her oldest one was of a dog, small and black and dirty. She'd found him in the park. She'd wanted to take him home with her, but her nanny had said no. Dolores St. Claire would not allow a pet to soil her priceless carpets or spotless upholstery. Chloe had wanted that dog so badly. She'd hugged him and let him lick her face until her nanny had pulled her away and taken her from the park.

Chloe had looked for the dog every time after that. In her heart she'd given him the same name she gave every stuffed dog she ever had: Charlie. A mutt's name, her father said, but Chloe didn't care.

Had there been a real Charlie somewhere in her forgotten past? And how old had she been at the time of that visit to the park? She wasn't yet in school, Chloe was almost certain. Once she'd started first grade, she'd had a different nanny from the kind older woman who'd let her hug Charlie for a long time.

Wow. She hadn't thought about Charlie in years.

Restless, Chloe swung her legs over the edge of the bed. No more napping—time for action. She had sisters to find.

At the thought, the most compelling image of her uneasy nap strode to center stage.

Vince. He'd offered to help her with the name of an investigator. But that was before he'd shoved her away.

Why had he pushed her away? When the air between them crackled every time they met, when his touch made it obvious that he wanted her as badly as she wanted him? Chloe stared out her bedroom window without seeing anything, lost in the sensation of being cradled in his lap and comforted in a way she'd have given anything to experience as a child. Of his hard body against hers and the staggering power of his kiss. Of the instinct she had that, once released, his intense sexuality would take her to places she'd never even imagined.

Then she recalled his shock at learning that she'd never had sex before.

Chloe smiled. Vince Coronado had probably thought he couldn't be shocked. There was a certain power in the knowledge that she'd managed to do what no one else had.

Her smile faded. She should never have told him. He might be rugged and unpolished, but within him was a core of decency and honor that would stop him cold, now that he knew. In this day and age, virginity meant little to most people, but to a man whose mother had been a prostitute…it might mean too much.

Suddenly, his reaction made sense. He'd been all too ready to put his hands on her, to tease her, to see where things might lead. His interest in her help in wallpapering had been a blatant ploy to spend time together; the idea to play darts had also been his. She'd had a feeling that they were on the first steps down a long road that could lead to more—until she'd opened her mouth about her inexperience.

Instantly, Vince had backpedaled as fast as he could.

It was such an old-fashioned reaction, so unlike his reputation as a hell-raising cowboy of a cop who paid scant attention to the rules. But, Chloe realized, it was exactly like the man who defended women and children, who talked prostitutes into shelters and bought toys for their kids.

She hugged the pillow closer, wishing it were Vince.

He would never seduce her, now that he knew. His sense of honor wouldn't let him.

But that didn't mean that she couldn't seduce him.

Maybe she didn't have experience with seduction because she'd never wanted to tempt a man before, but her body was coming out of long years in the deep freeze, heating up with a vengeance.

The new Chloe, whoever she was, would break some rules, she thought. And enjoy doing so.

But first, she sobered, there was something else she had to do. She had sisters to find, and she wanted—needed—to understand why her adoptive parents had chosen this path. As a daughter, she was still shaky and unsure of how to regain footing for their badly damaged relationship. The professional in her, however, was curious, knowing there must be powerful motivation behind a decision with so much potential for disaster.

Why they had made the choice and how they had managed to hide it from her for so many years were only a few of the multitude of questions Chloe had for the man and woman who'd raised her.

She rose from the bed and headed for the shower, determined to uncover the truth. No matter what it was.

HE'D TOSSED AND TURNED as morning softness yielded to glaring heat. Finally, the purring cat on his chest had tipped the balance. Vince had given up on sleep.

Now here he was, driving aimlessly through old scenes from old crimes, the stark landscapes of man's ability to prey on his fellows. A shadow world of night creatures turned ugly by day.

This neighborhood's only relief was the park covering a whole city block, shady expanses filled with families who feared to leave their homes when sundown came. Even a laid-back college town couldn't escape it, and this part of Austin had suffered more than most. So often required by his job to be a creature of the night, Vince warmed to the picture he saw now, of families and children and hope.

A young boy chased after a Frisbee, running backward, not watching where he was going. He bumped into a woman, who reached out to steady him.

Gloria.

Vince squinted, trying to be sure the woman he saw was not just a figment of his wishes. No, it was Gloria, he was certain. He scanned the street, looking for a quick place to park. Just as he was about to abandon his car where it stood, he glanced back to see her joined by a man who was facing away from Vince. Something familiar niggled at Vince's mind.

The man turned slightly, arm raised as if making a point.

Newcombe. Vince's breath caught. He slammed on the brakes, taking a glimpse in his rearview mirror to see if he blocked traffic. Not yet. He stayed right where he was, itching to leap from the car.

That would be the height of folly. Whatever he was watching, it wouldn't do for Newcombe to know he was there. He'd observe, then talk to Gloria after she and Newcombe parted.

The two were arguing, Newcombe with a menacing stance, Gloria gesturing wildly. Newcombe's body language said he had the upper hand; Gloria's said she didn't like it one bit.

He'd been right. Newcombe had played a part in Gloria's change of story. But why? And how?

How wasn't such a mystery as why. Newcombe was a cop; he had the ability to make her life hell. He might even threaten her with losing her son. Why might not be a mystery, either. Newcombe wanted Vince in ruins; Gloria could help.

Horns honked behind Vince. Cursing under his breath, he hit the gas. He made a left turn and parked in a nearby alley, then carefully walked back to the edge of the building to watch the two from a distance.

Newcombe shook one threatening finger at Gloria, then stalked away, angry determination on his face. Gloria's face crumpled. She whirled and ran across the open space and into the trees on the other side of the park.

Vince wanted to follow her, but Newcombe's path lay between them. Until he had more information, Vince wasn't ready to confront his nemesis. He wished Newcombe would hurry up, before Vince lost Gloria in the crowd.

Finally, Newcombe veered off toward a side street. Vince raced across the pavement, his gaze fixed on the last spot where he'd seen her. His long strides rapidly covered the open space, but as soon as he neared her last location, he already knew it was too late.

She was gone. Vince gritted his teeth in frustration.

Maybe that was just as well; whatever hold Newcombe had on her, Vince wasn't sure he could break it. He couldn't be certain that their odd friendship would supersede her fear. No matter how much he'd done for her in the past, Vince had no carrot to offer Gloria now.

Damn. One chance sighting. Not much to hang his career on.

Just let me catch one break, Newcombe. Then you're toast.

CHLOE'S MOTHER was nowhere in evidence when the houseman let her in. "This way, Miss Chloe." He gestured. "Your father's in his library."

Chloe walked past him into the room that, with its rosewood paneling and thick carpets, massive furniture and shelf after shelf of leather-bound books, perfectly represented John St. Claire's power and influence. At the huge mahogany desk, her father sat working. Before he saw her, she paused, feeling, for the first time, a stranger in this house.

Their gazes met. Chloe had always been the good daughter, trying with everything in her to make this man proud so that he would at last take her in his arms and swing her around the way Jenny Sadler's father had, letting her hair fly as she squealed. Or snuggle her on his lap the way she'd seen Meggie Albert's father do on sleepovers, before reading them story after story, then tucking them both into bed.

The young Chloe had longed for a jovial dad, free with affection, and blamed herself that hers wasn't. The therapist Chloe understood intellectually that he was a reserved man who nonetheless loved her deeply, that he had demonstrated his caring in other ways with his fierce protectiveness, his hard work to give her a good life.

The Chloe she was now, split in half by his stunning revelation, knew only that she understood nothing, but she wouldn't leave until she did. "Why?" she asked. "You said you weren't ashamed of my past, so why did you hide it?"

He remained silent, and she saw the cost to him. Maybe she shouldn't be asking anything of him when he was so obviously ill. Deep within Chloe, terror stirred. Through all the years of her memory, she'd counted on an unspoken assurance that whether or not she ever lived up to his expectations, he would not let harm come to her.

To think that the greatest threat she'd encounter would come from him would have been unimaginable.

Uncertainty dogged her. He was fighting off an invisible predator inside his body. Maybe she should wait; maybe she didn't need all the facts right now.

But she did.

"I'm sorry, Chloe." He spoke before she could summon the words. "I was aware when we embarked on this course that there were pitfalls in it. I told myself that you didn't need hurtful information, and as the years went on, it became easier to believe that it didn't matter. That you wouldn't care, that you'd even be glad if you knew, because we'd given you a good life and all the advantages so many children don't have." He paused, and she saw a new vulnerability in him. "We did give you a good life, didn't we, sweetheart?"

Torn, Chloe cast about for the right answer. No matter

what he'd done, the price of it was plain on his face. She wouldn't add to it by discussing the father she'd wanted him to be. "You gave me every advantage money could buy," she answered honestly. When he winced, she hastened to add, "You made me feel safe. I always knew you would take care of me."

"But it wasn't enough, was it?" he asked with surprising insight. She had no idea he'd seen into her heart. "You always wanted a sibling. Never a brother, though— you used to make up names and play imaginary games with a sister. Remember that?"

"Not the imaginary games, but I do remember always wanting a sister. I didn't realize that you were aware of it."

"You were such a solitary child, Chloe, and almost frighteningly bright and perceptive. We were aware that you missed your sisters, but we thought the best thing to do was to close off your past and concentrate on the future." His eyes grew sad. "You cried yourself to sleep every night for six months. In the daytime, you were so withdrawn that we despaired of ever getting you past it. We consulted a psychologist in Dallas and kept her on retainer."

"Why Dallas?" was the first question Chloe could sort out of the jumble of all she wanted to know.

He looked uncomfortable then. "Please." He gestured. "Sit down. This is going to take some time to explain."

Chloe didn't want to sit, but she could see him flagging, so she obeyed.

"It's hard to figure out where to start," he said. He

sagged against his chair. "I suppose with your mother and me. You can't be surprised to learn that we were not a love match. I was first attracted to your mother's money."

Chloe stifled a gasp at the harsh statement.

"She understood that, though we never discussed it then. The alliance suited us both. I was ambitious but poor, and she was well on her way to becoming what was once called a spinster. She'd always been aware that the wealth she'd inherited upon the death of her parents made her the object of fortune hunters, and she'd learned caution early on. I was a pretty good catch, though, if I do say so myself. To make a long story short, she fell for me, and I found much to admire in her. We were compatible, which is a far sounder basis for marriage than passion. People make mistakes when they let passions rule."

There, in a nutshell, was Chloe's life. If Vince could hear this conversation, he'd understand how she'd remained a virgin this long. "Maybe they do, but a life without passion is colorless," she said.

His smile was fond. "You think that now, sweetheart, but I promise you, passion doesn't last. Your mother and I were older, and we understood the world beyond the rush of heated blood."

Chloe opened her mouth to argue, but closed it without saying anything. They would never see eye to eye on this, and she was relieved to understand why.

"I'm sorry to say, now that I know the joy of it, that we never planned to have children. Over time, though, your mother came to want a child desperately—" He stopped, clearing his throat. "And I couldn't give her one. I'd had mumps as a teenager, and I was sterile."

Chloe felt his discomfort and squirmed herself at such an intimate revelation. "So you agreed to adopt. Why hide it?"

He grimaced. "That was more your mother saving my pride than anything else. And since we'd moved to a new place and neither of us had extended family, it was easy enough to go along with assumptions that you were our biological child. And that's why the psychologist in Dallas with ties to no one here."

He placed both hands on his desk and leaned forward. "You're ours, Chloe. Make no mistake about that. No, it wasn't me who wanted to be a parent and I never expected to care for you so much, but it didn't take long before I knew I'd die for you." His eyes grew fierce. "Hate us—hate *me,* since I was the reason your past was hidden—but *never* think that we don't love you. You quickly became everything to both of us."

Chloe jumped up from her chair and began to pace, unable to withstand the onslaught of emotions—love tangling with fury that this man had played God with her life as though he had the right.

One thought leaped past the others. "The psychologist can't possibly have condoned what you did."

He looked abashed. "No. As a matter of fact, she'd feel smug right now. She warned us that we'd never get away with it for a lifetime, that the longer we waited to tell you, the deeper and more permanent the estrangement would be." He lifted haunted eyes to hers. "We waited too long, but we believed we'd have time…and then our lives were so good that it was easier to just keep going. As the years passed, we seldom thought about it because in our minds, you were our daughter and only ours. When we did consider it, we worried that we'd lose you if you found out.

"Was the psychologist right? Have we lost you, Chloe? Please, don't blame your mother for this. She only went along for the sake of my pride."

"How could you—" She whirled away, unable to sort out so many conflicting impulses. Then she whirled back, hands clenched. "I don't know what to do. I never fit, and I always wondered why it was so hard. Part of me wants to punish you for what you've stolen from me." Tears stung her eyes. "Part of me feels terrible about that anger because you're—"

His smile held no mirth. "Dying?" He shook his head. "Maybe this is my punishment, Chloe. Maybe the idea of karma is real, and I'm reaping mine now." He leaned forward, his gaze intense. "But regardless of what happens to me, I'm concerned about you, sweetheart. Angry with me or not, you've depended on me most of your life to protect you, and the desire to do that doesn't just vanish. Even if the one you need protecting from is me." He rose and took a step toward her, then halted. "Tell me what you want from me, Chloe. If it's within my power, you'll have it. I'll move heaven and earth to make this up to you."

Anger shot past weakness. "You can never make this up to me. You've taken my life from me. Worse, you've made me spend twenty-three years trying to become someone I'm not. And in doing so, I've lost who I really am."

He recoiled as if from a physical blow and grasped the desk for support but somehow remained standing. "You may be right that I can never fix this, but that doesn't mean I can't do something." His body might be failing, but his eyes held the ferocity of the lion he'd always been. "I had the resources to hide this from you for all these years. I can use them to help you find your sisters now."

Chloe had come here expecting to have to fight her parents on this, to have to dig for every morsel of information. "You would do that?"

"Sweetheart," he said, his face drained and gray, "I would open up a vein and give you my lifeblood if that would help." His mouth twisted in a rueful shadow of a smile. "If my blood weren't tainted with this damn disease." He shook his head but returned his gaze to hers. "It won't take long to locate them. I've had someone watching for them all these years."

"What?" She stared at him. "You know where they are?"

"No, not specifically. I wanted to forget they existed. But I've paid someone to alert me if—"

If they tried to find me, Chloe finished silently. "But they haven't tried, have they?" she said, voice hollow.

"I don't know that. We covered our tracks well. What I've paid him for is to make periodic checks on them and to also let me know if there had been inquiries to the doctor or the judge who helped us out. They could be searching, but they're not close to finding you yet."

Hope stirred. Maybe they did care, these sisters she could barely imagine. "Do you know what they look like?" *Do they resemble me?*

His eyes were dark and defeated. "No. I didn't want to."

Suddenly, Chloe couldn't be angry with him any longer. More than anything, she was sad. And lonelier than she'd ever been in a life filled with solitude. They couldn't go back to what they'd been, and she could take no comfort in the illusions that had comprised what she'd thought to be the truth of her life. But the man before her was offering to help her find out what the truth in fact was, when he could have fought her on it.

"Sit down," she said, grasping his elbow.

He stiffened in pride, leaning against his desk.

"Please, Daddy," Chloe said, and tightened her grip on his arm, feeling exhaustion tremble in his big frame. She lifted her gaze to his. "I do want your help. I want everything you can get on them. But the first thing we have to do is take care of your health. Please…let's sit down."

"You'll stay?" The uncertainty in his eyes nearly broke her. Not once in her life had she seen this man be anything but supremely confident.

"Yes," she answered. "I'll stay for a while."

They walked to the sofa, side by side, for the first time with Chloe as the stronger.

CHAPTER ELEVEN

SOMETIME AFTER MIDNIGHT, Vince pulled up in front of Leticia's apartment, not surprised to see lights blazing inside. Tino's son was like him: a night owl. Leticia worked swing shift at a nursing home while her mother kept Tino Junior. Maybe the kid had been trained to it; Leticia admitted that she'd often wake Tino Junior up to play with him for an hour or so when she got home most nights. That way he slept later, too.

Not a smart habit to form; she'd have problems once the boy started school. But Vince knew how few families led storybook lives. Leticia did the best she could with few resources and next to no help from the boy's father.

Who was, of course, the reason Vince was here at this hour of the night. With a sigh, he knocked on the door.

"Who is it?" Leticia asked.

"Vince."

After a moment's hesitation, she opened the door but stood in front of the gap, her son on her hip. Leticia Martinez had once been a pretty, bouncy girl, brown eyes filled with mischief and more than a little sensual allure.

She was still pretty, but she didn't bounce. Life with Tino had worn her down. "Hi, Vince."

"Leticia." He nodded. "How are you?"

"Vee—" Tino Junior's chubby cheeks dimpled.

"Hey, buddy." Vince smiled back, gesturing toward the door and addressing his remarks to Leticia. "Gonna let me in or are we going to pretend Tino's not here?"

Her head dropped. She stepped away. At that moment, Tino Junior launched himself toward Vince.

Vince caught him and tossed the boy over his head, enjoying a moment of pure pleasure as the child's laughter rolled over him. He took a minute to engage in gentle horseplay, tickling the boy, swinging him around, then drawing him close for a hug.

As the little arms squeezed his neck, Vince knew a moment's doubt about his course. If anything happened to this boy because he'd involved Tino...

Nothing would happen, he vowed. Tino had told Mike he'd found a guy Vince should talk to. If the guy checked out, Vince might have what he needed to drive the first nail into Moreno's coffin. The first was the hardest; after that, things would tumble into place. He was so close he could smell it. Taste it.

And he was more than ready to finish this. He'd lost his hunger for vengeance, he realized.

Because he'd found something he wanted more.

Chloe.

But justice had to be served. Carlos had been murdered and his integrity questioned. If Vince didn't clear him, or let the murderer go unpunished, it would be poor repayment for Carlos's saving his life.

"Tino, get out here," he commanded, suddenly eager to move on. With Tino's son still tight against his chest, Vince watched his old friend saunter into the room, no trace of penitence in his gaze.

"Hey—" Tino's shoulder lifted in nonchalance. "Whassup?"

Vince shook his head. "Let's take it outside." Though furious with the boy's father, he gently pried Tino Junior from his embrace and handed him to Leticia. Without glancing back at Tino, he nodded to Leticia and walked out, assuming Tino would follow.

Knowing he'd drag him out by force if necessary.

Tino took just enough time to make sure Vince saw that he wasn't cowed. Outside the doorway, he stopped, arms crossed over his chest.

"Want to tell me what the hell you thought you were doing?" Vince asked in a growl.

"I don't answer to you, man. I'm all grown up, see?"

Vince merely stared at him. "Yeah. Looks like it."

"Hey, it was only weed," Tino protested. "A guy's got a right to a little fun."

Vince's hand whipped out and grabbed Tino by the collar. "Not when you expect me to bail you out, *carnal.*" The emphasis on the last word made it clear to them both just how little brotherhood he felt. "I don't need this, Tino. We're in the big show now. Your bush-league antics won't wash. You get your act together or forget having any help escaping them."

Tino's eyes flashed with rebellion and something that looked a lot like contempt, but it was gone so quickly

Vince might have imagined it. He jerked free of Vince's hold. "You need me as cover for your vigilante act on Moreno, remember?"

Vince stiffened. "I'm no vigilante."

"Then why you sneakin' around?" Tino wasn't the brightest guy, but he had a craftiness obviously honed in the joint. "See, way I figure it, you got just as much at stake in not ticking me off 'cause I can make some trouble for you if I talk around that maybe you be in places you not supposed to be. I don't think you need more trouble right now, eh, *carnal?*"

Ice formed a ball in Vince's gut. "You think you can play me, Tino?" He advanced on the younger man. "You care that little about your boy and Leticia that you'd screw around on both sides of the fence?"

"No, Vince—" Tino's retreat was instant and insistent. "Hell, no. I—" He exhaled loudly and looked away, then back. "Listen, it's been a lousy few days. I don't like this undercover crap—Moreno's boys make me nervous, you know?" Entreaty filled his voice. "You do this stuff all the time, but not me—I never did nothin' like this before." He raked both hands through his hair. "I just needed a little downtime, that's all. The guy I was with didn't make that cop. I never intended anything to happen."

Vince was forcibly reminded of an aspect of Tino he'd managed to forget: Tino didn't ever mean to do anything wrong, he'd swear with total belief to anyone who would listen. It was always lousy luck at fault, if not someone else. Never Tino. Obviously, prison hadn't changed everything about the man who had yet to outgrow irresponsibility.

He sighed. "It better not happen again. My stack of chips is about gone, and I can't be wasting them on your mistakes." He cuffed Tino gently on the shoulder. "Now, let's forget it and move on. I want you to set up that meet." After a few minutes of explanation and wrangling over logistics, Vince left. He glanced back as he slid into his car, seeing Tino's silhouette against the porch light, his stance sagging.

Tino was his weak link. Vince was standing waist deep in quicksand, trying to climb out with the help of someone who would turn and run at the slightest provocation—but he didn't have a lot of choices right now.

And though the cop in Vince understood that some people couldn't be saved, a part of him that no one else knew had lived through some very rough times with Tino, times when he was just as scared as that little boy, only he couldn't admit to it. He'd had to be strong for both of them, and he'd never let Tino see that having to scramble to keep them both fed and warm and safe had sometimes been all that had kept Vince from giving up. He and Tino were bound in an odd symbiosis, Vince the strong older brother and Tino the younger and weaker.

But without the need to keep up a front for Tino, Vince couldn't be sure he would have held on long enough to meet Carlos Quintanilla. Actually, a shoplifting expedition because Tino was sick had resulted in Vince's getting caught by Carlos.

So though Tino owed Vince, Vince owed Tino, too. And for the sake of that bond, Vince had to try, lousy as the odds might be, to give Tino one more chance. To salvage him in the name of the man who'd tried to save both and managed to rescue only one.

But Vince was only too aware that the rope that was Tino was frayed and might not bear his weight long enough to get him to safe ground.

Vince thought of Chloe then. *I guess you don't choose safety, do you?* she'd asked.

For the first time in his life, though, Vince realized that he had a reason to avoid dancing on the edge of danger.

CHLOE WALKED DOWN the hall to her office Monday morning after having seriously considered calling in sick. The weekend had been grueling emotionally; she was far from sure she had the resources left to do her job properly, and she had another appointment with Danielle late this afternoon at the shelter. It wasn't likely to be an easy session.

But her sisters wouldn't be found any sooner if she stayed home from work. Her father was going to use his influence and expected quick results. Unlike her, no one had taken pains to hide them.

Caroline and Ivy, he said their names were. Chloe tried to picture them. Would they be blond and tall like her? Would they have brown eyes?

Her heart twisted. Maybe they didn't want to know her. Maybe it wasn't how well she'd been hidden but that they'd gone on with their lives, too busy for a baby sister.

"What's up, *chère?*" Wanda asked. "You okay?"

Chloe stopped just inside the suite of offices. Ingrained habit had her demurring, "I'm fine. How was your weekend?"

Wanda's eyes rolled. "Lester's decided he wants to make up. Says he'll be my slave if I'll take him back. Like I couldn't find me a slave boy with a cute butt instead of his raggedy ass."

Chloe burst out laughing, intensely grateful for the distraction. "Lester's butt isn't cute?" She couldn't believe she was talking this way.

"It's not so bad, but maybe I want fresh meat." She winked. "You know—someone young I can train to please me."

At that moment, Chloe remembered that she was in the presence of an expert, maybe lousy at picking men but far more experienced at dealing with them than Chloe would ever be. "Wanda—" She couldn't believe she was really considering asking this. Then she charged ahead. "What do you do if—"

"If what, *chère?*"

"Never mind."

Wanda waved Chloe into her office, gaze piercing. Closing the door behind her, she leaned against it. "You got a man you want, Chloe?"

Chloe glanced away. "Maybe."

"Wouldn't happen to be a certain cop with an attitude almost as big as his—" Wanda halted, grinning. "Not that I know from experience, you understand. Wouldn't mind finding out, of course. Man's sex on the hoof if ever I saw it."

Chloe stiffened. "I don't know who you're talking about."

Wanda shrugged. "All right. Whatever you say. You want to talk, I'm happy to. Just keep in mind that the certain detective we're not talking about may be a hard case, but he's the genuine article—hero stuff. You don't want to confide in me, no problem, but don't mess with him if you're not serious, because he's getting in deep with you, Chloe. Don't hurt him."

Chloe was stunned by her vehemence. "I—how could I hurt him? He's—" *The strongest man I ever met,* she thought.

"That man we're not discussing got burned bad by his divorce. I'm talking out of school, so we'll let it go at this—I know too many women who'd have jumped at the chance to land him, but he's never taken a tumble since." She paused. "Until you. But the man's no fool. He sees that you come from this lily-white background, whereas his ain't so pretty. Seems to me, he's gonna be gun-shy, expecting you to run back into your safe little world even if you walk on the wild side for a bit."

"I don't think it's appropriate for us to discuss this, Wanda." Shaken by a new view of Vince, Chloe skittered away from a conversation that hit too close to the bone. She wasn't prepared to go into how blue her blood really was.

"Fine. You're the boss—"

"I'm sorry. It's just that—"

The older woman's eyes weren't quite so soft anymore.

"I'm glad to listen. I mean that. But if you're just playing rich girl out for a good time before you marry the King of Hair Spray, count me out." With that, she headed back to her desk.

Chloe was still trying to frame a response, when Don Newcombe poked his head into the doorway. "Got a minute?"

She stirred from her confusion. "Sure. Have a seat. Want some coffee?"

"No, I've had plenty already. Wanted to discuss this report." He gestured to the papers in his hand. "Coronado."

Her stomach jittered. "Oh?"

He watched her for a minute. "Your remarks seem a little…" His gaze sharpened. "Sympathetic."

She kept her voice carefully neutral. "In what way?"

"The guy's been in trouble more than he's been out of it, Chloe. He's in hot water now, and his career is check-ered with chances taken that could have gone south."

"But they didn't, did they? His arrest record is ad-mirable, and his clearance rate is the best in the depart-ment." Rare temper stirred, and she remembered what Vince had said about their past conflict. "Could it be," she asked in a pointed tone, "that your reaction to him is personal?"

Newcombe's eyes narrowed. "What did he tell you?"

Careful, Chloe. You aren't doing Vince any favors to rouse Don's suspicions. She strove to soothe. "A well-run department requires a wide range of personalities.

Perhaps you and Detective Coronado simply have a personality conflict, is all I'm saying. I don't doubt for a minute that you're trying to do your job as thoroughly as always." She watched for his reaction.

Guarded now, he was. And defensive. "Coronado and I had a run-in early in my career. You want my version?"

"If you'd care to tell me."

He glanced away. "Not really." He looked back. "I made a mistake about the facts in that case, but I've kept a close eye on him ever since. He's the type, Chloe—I've got plenty of experience now, and I've seen cops go bad. Coronado is one who could do it."

Chloe couldn't disagree more. "I think," she said carefully, "that you could be confusing a willingness to take risks in the service of justice with a true criminal bent."

Her voice strengthened with her convictions. "I've had several far-ranging and serious discussions with Detective Coronado, and I honestly do not believe his tendency to push the boundaries of accepted procedure is motivated by anything but a sincere desire to take down the bad guys. He doesn't mind stretching the rules as far as they'll go. However, he would never break them, Don. There are confidences I cannot betray, but I must tell you that he has had experiences that demonstrated amply to him the cost of that life outside the boundaries, and he's out to buttress the barriers that protect the good and the innocent, not destroy them."

Newcombe stared at her, his cynicism barely hidden. "You haven't been in this world long, Chloe," he said.

"I have. I know that you've got training and mean well, but you're still naive about human nature, for all your education." He slapped the folder in his hand against his lap and rose. "Coronado has something to hide besides the Krueger bust—I feel it in my gut. And when I put all the pieces together, I'm taking him down, for the good of the force."

Without waiting for her response, he walked away.

And Chloe watched, stung by his remarks and wondering what he'd say if he knew Vince agreed with him about her naiveté. Maybe both were right; her parents had lied to her all her life, and she'd never had a clue.

Was her judgment of Vince just as flawed?

CHLOE APPROACHED the secure doors of the Women's Shelter and waited to be buzzed in. As she signed her name, the volunteer on duty spoke to someone behind her. "Hey, Detective, you leaving? The kids will be sorry to see you go."

But Chloe hadn't needed the woman's comments to know that Vince stood only a few feet away. The very air had changed when he'd come near. She set the pen down and backed away so he could sign out.

He didn't move, his gaze sliding over her with a hunger that called forth an answering need in her. "Doc," he greeted in a voice more neutral than the laser intensity of his blue eyes. "How are you?"

"Fine." She swallowed against a throat gone dry. "How about yourself?"

He was about as fine as she was, Chloe thought. She

had to get away before she did something stupid. "I—I'd better go. I have an appointment."

His jaw locked, but his voice didn't betray his emotion. "You got a minute?" He nodded toward the outside.

She wanted to accompany him, much more than she should. Glancing at her watch, she saw that she had no time left before she was due to meet Danielle. No matter how badly she wanted to clear the air between them, she couldn't do that to a woman who was in such a vulnerable state. "I'm sorry," she said, and meant it. "I—this client is fragile, and I can't let her down. I mustn't be late, not today."

Probably as aware as she was of the volunteer avidly listening, Vince shrugged. "No big deal. Some other time, maybe." But his eyes said something completely different. "See you around, Doc."

Chloe watched him leave, torn between a client who needed her and a man who already meant more to her than he should.

CHAPTER TWELVE

THE BROKEN WOMAN Chloe had held last time was no-where in sight. In her place was a hard Danielle, defiant and spitting, daring Chloe to let her down. "You can't understand, a rich bitch like you. I see your fine clothes, smell your expensive perfume. You have no idea what my life is."

She would push, she would shove, she would test Chloe six ways from Sunday. It was expected; survivors of child sexual abuse lived their whole lives unable to trust anyone. Why should Chloe be the exception for Danielle?

Trust is the first casualty of abuse, but a child's will to survive is strong. To make it, the child must find ways to cope, to tiptoe around the heinous wrong that has been done. Children learn the world through the adults around them. Danielle's most lasting lesson had been that she could depend on only herself.

Chloe dug deep for the patience she would need. This would be only the beginning of the challenges. For Danielle to have a chance, Chloe would have to hold fast and prove to her that despite Chloe's knowledge of what had been done to her, Danielle was not despicable in her eyes.

"None of us can truly understand another person's reality, that's true. You have no reason to trust me—yet. But I'm going to stick with you, Danielle. I don't expect you to believe me. I realize I have to earn it."

The younger woman glanced up, hope peering out from the heavy drapes of fear. "I'm just a whore."

"That's simply another way of making yourself a victim. Is that what you want?"

Anger blazed from her eyes. "I'm no victim."

"That's right, you're not. You're strong enough to face what's been done to you. You have enough courage to come here and talk to me."

Chloe leaned closer. "You did what was necessary to survive, Danielle. Honor that. Credit that while others drowned in their misery, you had the courage to fight for life."

Carefully and slowly, Chloe reached out to a woman whose world had been the polar opposite of her own. Hand resting lightly upon Danielle's, Chloe spoke. "*I* honor you for getting to this point. You're going to make it, Danielle. I won't lie to you and tell you it will be easy—you'll never work harder. But you're a fighter, not a victim. You're going to win, do you hear me?"

A slight pressure squeezed against her hand, then almost crushed it. The broken heart of a child gazed up through Danielle's eyes. "I should have been able to stop him."

"You were a child. He had the power."

"But I'm not stupid."

"No, you're not."

"Why, Chloe? Why did he do it?"

The rasping ache in that voice clawed at Chloe's heart. "He's a sick man."

"He had no right—" Danielle keened, her body bending from the weight of her anguish.

Chloe knelt before the young woman, stroking the baby-fine wisps of hair.

"I can't feel—my body is numb. When I—when the johns touch me, it's like I'm dead. I feel nothing."

Pressing a kiss to the woman's head, feeling Danielle's tears on her fingers, Chloe held Danielle as she rocked in anguish. "But you will one day—" Moisture escaped Chloe's lids. "It will take time, but it can happen. And you're not alone in this, Danielle," she promised.

WAITING OUTSIDE, even though it made no sense, Vince couldn't help glancing over at the oaks he'd stood under with Chloe. He scanned the parking lot for her car; when he spotted the small, unremarkable vehicle, he smiled.

He might not always choose the safe route, but he seldom set out to do something that defied logic; yet reason had been in short supply since he'd met her. Even if his life wasn't so screwed up now, what future could there be for them? Especially with Barnes in the picture. *The King of Hair Spray.* Vince chuckled at Wanda's description.

Unfortunately, however, Barnes presented a very real danger to him. Getting between Barnes and Chloe could only make Vince's life worse, but Vince found himself unable to care about the consequences as much as he should. She'd definitely gotten under his skin, and he wasn't sure what to do about it.

Nothing was the right answer. Now, if only he could make himself listen. He should stay away from her. That was better for her and what he needed to do to avoid distraction.

If lonely brown eyes would quit taunting him in his dreams, golden hair quit filling his vision…

Vince straightened and headed toward his car. When he got to the T-bird, he slid inside but sat there going over all that had happened, sifting for clues to get a handle on his situation. Tino had arranged the meet with Moreno's goon. Tonight Vince should have an important piece of the puzzle.

Lost in thought, he almost missed Chloe leaving the building. Something was wrong. Her gait was stiff and lacking in her usual grace.

He started from his car to see what was the matter, but she'd already gotten into hers and was driving off. Vince kept a careful pursuit, fairly certain by her path that she was returning to headquarters.

He followed her into the parking garage, searching for a spot close to the ones assigned to the Wellness Office and the D.A. When he couldn't find one, he abandoned his car at the edge of a row and strode toward her. "Chloe? Are you okay?"

She whirled, her face pale, her body somehow fragile again. "I'm—I'm fine."

"You're not."

"I said I'm—"

"Come here." He reached for her, and Chloe froze.

Then with a jerky step, she moved into his arms, and he felt her tremble.

Drawing her closer, he tightened his hold, stroking her back and soothing her with nonsense sounds. Chloe's arms were trapped between them, her head nestled against his throat.

Slowly, Vince rocked her. Cheek brushing against her hair, he drew the scent of her into his lungs. "Ah, Chloe, you give too much of yourself to other people."

A shudder racked her frame. Vince placed a kiss on her hair, then to her temple, then lowered his mouth to the tender corner of hers.

Oh, God. How could he stay away from her until this was over? A slow groan escaped him; he wanted to shield her from everything, to take over the duty of guarding her tender heart from the world.

Chloe's head drifted back, exposing her long, pale throat. Tears leaked down her cheeks. He kissed her teardrops, tasting the salt of Chloe's compassion.

Chloe shivered, her hands clutching at his shirt. Need scorched him down to the bone. It wasn't just Chloe's body he wanted, though God knows he craved that. He wanted inside her heart, wanted to protect her. To make all this go away so she wouldn't get hurt.

And he longed to ease the ache that had been years building inside him with the balm of her generous heart.

CHLOE CUDDLED CLOSER. He was a champion. A good man who'd grown up with less to trust than she herself, yet he still tilted at windmills, still remembered, beneath that tough shell, what it felt like to be powerless—and to need.

She'd cried more with Vince than she'd done in her entire life. She tilted up her head to apologize, but the look in his eyes stole every word.

His head lowered, and his lips touched hers. The first breath of promise stirred within her.

"Chloe, what in God's name is going on here?" Roger Barnes thundered.

She jerked back to reality, the sound of Roger's voice a few cars over sending shock waves across her nerves. Grasping for a foothold in the present, mourning for what had been ripped away, she tried to tear herself from Vince's arms to face Roger.

But Vince wouldn't let go, bracing her against his side. Though Roger seeing them together could spell disaster for Vince, he never slackened his grip.

The two men bristled, the tension in Vince's frame matching the rigid lines of Roger's. "What are you doing here, Coronado? You're suspended from duty."

"It's a public place, Barnes. I'm a taxpayer."

This was a nightmare. Roger could destroy Vince, and she would have been the key to his downfall. From his body language, Vince was primed to defend her, but she couldn't let him do it. He was in too much trouble already; she had to defuse the situation.

She slipped away from the fingers tightening on her waist. She'd have to manage the negotiation of her life to spare him.

And he was the one man who'd never agree—who'd rather endanger himself than disappoint her.

They'd been standing in the shadows, and Vince's broad back had been between Roger and her. She prayed that Roger had only seen her too close to Vince, not drowning in his kiss.

"Thank you, Detective," she said in her best imitation of her mother's aplomb. "It was kind of you to help when I fell."

She forced herself to turn her back on him as though he'd served his purpose. "Roger." She brightened, composing her face into a careful mask. "I'm so glad to see you." Putting distance between her and Vince as fast as she dared, she kept her gaze trained only on Roger.

"Chloe, don't do this," she thought she heard Vince murmur. She prayed Roger hadn't. Closing her fingers on Roger's arm, Chloe walked fast.

She led Roger toward the stairwell, dredging up questions about his day as her face carefully assumed the contours of the woman Roger liked—cool, unemotional, controlled. While her heart cried out to the man she was desperate to save, Chloe hoped that he'd understand and not interfere.

She had to persuade Roger that what he'd seen was not what had really happened. If she hesitated, if she lost her nerve, Vince was doomed.

Halfway down one flight of stairs, Roger jerked his arm loose. "What in the name of heaven were you thinking?"

She had to make her explanation convincing. She let

the tears meant for Vince escape once more, hoping they would distract the angry man before her. God knows she'd never felt shakier. "Oh, Roger, I—I was just so unnerved after my session at the shelter. I don't know what came over me, but I wasn't watching where I was going and lost my balance. Thank goodness Detective Coronado was nearby when I stumbled."

Roger frowned. "It's foolhardy to even be seen with a cop like him. You're risking too much with that man, Chloe. Cut off your sessions immediately and issue your report."

Her knees went weak with relief. He hadn't seen enough. She would endure a lecture, grateful for Roger's tunnel vision. He was so self-absorbed that he wouldn't imagine her ever falling for someone like Vince. "I've already done it."

"Good. Stay away from him from now on. You can't taint your whole career over a rogue cop."

She bit back the defense that leaped to her tongue. "I'm always careful." She held her breath as he studied her.

Finally, he nodded. "You must keep proper distance from this work, Chloe, or it will get you into trouble. Your family's reputation is too important."

It was all she could do to bite back a retort. Her family's reputation was important to *him,* he really meant. If he only knew… He'd find out soon enough, but meanwhile, whatever strands of obligation she'd felt toward him snapped.

"Coming?" he asked, gesturing toward the stairs. "How about dinner this evening?"

I'd rather starve first. "I'm sorry, I can't. My volunteer session ran overtime. I have a mountain of paperwork to do."

"Very well. I'm due in the chief's office. See you later, Chloe. Remember what I said."

When he turned in the opposite direction, Chloe fought off conflicting urges to sink to the ground in relief or stick out her tongue at his retreating back. Pompous ass.

Then Chloe smiled. Vince had had more impact than Roger could ever imagine. She waited until she heard the elevator's ding and the doors close behind Roger to head for her office.

VINCE LEANED against the stairwell, adrenaline pumping. Every muscle had strained to intercede, to shield her from the consequences of his lack of self-control.

The only thing that had stopped him was the plea in her expression. He saw what she was trying to do but couldn't imagine that Barnes could be so dense. Was he so blind that the power of their emotions hadn't slapped him in the face?

When she'd practically dragged Barnes down the stairs, Vince had wanted to jump out and pull her back, daring Barnes to intercede. He'd followed them down the stairs, intent upon his goal, then stopped dead in his tracks as he heard Barnes's words.

Good God. If he forced Barnes to recognize their connection, Chloe could lose her job, maybe her license.

Listening to Chloe argue, Vince hadn't known whether to kiss her or yell at her. She risked too much for her own welfare. Yet even as dismay surged, he felt warmed throughout that she would leap, however unwisely, to his defense.

But when she and Barnes parted ways, Vince held himself back from going to her. Too brave by far, Chloe deserved better than to be dragged down to share whatever dark fate could still come his way.

Drawn toward her, wanting badly to feel her against him and to reassure himself that she was all right, Vince nonetheless forced himself to turn and retrace the steps to his car.

HECTOR BALDERAS WAS a typical bottom-rung gangbanger, swaggering and posturing to cover up for being so far down the ladder that he'd probably never even met Moreno, much less had any part in doing a job for him. Vince had seen so many losers like him that they blurred together. He shot Tino a glare over Hector's head that clearly said, *What kind of fool do you take me for?*

But Vince remained, even though it might be a waste of time, because he'd also learned over the years that you never knew where the key piece of the puzzle would turn up. Often, it was some small, seemingly unimportant tidbit that made everything fall into place. So he resisted a sigh and concentrated on giving this lowlife his due. "Buy you a beer?"

"Yeah, okay," said the clearly uncomfortable Hector. His gaze kept straying to the half-naked woman making love to a shiny chrome pole.

"Corona all right?" Vince asked with one quick nod to the waitress.

"What?" said Hector, his tongue all but hanging out of his mouth.

Tino laughed. "Beer, *ése*. That piece of tail is messin' with your mind."

"Oh—yeah." Hector glanced at Vince, but his gaze kept straying back to the stage. "I guess Corona's all right. With a shot." He struggled to act unaffected, but despite the meat-locker air-conditioning, sweat popped out on his forehead.

Vince gave their order and leaned back, his own gaze darting toward the stage. He must be getting old. The fake tits and stiletto heels would once have had his eyes bugging, too, but here, surrounded by women prepared to offer a man whatever he wanted, he was unmoved. Yet, a glimpse of Chloe's vulnerable nape had the power to make him rock-hard in the blink of an eye.

The legs of Vince's chair hit the floor with a thud. Even as the thought of Chloe intruded, he shoved it away. To think of her while in this place almost seemed a sacrilege.

What was he going to do about her? He'd never made love to a virgin in his life; now it was all he could think about now—and not, as would once have been the case, because she was a challenge. She was more than that— she scared the hell out of him. The responsibility of initiating her into lovemaking broke him out in a cold sweat worse than anything Hector Balderas could possibly feel.

With ruthless force, Vince dispatched thoughts of Chloe St. Claire. He had no business focusing on her now. Moreno was what had to matter.

The beers arrived, and Vince endured a conversation, if you could call it that, with Hector and Tino that would never have bothered him before, comparing the body parts and probable sexual skills of the various dancers while he bided his time, softening Hector up, giving him a chance to relax.

Vince tuned out Hector's negotiations for a lap dance and let his gaze scan the room.

And froze as he saw Jerry Akers across the way, staring at him, obviously wondering why he was in here with a couple of lowlifes when he wasn't cleared for duty yet.

Lousy damn luck. They'd come to a place not favored by a local gang on purpose. Why Akers was in this bar, Vince didn't know, but he'd still wonder about Vince's companions.

Playing it cool, Vince nodded and turned away. He leaned forward. "All right, enough," he ordered. "Bye, babe," he told the dancer, who shrugged, removed Hector's hands from her hips and strolled off.

"Hey," Hector complained, obviously half-gone from too many beer-and-shot combinations. He turned glittering eyes to Vince. "I wasn't finished, *cabrón*." His voice got louder as he leaped to his feet. His chair clattered to the floor, and heads turned. "Who the hell you think you are? You're just a damn—"

"Outside. Now." Vince rose and walked out, ignoring

Hector's outburst, hoping he'd shut up before he drew any more attention.

He didn't. Instead, Hector grabbed Vince's arm and jerked. "You don't tell me what to do, man. You need me. I don't need you." He doubled his fists, wire-tight with insult.

Vince longed to coldcock the little worm but merely lifted an eyebrow. "You want my help with your brother or not?" The last thing he needed was the spotlight.

Hector looked confused, then frowned. "Yeah, but—"

"Then get the hell outside. Now." Vince gave Hector his back again.

After a long moment, Hector followed.

WHAT A WASTE, Vince thought an hour later as he pulled into his driveway. He leaned his head against the seat and rubbed eyes raw from cigarette smoke and too little sleep.

Once on the front porch, Vince stuck his key in the dead bolt. It wasn't locked.

He backed away, immediately alert. Stepping to the side, he listened carefully for sounds out of place. Then he slipped off the porch and rounded the house, staying well below the windows.

He hadn't left a dead bolt unlocked in years.

He crept across the back porch, every sense tingling. At the door, he tried the knob first, then slid the key noiselessly into the lock, turning it with intricate care. He eased into the kitchen, then paused. Absolute silence greeted him.

Something didn't feel right, though.

Eyes adjusting to the moonlight spilling through the windows, Vince scanned each room as he came to it. A small sound from the living room stopped him. He didn't recognize it.

His off-duty weapon was in the coat closet, too far away for him to reach.

That sound again.

Suddenly, Vince smiled and moved toward the source of the noise. Standing to the side, though it might be an unnecessary caution, he quickly opened the door.

"Mrrrr-oowwww," the prisoner complained, twining around Vince's feet.

Vince flipped on the nearest lamp. "What happened to you, guy?" He perused the room. Nothing obviously out of place, yet his scalp prickled.

Someone had been in his house.

The cat's ears twitched; his tail flicked back and forth. Vince bent over and picked him up. The tomcat growled, then turned, golden eyes blinking. Scratching the animal behind his ears, Vince felt the cat relax by inches; finally, he purred.

"Sure wish you could talk, fella. I'd like to know what you saw." He stared into the closet and thought. It took a minute for something to register.

His weapon was gone.

"Hell." His heart sank. Setting the cat down, he observed the room again. Everything looked as it had when he'd left this morning.

But it didn't feel the same.

He saw nothing else missing as he moved through the house. When he opened his bureau drawers, subtle disarray greeted him. His place had been tossed by the best. They'd been thorough. What were they looking for?

And who were they?

He could only think of bad scenarios to explain the missing weapon. His fingerprints were all over it; a careful thief could use it in the commission of a crime and no other prints but Vince's would show up. The back of his neck tingled in horror. Who had been here, and what was the agenda?

The obvious thing to do was to report the break-in; yet something within him resisted. He'd dust for prints himself, but he already knew what he'd find—

The absent traces of someone who did not wish Vince Coronado well.

The suspects were legion.

Moreno and Don Newcombe were good places to start.

Vince headed for his car to get his gloves and fingerprint dust. Just as he opened the front door, the phone rang.

His hand stilled on the door frame. His heart sped up its pace. He debated not answering.

Three rings. Four. Swearing under his breath, Vince crossed the room quickly, and snatched up the receiver to his ear.

He didn't say a word, though. Just waited.

A tinny, mechanical whine spilled through the line. "It can get worse." The too-even cadence of an artificial voice grated on his ears.

Vince said nothing.

"Back off." *Click*.

Vince stared at the receiver long after the dial tone began. Then he looked out at the darkness and felt bleak certainty claw its way up from his belly.

It can get worse.

Though he didn't know how, he never doubted it would.

CHAPTER THIRTEEN

"CHLOE..." Her mother stood in the doorway, silhou-
etted against the marble entry, her posture, for a change,
not so regal or commanding.

Chloe managed a smile born of honest sympathy.
Her father's illness and the revelation of her adoption
had taken their toll on her mother. "It will be all right,
Mother. I promise." Then she did something out of character for the two of them. She retraced her steps across
the porch and hugged her mother.

And Dolores St. Claire, for once in her life, clung. If
Chloe had needed proof of how afraid her mother was
of losing her, she didn't anymore.

She drew back to a safer distance but grasped her
mother's hand in hers. "I want to meet them. I want
very much to know them." How much that was true
betrayed itself in her voice. There was a hunger growing
within Chloe by the day to find these lost traces of who
she really was. "I try to understand why you lied to me
about my past and not feel so angry—" Chloe clutched
in her hand the piece of paper on which her father had
jotted her middle sister's phone number, glancing away
until her voice was once again under control. Then she

continued in a careful tone, "I want to forgive you. I just—" She was forced to pause a second time.

But instead of calming, her agitation increased. The sense of betrayal overwhelmed her. "I'm sorry, it's too soon."

Before she could say something she'd regret, Chloe dropped her mother's hand and fled.

FIRST, she sat at the graceful Queen Anne writing desk, ankles crossed, back straight, and picked up the phone to dial.

She got through six digits, but her hands were shaking so much she missed a number. With a quick stab, she hit the Off button and dropped the phone to the desktop. She sagged against the back of the chair, breathing too hard.

Ivy's name was Galloway now—she'd married a wealthy man named Linc Galloway and had a baby, the investigator had said. A little girl named Amelia Caroline Galloway, for her other sister.

Not after me, Chloe thought. But why should she be? Ivy didn't know Chloe. Maybe she'd even forgotten her younger sister existed.

Please. Please want me. Chloe stared at the phone. It would be so much easier to take her father up on his offer to make the first approach. Then she could know without having to face any rejection firsthand.

I never took you for a coward, Doc. Vince's smiling challenge rose in her mind.

I'm scared, Vince. Really scared. Chloe bent over,

sucking great gasps of air in and blowing them out, seeking a calm that had never felt more distant.

Do it now. You have to know, either way.

She jumped up from the desk and grabbed the phone, heading for the safety of the chair in which Vince had held her while she cried. Clasping the bedraggled scrap of paper in her finger, she huddled against the cushions and wished they were Vince's comforting embrace. Before she could let herself think too hard, she punched in the numbers and listened to the phone ring, gripping the receiver in her hand.

A man's deep voice answered. "Hello?"

Chloe could hear a baby's gurgling laughter.

"Ow," the man yelped. "Let go of Daddy's ear, Amelia, honey." He exhaled as if in relief. "Hello?"

Amelia. The baby was real. Her *niece*.

"Is anyone there?" His voice grew impatient.

Linc. His name was Linc. Chloe sat frozen.

Then a woman's voice sounded in the background. "Who is it? Want me to take her?"

Ivy. Was that Ivy?

"It's no one," he answered, his voice fading, as though he was about to hang up.

"Wait," Chloe said softly, then louder. "Wait, please—hello?"

"Hello?" he said again. "Who is this?"

"It's—" Chloe's throat closed up tight.

"Forget it," he growled. "Prank call someone else."

"No, wait, it's—I'm Chloe. I'm—" How could she explain to this stranger she'd angered?

"Chloe?" He sounded dumbfounded. A long pause

ensued. "My God. We've been looking everywhere for you."

It was her turn to be stunned. Words wouldn't come.

"Hello?"

"I—" She cleared her throat. "Do you mean it?"

A soft chuckle emerged. "Ivy has been frantic to find you. She'll be—" A woman's voice sounded in the background. "Sweetheart, it's your sister. It's Chloe."

Chloe strained to hear her sister's voice. She chewed at her lip, barely daring to breathe.

"Hold on. For the first time since I met her, Ivy is speechless." Amusement rang in his tone. "Wait—here, love, let me take Amelia—" His voice faded.

But Chloe was still trying to absorb what he'd said. *We've been looking everywhere for you.*

"Chloe?" The woman's voice came on the phone now, sweet and tremulous. "Is—is it really you?"

Chloe swallowed. "Yes, it's—" Her throat closed up again.

"How did you find me—oh, Chloe, I've missed you so much. My word, Caroline will be pea green with envy. We have to come see—where are you—oh, Linc, it's her, it's—"

Then she laughed, but Chloe could hear tears, too. "I'm sorry. I'm babbling. I'm just so thrilled…." She paused. "Are you still there?"

"I—" Chloe could barely speak past her own tears. "You—you wanted to find me? You didn't…forget me?" She clapped one hand over her mouth, stifling the sob trying to break free.

"Forget you? Never—oh, where are you, sweetie? Where have you been? It was as if you'd vanished from the earth."

"I didn't know," she whispered. "I—I only was told two days ago that I had sisters, that I was adopted."

"Oh, my word. You poor thing. Caroline and I were separated, too. We only found each other recently." Ivy paused. "I've thought about you every day. I tried to stop them from taking you, but they said that I was selfish for keeping you from a family who'd shower you with everything Caroline and I could never provide. Maybe I should have run away with you, but I was only thirteen and they wouldn't—there hasn't been a day since then that I haven't regretted not finding a way to—" Ivy's voice broke.

Ivy wanted her. Had always wanted her. The enormity of that had Chloe reeling. "I'm sorry," she said, tears flooding. "Sorry I—I forgot you. I don't know how that could have happened. I always wanted a sister, and all along I—" Her throat became too full to continue.

"Oh, honey." Ivy's voice was all tenderness and no rebuke. "You were so little. You can't be expected to remember things that happened then. I should have been able to find you—"

"No. You couldn't have," Chloe said. "My...parents made certain of that."

"Why would they—" Ivy broke off. "I apologize. Of course they had the right and it's not my—"

"Pride," Chloe said, aching. "He couldn't father children and didn't want anyone to know. My mother did it to protect him."

"So many years…" Ivy trailed off, and once again they were silent, pondering.

"Are they good to you, Chloe?" Her voice was strained. "Was your life—"

Chloe thought of what Ivy had said about letting her go so that she'd have a better lot and knew that whatever her reservations, she couldn't let them show. "I've been sheltered and given every luxury. I've had so much—too much, really." *Except my family. My past.*

"Oh, I hope they've treated you like a princess. You were such a beautiful little girl, always so sweet and serious."

Chloe tried to absorb the idea that here was someone who knew her before she remembered herself.

"I've got a million questions. Where are you? What's your last name? I want to know everything that's happened over these years, and I want to see you—oh, my goodness, Caroline's going to be so amazed—"

Chloe smiled as Ivy's enthusiasm bubbled over again. "My last name is St. Claire, and I'm a psychologist with the Austin Police Department."

Ivy gasped. "I lived in Austin for five years. How could I have been in the same town and never—oh, Chloe…"

"We're not far apart now, just a couple of hours away. Where is Caroline? I want to see you both."

"Caroline's…well, some of the time she and Diego are in Dallas and sometimes in a little village in far West Texas called La Paloma. She's a doctor."

"Diego's her—"

"Husband. He's an amazing man. Once he was a

Special Forces medic, but he's also into alternative-healing methods. She was in an accident, and when she met him, he was taking care of the poor people in La Paloma, while she was a high-powered cardiac surgeon at Mercy Hospital in Dallas. They've joined forces now and have clinics in both places. He's so good for her."

"I'm glad. What about you? Linc sounds wonderful."

"He is. He's, well, he's just…everything. I can't wait to introduce you. Oh, Chloe, when can I see you?" Without waiting for an answer, Ivy rolled on. "I'm going to call Caroline and then I'll pack up my family and we'll be on the road—" She stopped suddenly. "That is, if it's okay." She sounded as uncertain as Chloe had felt.

"You can't know how much I want that, but—"

"It's all right," Ivy filled in quickly. "Maybe it's too soon."

"No, Ivy, I desperately want to see you. It's just that things are…complicated right now. My… parents…and there's this man, and he's in trouble—"

"I'm sorry." Ivy's voice held both tears and laughter. "Of course you have a whole life without us and naturally your…parents must be considered."

"I want to know you, Ivy. So badly."

Ivy's tone was warm and comforting. "I believe you, and we'll be there just as soon as you're ready, or you can come here if you'd prefer. You decide what's best for you."

"I can't begin to convey what it means to me that—" Chloe's voice broke. "I have a sister. You're real, not imaginary," she whispered.

"Oh, honey, you have a whole family now. Two sisters, two handsome new brothers and a little girl who looks a lot like you did as a baby."

"Really?" Chloe's eyes overflowed then.

"Truly. I love that about her. What do you look like now? I know your eyes are brown, but is your hair still blond? How tall are you?" Ivy was picking up steam again, when a shriek sounded behind her. "Oh, dear. Amelia thinks that her needs take precedence. I have to nurse her, Chloe. I don't want to stop talking, but she'll never settle down if I'm on the phone and so excited."

"Go ahead," Chloe urged. "I could visit with you all night, but she has to come first. Hand the phone to Linc, and I'll give him my phone number. I want to see you, Ivy, all of you, as soon as possible. In the meantime, call me at any hour."

Ivy laughed. "I'll try my best not to call you in the middle of the night, but I'm not sure how much sleep I'm going to get after this. Thank you so much for finding me. I've missed you like the dickens." Her voice thickened. "Oh, dear, here I go again. You get some sleep, sweetie, and I'll talk to you tomorrow. I love you, Chloe." Then she was gone.

I love you. Chloe bowed her head and let the tears fall.

"Chloe?" Linc's deep voice was kind and gentle now. "You all right?"

She sniffed and wished for a tissue. "I've never been so happy in my life."

He laughed, and she thought she was really going to like this man who was now part of her family. Her *family.* "Ivy's over the moon," he said. "She's wanted this for so very long. Family is everything to her. I'd be one lonely, bitter man if I hadn't met her. Instead, I'm rich because I have Ivy and Amelia, and now our circle can be complete."

"Oh, Linc, I can't wait to meet all of you. I was so afraid—"

"You never have to fear Ivy. She's got enough love for the whole world. Your heart will be in good hands."

Somehow Chloe believed that. She and Linc spoke a little longer and exchanged phone numbers, office, home and cell, before she reluctantly let him go.

She curled up in the chair, cradling the phone to her chest as if it held her new family in it. Her heart was so full she felt it might explode. Overflow with the riches of knowing that soon so many questions would be answered. She sat there for long moments, alternately smiling and crying, trying to make herself go to bed and rest up so that she could tackle figuring out how to carve time in her caseload so that she'd be free to meet her sisters.

Sisters.

She couldn't go to bed yet. She craved lights and people, not the too-quiet walls of her house.

She was going to get that dog and name him Charlie. She needed a companion.

Even in her present state, Chloe could smile at the idea. She didn't really have time for a dog, but she wanted somewhere to expend this love that had been buried inside her so long that she'd thought it dried to dust.

Then it hit her. She had sisters to love now, and a niece. Two brothers-in-law. Chloe swiped at her cheeks, wishing she had someone she could talk to about this new and terrible longing that threatened to eat her alive.

And suddenly she knew exactly where she was going.

Even if it was too late at night. And he might be entertaining a female companion. Given that he was a walking female fantasy, it was entirely likely.

At the thought, Chloe almost turned back. She could wind up humiliated.

But for once she was going to take a risk.

In minutes, Chloe was in her car, nearly to Vince's house, telling herself that she'd just drive by. If the lights were off, she'd keep going. If the lights were blazing...

Maybe. Maybe she'd stop.

Only one faint light glowed. No convenient signs left by fate as an inescapable decision.

Chloe pulled to the curb but didn't cut off her engine. For the first time in years, she chewed at a fingernail, pondering the idiocy of going any further.

Do you always choose safety?

After ripping the nail away, Chloe turned the key and let the silence swell and overtake her. Knuckles white on the handle, she opened the car door and stepped out. Before she could lose her nerve, she hurried up the walk, concentrating on the concrete sidewalk beneath her feet, then the porch steps. She lifted her hand to knock—

A hand closed over her mouth. She was bodily lifted from her feet and torn from light into darkness.

A scream clawed its way up from her throat.

"What the hell are you doing here?" Vince whispered harshly.

She tried to speak, but he trapped her between his body and the house, his hand still over her mouth as he scanned the area.

"Don't say anything," he warned. He continued to scrutinize the lawn and the street. "Someone broke into my house."

Chloe gasped.

Then he pinned her with those laser eyes. "We have to be quiet." His seriousness rubbed off on her.

She nodded her understanding.

His hand dropped, but he didn't move away. He listened to the night sounds.

After a few moments, the tension drained from his frame. "I'm pretty sure they're gone. I just—" He focused on her. "Sorry. Did I scare you?"

"It's all right. I know you'd never hurt me."

Vince's eyes widened. A different tension invaded him as they regarded each other in the moonlight.

New sensations took over: his muscled chest against her breasts...the unyielding wall behind her...his erection against her belly...

Chloe saw his pupils darken as his gaze dropped to her lips. Her body softened, her pelvis tilting slightly in welcome.

"Don't," he warned. But it came out a groan.

"Kiss me," she said.

"No." He licked his lips.

She stared, fascinated, at his tongue, then tried to lift herself to his mouth. His hands imprisoned her upper arms, holding her in place. "Why not?" she demanded, amazed at her daring.

His features went still, but his eyes burned. He didn't answer.

She shoved at him. Like a boulder, he couldn't be moved.

"No." His eyes locked on hers.

"No what?" She glanced away, already regretting her impulsiveness. "If you don't want me, just say so and get out of my way."

His shoulders began to shake, and a rough laugh rumbled up from his throat. He pressed his groin against her, and it was the most erotic and glorious sensation she could imagine. "Does that feel like I don't want you?"

"I'm female. You're male. You can't help a simple physical reaction."

"Christ, Chloe, I've been hard so much of the time since we met that the damn thing should have broken off by now." He clasped her chin and turned her face up to him. "I want you so bad it's making me crazy."

"Then why—" She couldn't finish.

"Because you're—"

Then she got it. "Because I'm a virgin? You jerk. You impossible, arrogant jerk. You think that because I haven't had sex with anyone at my advanced age that somehow I need to be treated like some fragile little flower?" She smacked at his chest and pushed again. "Let me go. I'm leaving."

But he didn't budge. Instead, he clasped her wrists and trapped them above her shoulders. "What the hell do you expect, Chloe? A woman's first time should be special. It should be romantic, with flowers and wine and candles and—"

"Maybe I don't need those. Maybe I don't want gentle."

Fury sparked. "So that's why you're here? To let the mongrel teach you to do the nasty?" He thrust away from her.

And she mourned the loss of him. Scrambling to figure out where this conversation had derailed, she was opening her mouth to argue, when he whirled.

"Well, to hell with that," he said. "Just to hell with that. You go find some other mutt to sully your lily-white body, because this bastard isn't bastard enough to do that. I don't play stud for anyone, not even spoiled rich girls—"

"Stop it." Chloe closed the gap, grasping his head in her hands and standing on tiptoe to press her mouth to his. He stiffened, and she nearly lost her courage.

She forced herself to persist. "You matter, Vince. I came here tonight because you matter. Make love to me. I want my first time to be with you. No one's ever made me feel as you do."

A shudder ran through Vince as he stared down at the woman who'd crowded all others out of his mind since the day they'd met. When she tried to pull him close again, he balked. "You have to be sure," he warned. "I'm not doing this if—"

"I'm sure." She slid her arms around his neck, kissing

him until he could barely remember his name, much less resist her.

So he wrapped her tightly into his embrace and turned the kiss hotter. The top of his head was going to blow off, and he couldn't care less. Everything in his life shrank to nothing in comparison with how much he wanted Chloe, how much he needed—

Vince went still. He couldn't need her. He wouldn't.

"Shh," she said, and ran her tongue over his lips. "Forget everything but me, Vince. Please…let us have this one night without the world interfering."

Her eyes were huge and dark and so damn beautiful he couldn't do anything but hold her closer. "I don't know if I have any candles," he murmured, sliding his mouth to her jaw, nibbling at the tender underside of it and hearing her sigh.

"Maybe the dark is better, anyway."

He heard the nerves and drew back a few inches. "Oh, no, you don't. I want to see every last gorgeous inch of you."

Chloe's fingers trailed across his chest. "I want to see you, too," she murmured. There was mischief in her eyes. In the curve of her lips. "Every last inch."

He groaned. "You're killing me."

"I am?" She sounded thrilled.

Vince couldn't stop a chuckle. He swept her off her feet and headed for the front door. "But I'm not anywhere near dead yet." Using his shoulder, he eased inside, then closed the door with his heel and locked it behind him.

Just then, Chloe fastened her mouth to his throat.

He almost dropped her. Tightening his grip, he made short work of the distance to his bedroom.

But once there, he slid her slowly down his body until her feet touched the floor. Then he stepped back, somber. "Why did you come here tonight, Chloe?"

Her eyes a little glazed, Chloe frowned faintly. Then it was as though the sun had come out after long, cloudy days. "I found my sisters."

He goggled. "Already?"

"They want me, Vince." Her eyes were warm melted chocolate. "They've been looking for me."

"I'm glad," he said. She wouldn't be so alone anymore.

And she wouldn't need him. He should be happy about that.

Chloe's gaze dipped as if suddenly shy. "I was too excited to sleep. I wanted to tell you, but I was afraid you might have—" She glanced around the room and shrugged. "I thought you might not be alone."

Just like that, the day's events crashed in on him. "Chloe, you shouldn't be here. You have to go," he said. "Barnes is right. You can't afford to be anywhere near me."

Her eyes fairly crackled then. "Roger is a pompous jerk. He has no idea what I need—" She looked Vince over with a thoroughness that should have made him uncomfortable.

It only made him stone hard.

Vince took a step back, grasping for the lost reins of his control.

Chloe advanced. "Don't change your mind, Vince. Please." Her tongue took a nervous swipe over her lips, and he barely stifled a groan. "I want to know what it's like, and I want you to be the one to teach me."

"Chloe—" His voice came out strangled. "I'm trying to save you, and you're not helping."

The woman who'd challenged him at darts smiled, eyes sparkling. "Maybe I don't want to be helpful." Then she did the one thing he couldn't fight: she visibly lost her nerve. "You said you wanted me," she whispered.

He saw just how vulnerable she was but tried to keep perspective. "One of us has to have some sense. There's no percentage in anything between us. You know that."

"Do I?" she asked softly, and placed her hands on his chest, sliding them up to tangle in his hair. She rose to tiptoe and paused a micron away from his mouth, throwing his challenge right back at him. "I never took you for a coward, Detective."

Then her breasts pressed into him and that fallen-angel mouth closed over his. Vince scrambled to hold on to his rapidly vanishing logic.

She slid her tongue inside his mouth, moaning softly, and logic went up in smoke.

Chloe felt it when Vince gave up on protecting her from himself. The kiss turned so carnal and consuming she had to fight for breath.

Oh. Oh, my— Had she ever dreamed anything could be like this? Any pretense of distance vanished, and Vince's desire rolled over her like the last wave before drowning.

And all Chloe could do was hang on for dear life.

Inside Vince pounded a drumbeat of possession.

Mine. She's mine.

For one wavering second, Vince glimpsed the faint possibility of pulling back, of remembering some trace of why he should resist her.

Then the riptide swept him under, and all he could do was try not to devour her whole when every beat of his heart shouted for him to take her and keep her and never, ever let her go. "Wait—" He tore his mouth from hers. "I'll be right back."

Chloe froze as he left the room, unsure what she'd done wrong. Ready to bolt.

Then she heard the soft, sensual music. *Sade.* The man continued to surprise her. Something inside her took a tumble.

Vince walked back into his bedroom with one single stubby candle in his hand, feeling like a fool. At the sight of her, he stopped, wondering how he'd ever gotten so lucky.

"Puccini to West Africa—you're a man of diverse tastes. Was it a woman who taught you about opera?"

Vince grasped at the distraction. "Yes." The older woman's face rose in his memory.

"You loved her," Chloe said.

He started to deny it, but the time for playing games was past, and Liliane deserved better, anyway. "Liliane saw something in me no one else ever had," he admitted. "She convinced me that I could make up for my slow start, that my world could be as big as I dared reach."

"I'm glad. You're as smart a man as I've ever met.

You shouldn't sell yourself short." Her lips curved at the corners, and the need to trace them with his tongue overshot the discomfort of her too-keen perception.

He crossed the remaining steps and set the candle down on the night table, lighting it with a hand that wasn't quite steady. "I don't want to talk anymore, Chloe."

Her eyes went wide and dark.

"I won't hurt you, I promise."

"I'm not afraid of you, Vince. I only want to be enough, and I'm worried that I won't be, that I can't—"

With a kiss, he hushed her.

Fingers clumsy with a longing that was more than physical, Vince slid the straps of her sundress down her shoulders, tracing the sweet line of her collarbone and tasting her skin on his tongue.

Peaches. The good doctor tasted of peaches, sun warmed and ripe for the picking.

Her fingers slipped beneath his T-shirt. He flinched when her nails grazed his belly. She jerked her hands away. "I'm sorry," she whispered.

Vince grasped for what was left of his self-control. "That wasn't wrong," he barely managed to say. "It was—" He picked up her hand and kissed her fingers one by one, then lowered her hand to the front of his jeans. "Just about more than I can handle."

Her eyes widened as she felt his response. "Oh." She worried at her lower lip.

"That mouth," he growled. "I wanted that mouth the first time I laid eyes on it." He bent down, and when her hand closed over him, he couldn't stifle the groan. "Chloe—" he said against her lips. "I want to take this slow, but you're making it too—"

He squeezed his eyes shut and tried to think about anything besides how she smelled, how she tasted, how he never wanted her hand to move, but—

"Hard?" Chloe asked, and he heard the smile.

He looked up. Her eyes still held jitters.

Vince shook his head, drawing her down to the bed. "I should have known after you almost whipped me at darts."

"Known what?" Her voice was breathy and threatening to drive him out of his mind.

"You don't play fair. And you're never what I expect." He rolled onto his back and put one arm over his eyes, struggling to back down several notches before he ruined everything.

The mattress moved. Her warmth left his side.

Vince sought her out. She was pulling up the straps of her dress, searching for her shoes. "I'm sorry," she said. "I'm—I tried to tell you I wouldn't be good at this."

Vince bolted up straight. "What?" He vaulted the footboard and grabbed her. "What are you talking about?"

She wouldn't meet his gaze. "Passion. I'm not a passionate person. I can't be what someone like you expects."

Vince knew he didn't dare smile. Part of him felt more like howling, anyway. "Darlin', if you were any more passionate, I'd be terrified."

It was her turn to be startled. "What?"

"Chloe, you've singed every last nerve ending I ever possessed. You're so responsive it's all I can do not to be a complete animal with you."

Color rose in her cheeks. "Why shouldn't you?"

"Oh, sweet mercy." Vince swallowed hard. "Because—"

Her chin jutted, and her eyes spit sparks. "If you say because I'm a virgin, I'm going to scream. Stop treating me as if I'm crystal. Make me feel like the women in all those books I've read, Vince. I never thought a man would ever make me want to—" She stopped.

"What?" he prodded. "Tell me."

Cheeks flaming, her eyelids fluttered down, then defiantly rose again. "Moan," she said. "Claw. Act like anything but a lady."

Every word flashed through him like chain lightning. One more time, Vince tried to remember all the reasons they had no business doing this, all the reasons he had to take it slow and easy.

Chloe backed away from him.

Vince squeezed his eyes shut and told himself it was for the best. She'd finally regained her senses.

Then he heard the whisper of fabric sliding to the floor. He opened his eyes, and there she stood, clad only in the tiniest pair of pale yellow panties he'd ever seen, back straight but hands clenched into fists, while her eyes swirled with a mixture of need and bravado and an uncertainty that broke his heart.

"You really don't play fair, do you?" he asked, advancing on her. "But I was right. You're no coward, Chloe St. Claire," he said, stripping his shirt off over his head and reaching for the snap on his jeans as he came within a hair's width of her body and wondered if he'd ever draw a solid breath again. "I'm still going to try to be gentle with you, but that's seeming pretty damn impossible right this minute, darlin', so if I fail, I'm just gonna have to give you a rain check and try again. That all right with you?" he asked as he lost the last of his clothing and pressed full length against her.

Chloe wanted to purr as his naked skin and rock-hard muscles electrified her flesh. "Yes," she barely managed to say before he swept her from her feet and covered her mouth with his, returning to the bed.

He proceeded to do things to her she'd read about in books—

And others she had not.

Despite his hunger, he patiently lured her along with him, teasing, tormenting…honing her own craving to a razor-sharp edge.

Featherlight, a finger traced the tender crease where thigh met hip, the silken hollow beneath her breasts. His palm caressed her mound, a slow, tantalizing press against the heart of her…

His tongue, his lips everywhere, whipping her nerves to fever pitch until she was ready to beg.

"Vince," she gasped. "I—I want—"

He grappled at a drawer of the nightstand and knocked half its contents to the floor before emerging with a condom in his hand and a pirate's gleam of triumph.

Chloe was torn between smiling and crying and giving thanks that this man had come into her life and taught her that she could understand passion, that she could feel—

Love. Even before he did more unspeakably erotic things to coax her body to singing, weeping, screaming bliss, she knew that she was falling in love with Vince Coronado, whether he would welcome it or not.

"Please," she begged him. "I can't—"

But Vince slid his mouth lower and showed her that she could.

And then he showed her again.

Too dazed to move, Chloe could only look at him, at the strain on his features as he held himself in check, and she knew that she'd found her hero, her knight in shining armor, no matter what he called himself. "Now, Vince," she begged.

His eyes were troubled. "I don't want to hurt you."

"You won't," she murmured, and drew his head down for a kiss, arching her body into him with a new and sure knowledge born of this remarkable night and this unique man.

Though aroused to the point of pain, still Vince attempted to go slowly, but Chloe wouldn't wait, wrapping her legs around his waist and opening herself deeper until he was too far gone to resist.

The power of the joining jolted both of them.

"Chloe—" Vince wished for a poet's tongue so he could tell her in beautiful words about this place she'd taken him when he was supposed to be guiding her. Lacking the words, he bent to her and let his body speak for him.

As she moaned his name and wept with his kisses,

Vince knew a knife-edge of longing to stay with her in this moment of rapture where the world couldn't touch them. Where his heart knew her heart and deserved all the goodness that was Chloe.

And when they tumbled together into bliss, he held her more tightly as if somehow he could keep the world at bay.

Until he could find the magic that would bind her to him forever.

One more kiss that felt like sliding into a cool river of peace. Before sleep claimed him, Vince told her in silence what he could never dare say.

I love you, Chloe. In another time, another world, they would have been perfect together, he thought as he rolled and kept her against him, feeling her warm breath as benediction.

But this was the real world, where she was a princess, cherished now by two families.

While he was a cast-off child no one had ever claimed.

VINCE JOLTED AWAKE at the pounding on his front door. "Coronado, open up! Police!"

He leaped from the bed, automatically reaching for a weapon. Coming up empty, he blinked, trying to remember—

Chloe. "What is it?" she asked, voice rough with sleep.

"I don't know," Vince said, jerking on clothes, searching for shoes.

But his heart sank. *It can get worse.* "Stay here," he

ordered. "Don't leave this room, no matter what you hear."

"I'll come with you," she said.

"No," he snapped.

More banging. "Coronado, open up now!"

He fought to mute the dread making him edgy. "Please. Let me handle this." He stared at her, memorizing her naked curves beneath the sheet, her hair all sleep rumpled and sexy, and wanted the power to turn back the clock. Vowed to protect her from whatever this was.

"Get in the bathroom and lock the door," he said.

"What?"

"Do it, Chloe." He wished to hell he could kiss her again, just once. Instead, he forced himself to turn away. "All right, I'm coming," he yelled. He strode to the door and opened it but stood in front of the gap. "What do you want?"

"Vincent Coronado, we have a warrant for your arrest for the murder of Hector Balderas." Jim Thompson from Homicide moved toward him. "You have the right to remain silent. Anything you say can and will be used against you in a court of law…." He continued the Miranda warning, but Vince tuned out the words as he saw who stood behind Thompson.

Don Newcombe, face grim, contempt burning holes through Vince.

Then Newcombe's gaze shifted to something behind him. Vince's gut seized.

He looked over his shoulder, and there Chloe stood, clothes hastily donned; she was so clearly fresh from his bed that he nearly groaned, wondering how in the hell he'd save her now.

"Don?" she said. "What is this?" But confusion slowly gave way to horror. "He couldn't have done anything wrong. He was with—"

"Get the hell back in the bedroom, Chloe," Vince ordered. "You don't understand—"

"Coronado, answer me—do you understand your rights?" Thompson grasped Vince's arm.

Vince reacted on instinct, ready to fight to protect Chloe.

Thompson and the patrolman beside him both grabbed at Vince. Thompson caught his arm and yanked him around, bending one elbow behind him. The sharp edge of metal bit into Vince's wrist as the cuff tightened.

A sharper edge of fear sliced deep. Vince forced himself to still, mind racing over how to keep Chloe out of this.

Hot on the heels of that thought came a question: Who wanted Balderas dead and him framed for it? "It was my weapon, wasn't it?"

Thompson's grim look was all the confirmation Vince needed.

Chloe was pale but shook herself as if emerging from a dream. "You don't understand. He was with—"

"No," he shouted over her. He couldn't let them taint her. He appealed to Newcombe. "She has nothing to do with this. If you care anything about her, keep her out of it."

"Vince, you couldn't have—" Eyes stark with terror, Chloe took a step toward them.

"Let's go," Vince ordered. *"Now."*

Thompson shifted his gaze between them. "Doc, I think you'd be wise not to get involved." With a firm hold, he turned Vince to face the door.

Newcombe's smile was chilling. "I told you to stay away from him, Chloe. He's dirty, and now he's killed twice."

"Shut the hell up, Newcombe. You won't get away with framing me."

Newcombe stepped toward Vince, fists clenching. "Resist, Coronado—come on, give me a shot, you lowlife—"

"Back off, Newcombe." Thompson intervened, leading Vince away.

"Vince, I'll be there as soon as—"

He spun around. "No. I don't need you." His voice rough with desperation to spare her, he saw the barb hit, saw her flinch. Saw her naked heart in her eyes, pleading with him for answers.

Dear God. Vince could hardly breathe. Everything in him strained toward the woman he needed to protect. *Not now, damn it. Give me a minute to—*

A sharp yank on his strained shoulders reminded Vince of one irrefutable fact.

He no longer had control of anything.

JAIL SMELLS: disinfectant, fear. Hopelessness.

Vince had known them for years, had felt them scorch his nostrils, curl up inside him and poison his lungs.

But he'd never expected to become one of *them,* the dregs, the lost. A part of society he'd crawled his way out of—a cesspool he'd known, from his earliest days, waited to suck him under its black surface. A hell he'd fought with everything in him to escape.

The stares of the booking officers scored deep gouges into his pride. The pity of the cops who'd brought him in, embarrassed to be cuffing one of their own. The silence in the squad car had pulsed with shame…and distance. Already, he was on the outside. No longer one of them. A pariah…a leper. A scumbag in the making.

Thompson had jerked him from the car with the rough haste they all used, as if prolonged exposure would taint them, too. As they rolled his fingers in the ink and printed him, Vince felt dirtied…diminished. Nothing separated him now from the slime he chased on a daily basis. The grime of his life had settled into its natural resting place.

This was where he'd been headed since birth. The son of a whore hadn't escaped after all.

No. For blessed seconds, rage warmed him. He was innocent. Damn it, he *was.*

But the looks of those around him pronounced judgment.

Guilty. Handcuffed. Photographed. Fingerprinted. Doomed.

Why? Who wanted him this badly? Moreno? Newcombe?

Then he entered the holding area filled with prisoners cuffed three together, and reality slammed into his gut.

Jeers and catcalls. Word traveled fast. "Come here, cop." Smooching sounds. "Come to Papa, lawman. Let's welcome the detective, boys."

"We'll be questioning you in a few minutes, Coronado. Make yourself comfortable."

Menace rolled over Vince, choking off his breath. A sharp tingle between his shoulder blades grabbed his attention. Out of the corner of his eye he saw Darden Whalen, the knife-wielding dealer who'd already served one long sentence, thanks to Vince.

"You look good in jewelry, Coronado," he sneered. The gleam in his eyes promised retribution. "Ain't that right, boys? No one we like to see in here more than a cop. So you dirty, eh, Coronado?" Malevolent eyes glowed as Whalen clucked dismay. "My, my...who gets to be your roommate, Vince?"

The officer beside Vince shifted. "Shut the hell up, Whalen."

"What you gonna do, Officer?" A contemptuous stare raked over Vince. "This place is full—no luxury suites available for the lawman." He nodded at Vince. "Me, I don't think too much of anyone who'd shoot a man in the back."

Vince stared stonily ahead. It wouldn't do him any good to remember all the stories he'd heard of cops dying in jail at the hands of those they'd taken down. He stood straighter, impaling the convict with his glare. "Too bad they won't let me be your roomie, Whalen. I'd like to be here to wave goodbye when they drag your ass to Huntsville."

"You gonna be right behind me, Coronado."

A spike of dread drove deep into Vince's gut. Whalen could be right. How high would they set bail? Could he make it? And could he clear himself while still in jail?

A vision of brown eyes welling with tears rose up before him. *Ah, Chloe. Why did I think I could protect you? I can't even protect myself.*

CHAPTER FOURTEEN

HOME NOW, alone and frantic, Chloe paced her living room, trying to figure out how to help Vince. He couldn't have done it. Why didn't they see that? What on earth was happening? Had everyone gone mad?

She grabbed the telephone to call Roger and insist that he fix this travesty.

But it was still dark, and Roger would be the last one to help. He probably already knew and was no doubt jubilant. He'd remind her that he'd warned her to stay away from Vince.

She needed someone who believed in Vince, someone with standing inside the system. Once, she would have asked Don's advice, but no more. He, too, was part of the night's disaster.

Whom could she call? Suddenly, she remembered Mike Flynn, Vince's friend, and his calm manner, his cool head with Vince after the Krueger shooting. He would know what to do, how to work the system to get Vince out right away.

She dialed the station, identified herself and requested Mike's cell-phone number. Punching the numbers in quick succession, she mumbled prayers that he would answer soon.

He didn't. She left a message.

After setting the phone back in the cradle, Chloe wrapped her arms around her torso, huddling against an inner chill. The weather might be warm, but no amount of heat could dispel the fear that gripped her with bony fingers.

Vince was in serious trouble.

No matter what he might say to dissuade her, he needed her. If no one else believed in his innocence, she did. She *knew* that the same man who'd held her to comfort her, who'd championed children no one else cared about…

That man was no killer. So maybe she might not be the best help, but no way would she let him face this alone.

AN HOUR LATER, Chloe paced the first-floor lobby of the courts complex, waiting for Mike to emerge from Central Booking downstairs. Voice sleepy, he'd answered her message within minutes, horrified at the story Chloe related. He'd resisted letting her accompany him until she'd made it clear she would go by herself.

Hearing Vince's name in a murmured conversation at the control desk, she moved closer, hoping to glean something that would give her a clue to his fate.

"Never would have thought it of Coronado…"

"Did you catch what Whalen said? He wants a piece of Coronado bad."

"No surprise at that. He's already had one trip to the joint, courtesy of Vince. Now he's set for another."

"Yeah, but you know what happens to cops inside.

All kinds of people want to do them harm. Coronado's life expectancy just got shot to hell."

"I know we're overcrowded, but he should be in a separate cell."

One of the men walked away. Chloe stared after him, stomach clenching. Even in jail, Vince wasn't safe. If anything, he was in more danger.

Just then, the outside door opened, and Roger entered. He stopped in his tracks, his ever-present calm deserting him for once. "What are you doing here, Chloe?"

She drew a deep breath. "He's innocent, Roger. You have to stop this. You have to let him go."

Roger shook his head, pity warring with curiosity. "Do your parents know you're here? What will they think?"

Her parents. Chloe's spirits sank lower.

"You can't do this to them," he said. "Their position in the community is too important."

Her head snapped up. "Don't you mean it's important to you, Roger?"

The dart hit dead center. His eyes narrowed. "What does that mean?"

The events of the night caught up to her. "The only reason you want me in your life is that I complete the picture. 'A good asset,' I think Mother termed me." Her laughter was harsh to her own ears. "Well, I have a surprise for you, Roger. I'm not their child."

"What?" He frowned.

"I'm adopted. There are skeletons in my background that even I don't understand yet, but I can tell you this—

I'm not the princess you wanted in your campaign photos."

"That's nonsense," he scoffed.

"Oh, but it's not. Just ask my parents."

"It doesn't matter." But his eyes wavered.

"I suspect it will," she said. "Actually, it's somewhat amusing. Vince and I have more in common than we realized."

"What hold does he have on you, Chloe?" He seemed honestly curious. "Has he blinded you so much that you can't discern what he is?" His voice tightened. "Is he that good in bed?"

She sucked in a breath at the contempt on his face. "It's not about attraction, Roger." She plunged ahead, desperate to reach him. "This is about justice. Surely, you wouldn't stand by and let an innocent man—"

Rare emotion flooded his face. "He's killed two people, Chloe. He's a murderer." He reached for her.

Chloe stepped away from his touch.

Roger dropped his hands, the heat of the moment vanishing as though it had never occurred. "If he's innocent, he'll go free. The system is designed to take care of that."

Chloe struggled with her temper, fought off the despair creeping into her heart. "He didn't kill anyone last night. He—" *Was with me.* She barely stemmed the words, but the worst thing she could do was to draw Roger's attention back to where she'd spent the night. Instead, she focused on what she'd just heard. "You've got to arrange to get him out of here."

"What? You can't be serious. Do you realize the

outcry we'd hear if we gave him special treatment?" He shook his head. "He'll get his turn." He glanced at the elevator. "I've got to go. I suggest you leave, as well. You have no business here." He lowered his voice. "Think about whether you really want to get mixed up in this. I'd be within my rights to question you, too."

Chloe recoiled. "Me?"

"How do I know this is the first you've heard about it? I'm discovering that you've been spending a lot of time with Coronado, in and out of the office."

"He didn't do it, so he couldn't have told me. Anyway, you can't make me breach patient confidentiality."

His smile turned triumphant. "You have no exclusion, Chloe. This is a criminal matter. Even *if* he were your patient, a relationship that I'm beginning to suspect vanished long before you issued your report, you can't hide behind that. Consider whether you want your own reputation dragged through the mud, or worse yet, how much you'd like to wind up in a cell right beside him."

Blood pounding in her ears, Chloe could only gape. "You wouldn't."

"Oh, yes. If you force me, I most certainly would." He turned on his heel and departed, leaving Chloe staring after him.

When Mike walked out of the elevator a few moments later, the look on his face told her volumes. Rubbing one hand over the back of his neck, he shook his head. "It's not good, Chloe. Ballistics confirmed that the bullet came from Vince's gun. It was thrown into the alley near where Balderas died."

"But—"

Mike's voice was gentle. "He had motive. He was seen having a heated argument with Balderas last night."

"He didn't do it, Mike. He couldn't have."

"They've got a cop on Vince's detail who witnessed the argument just hours before the shooting."

"I told you he was with me."

"What time?"

She frowned. "From about midnight on, I think."

"Balderas was killed between ten and eleven."

Chloe grasped his forearm. "You can't believe he's guilty."

"My opinion doesn't matter if we can't prove his innocence."

Chloe struggled with despair. "If you won't help me—"

"I never said I was giving up on him. That doesn't mean we don't have to face facts."

She took her first deep breath in hours. Then she remembered what she'd heard. "He's in danger in that jail, isn't he? From the other inmates. I heard two of the officers talking. They said that if he—" She cleared a throat suddenly gone dry. "If he goes to prison, he's a dead man." Lifting her gaze to Mike's, she saw nothing to comfort her.

"Vince can take care of himself." But he shifted his weight from one foot to the other.

"When can I see him?"

"Not until he has his magistration hearing and posts bond."

"But if he's my client—"

Mike smiled, yet his eyes were sad. "No one who's

seen Vince when he talks about you is going to buy that you're his shrink." His voice grew softer. "Be careful, Doc. He's using what few chips he has to keep you out of this. So far Newcombe is cooperating. The mud on Vince is going to splatter everyone around him. He doesn't want any on you."

"I don't care."

Chagrin washed his features. "You're supposed to be smarter than a dumb cop. Go. Please."

"I can't leave him here," she whispered, blinking back tears.

"You're making things worse for him, not better. The harder you push Barnes, the more he's going to try to nail Vince. There's no love lost between them. If you really care about Vince, you'll go on to work and let me keep you posted."

"Mike—" She grew physically ill at the thought of deserting Vince in what now seemed like enemy territory.

"He can't concentrate on saving himself if he's worrying about you destroying your life by association with him."

Frustration and fear tangled inside her. "I don't want him to feel abandoned. I want him to know I care." She lifted her gaze to Mike. "I didn't get to tell him."

"You'll have your chance," Mike promised. "Assuming the magistrate grants bail."

She gripped Mike's arm. "What do you mean?"

"Never mind. Don't worry about it."

"Oh, no—" Understanding dawned. "They're going for capital murder? Does Vince have a good lawyer?"

"I don't know."

"I've got a trust fund, Mike. I'll post bond. I'll hire a lawyer. Tell me what to do."

Mike studied her for a long moment. "He won't want you any deeper in this, Doc."

Chloe straightened to the posture that had been drilled into her since childhood. "He said I was stubborn, and he was right. I'm not going away, no matter what happens. Fill me in so I can get to work."

Finally, Mike nodded. "Okay. He's gonna kill me, but he'll have to get out of jail to do it." He shot her a quick grin. "He'd tell you he doesn't deserve you, you know that?"

"It wouldn't be the first time we disagreed. Now, start talking."

He did.

"WHERE WERE YOU between ten and eleven, Coronado?"

Vince studied Jim Thompson, seeing the discomfort in the man's lanky frame. They'd worked some cases together. He respected Thompson, known all around for his evenhanded, steady touch with an investigation. He never jumped to conclusions but turned over every piece of a case slowly and carefully, preferring to see the pattern emerge rather than racing to a decision.

His presence might be Vince's only break so far.

Newcombe paced. "What's the matter? Decided to lawyer up?"

Vince cast him a glare. "I don't need a lawyer. I'm not guilty."

Newcombe snorted. Thompson merely sat in front of Vince, hands folded. "Nobody's going to say anything if you want one, Vince."

But I'll look guilty as hell. Didn't matter what the truth was, if he insisted on having a lawyer present, the assumption would be that he had something to hide.

"Have to get your story straight, is that it?" Newcombe jeered. "Why don't you take the easy way out and use Chloe's alibi?"

"Keep her out of this."

"How the hell did you sucker her in, Coronado? I thought she was smarter. She just want a walk on the wild side?"

Vince fought back the urge to launch himself at Newcombe. He refused to make eye contact, knowing Newcombe would love for him to lose his temper and say something stupid.

Thompson switched tactics. "Where's your Sig Sauer, Vince?"

Here it came. But he'd already laid the groundwork by asking his question when they arrested him. "It was stolen."

Even Thompson looked skeptical. "You reported the theft, of course."

Mentally kicking himself, Vince shook his head. "Somebody broke into my house and took it last night. I was going to dust for prints, but—"

"You're a cop under investigation, your off-duty weapon goes missing and you don't report it? Come on, Coronado, what kind of fools do you take us for?" Newcombe taunted.

Understanding that he'd been ten kinds of dumb ass didn't help Vince's temper any. "A fool who wants me any way he can get me," he retorted.

Newcombe slapped both palms on the table. "You don't have jack to back that up. You're the one who's under investigation, and I'm the one who's going to put you away."

"What's my motive?" Vince rose from his chair, leaning right in Newcombe's face. "You were wrong about me seven years ago, and you're wrong now, Newcombe. But you don't give a damn about the truth, do you? All you care about is how it makes you look." He wanted to bring up seeing Newcombe with Gloria, but he couldn't play that card yet. He had too few in his hand.

Thompson rose, too, grasping Newcombe's shoulder.

Newcombe shook him off and plowed ahead. "Your motive doesn't matter. Your weapon killed the guy, and yours are the only prints on it." He leaned closer. "You were seen earlier in an argument with him. You've killed before." He straightened, radiating confidence. "You're going down, Coronado. You know it, I know it, and now we've got proof."

He smiled. "And you're a dead man the minute you set foot inside the walls of Huntsville." He walked toward the door and paused with his hand on the knob. "Me, I say good riddance to bad rubbish."

After they left, Vince could only stare at the door, his mind doing cartwheels.

He had no alibi for the time of death. Akers had seen him with Balderas. So had a lot of other people.

And all they had to do was talk to Tino to realize that he was still working Moreno, even though he shouldn't be. Sure, it wasn't much motivation for murder that Balderas had been a disappointment. But only Tino, Vince and the dead guy were aware of that. And if they kept digging, they'd find out that he'd lied about Tino being his CI. They could say anything, draw any conclusion. Point was, his weapon had been used, and his prints were on it.

How did this tie into the missing evidence and Gloria's denials? Everything pointed to someone inside the department, but Vince couldn't accuse Newcombe without more proof.

And he was stuck in here with no way to clear himself. The web kept closing in on him, slender, sticky threads binding him at every turn. Some spider he couldn't see was hard at work on sealing him inside a prison of his own deceptions.

For the first time in this whole nightmare, Vince felt the cold bite of real fear.

"CHLOE, darling, what can you be thinking? Come home with us this instant."

Chloe winced as she saw her parents enter the lobby and mentally cursed Roger for calling them. "I'm not going anywhere, Mother."

"That man is accused of two murders," her father's deep voice rumbled.

"One," she corrected. "And he's innocent." She met her father's eyes. "He shot a criminal in self-defense. A man who preyed on children."

"Darling, don't do this," her mother pleaded. "I'm certain you mean well, but don't get involved in this sordid situation. It could have terrible repercussions for both you and Roger."

Her father placed one comforting hand on her shoulder. "We only want to help you, sweetheart."

"Vince is innocent." She heard her shrillness but couldn't stop. "Doesn't anyone but me care?"

"Chloe, keep your voice down," Roger said, reentering. "Everyone's listening."

Behind him she spotted the two officers at the console, eyes round at the spectacle. Shock washed over her parents' faces.

Careful Chloe would never make a scene.

Careful Chloe never drew attention.

Roger grasped her elbow and towed her toward the door. "I'm taking you home now."

Chloe dug in her heels, jerking her arm away from him. "Let him out now, Roger."

"I can't do that. He has to go before a magistrate."

"Then make sure he sees a magistrate immediately."

He cut a glance toward the officers. "I will not do special favors for a murderer, Chloe." His jaw tightened. "Not even for you."

"He's in danger. He could get hurt in there—I heard them say so." She nodded toward the two men.

"He won't get hurt."

Chloe didn't believe him. "You're only concerned about appearances, about how it will look to the press."

"He's guilty. He's going to prison for the rest of his life, at a minimum."

"You really are—" Her voice dropped to a stunned whisper. "You're going to ask for the death penalty."

He didn't answer, but she knew, and she was terrified for Vince. "You can't—he didn't do it, Roger. Something's terribly wrong here. Don't you have any regard for the truth?"

He stared while her parents looked on as if she'd grown two heads. "There is nowhere for you to go in this, except to make your life into a nightmare. I'm warning you for the last time—remove yourself while you can."

"And what about Vince? Who watches over him?"

"He'll get what he deserves."

Rebellion burst past all the decorum and control she'd been taught. She had to protect Vince however she could. She glanced at her parents, then back at Roger. "I am telling you right now that if you don't make sure he's in a separate cell and safe as a baby, I'm going to talk to every reporter in town."

Her mother's audible gasp didn't deter Chloe. "I'll make sure they know that a cop with a distinguished record is being persecuted by a D.A. who's jealous of the attentions his ex-girlfriend is paying to that same cop."

Roger's gaze narrowed. "I'll call it pure rumor and innuendo."

"They won't listen—it's juicy stuff. I don't think my parents would appreciate the negative publicity, either."

And Roger needed her parents' backing to make his political dreams come true.

Chloe's father gaped at her as if he'd never seen her before. Her mother recovered more quickly. "Roger dear, there's nothing wrong with what she's asking, is there? That's a simple precaution, isn't it—not special treatment? Wouldn't you give that to any policeman who found himself in jail overnight?"

For once, Chloe wanted to applaud her mother's Machiavellian mind. She'd given Roger the necessary out to preserve his pride.

But she knew…and he knew…

"It's not up to me," he said. "I don't run the jail."

"But those who do would listen to you," her mother continued. "You are a man of influence."

Chloe watched his pragmatism war with fury. For better or for worse, she'd cut the cords of their relationship, once and for all.

None of that was important. Only Vince's safety mattered.

And then his freedom.

"How much is his bond?" she queried Roger.

A muscle worked in his jaw. "Five hundred thousand."

She stifled a gasp. "Roger, that's absurd—he could be released on personal bond. He's not going to run."

"You don't seem to want to listen, Chloe. He's murdered two people." The look in his eyes told her Roger was all too aware that Vince didn't have that kind of money.

But she did. Not enough liquid funds for the whole

thing, but sufficient for a bail bondsman's cut. "Fine. I'll make arrangements."

Her father stirred at that. "Chloe, you can't mean to—"

A little more rebellion flared. "If he doesn't have the money, I'm posting it. He is not spending one more second in custody than necessary."

"Your grandmother would be—" Her mother's face was tight with strain.

"Proud. Grandmother would have been behind me all the way. She would never have let an innocent man go to jail to save face. I can't think of a better use for the money she left me."

Roger stared at her. "You don't mind who you hurt."

Chloe lifted her head high. "I haven't hurt anything but your ego, Roger. The rest of this is between me and my parents." Turning toward them, she continued. "You should go home and rest."

"What about you?" her father asked.

"I'll be fine." Every minute of the years she'd spent perfecting a cool exterior worked to her advantage at the moment. Vince needed her to be strong and smart. He had so much against him, so little on his side.

Anger uncoiled again. He'd had a stellar career, had clawed and scratched his way from nothing. Yet through the actions of unknown enemies, he stood to lose everything.

Even his life.

"All right," her father said. Then he paused, his gaze filled with concern. "Sweetheart, I'm afraid you're making a big mistake, but—" He drew in a deep breath, and she could see his fatigue. "If you need my help—"

Chloe bit her lip to keep sudden tears at bay. "I—" She stepped closer and kissed his cheek. "Thank you, Daddy," she whispered, holding firm against the longing to seek his shelter. "Just rest now. I'll call you later."

As she watched them go, weary and drained, Roger paused beside her. "We could have gone to the top together, you know."

The smile felt sad as it curved her lips. "I've never aspired to the top."

"How did I miss that?"

"You never asked what I wanted. You never noticed."

But she didn't blame him for being confused. She wasn't sure who this woman was, either.

THE NEXT MORNING, Vince felt eyes on him at every step. Presumption of innocence be damned; every Tom, Dick and Harry seemed to have written him off.

And the press vultures already circled the carcass.

The officer who held his arm regarded him uneasily. Pariah…leper…good cop gone bad. He could see it, could smell the questions that brimmed.

Oh, he'd gotten some sympathetic looks, and maybe some of his fellow cops had their private doubts about his guilt, but the distancing was already under way.

Vince stopped before the bench, shoving out of his mind how much he hated wearing the baggy prisoner's uniform, being cuffed, being stared at… judged without a trial.

"Vincent Coronado," the magistrate began. "You have been charged with capital murder in the death of Hector Balderas. Do you have a lawyer to represent you?"

"Yes, Your Honor." In the long, dark hours just past, Vince had wrestled with the decision. On principle, he found all defense lawyers scumbags; he'd never imagined having to choose one for himself. He'd thought about the sharks, the ones who could get Adolf Hitler off with a slap on the wrist. Maybe one of them should have been his choice, but Vince wasn't guilty. He wouldn't need a shark.

At least, that was what he told himself when the twist in his guts subsided and he could retain a grip on hope.

So he'd chosen to go for the only criminal lawyer he knew who might be worthy of a cop's respect. Gil Edwards won his share of cases, but he refused to have drug dealers as clients. That he had standards was a big point in his favor.

The magistrate read him his rights again. "Do you understand them, Mr. Coronado?"

Vince nodded, jaw tight.

"Speak up, please."

"Yes, Your Honor."

"Your bond has been set at five hundred thousand dollars."

Half a million bucks. It brought home, as nothing else had, just how intent Barnes was on putting him away. The big surprise was that he had a chance for bail at all, but it didn't really matter. He'd turned over and over how he could scrape up the money and had come up empty.

In between, Whalen's promises had whispered in his ear. The idea of waiting, night after night, for trial in the Travis County Jail, not in the relative safety of a holding cell, was sobering.

He'd endure it; he had no choice. He'd endured worse. By now, the art of turning off his feelings was second nature.

The gavel slammed down, and Vince's hearing was over.

The jailer led him back to his cell, pausing in an empty hallway. "I heard your bond's already been posted, Coronado."

His head whipped around. Nobody he knew had that kind of money.

Then it hit him. Chloe might.

Could it be? Would she have done that? He'd tried not to think about her, about their night together. Remembering it had been the worst kind of torture—the rich cream skin, the golden tumble of her hair…the way she looked at him, cried out in passion and made him feel like a god.

How she'd wept in his arms.

He couldn't let her be tarnished. Mike was supposed to keep her out of this mess. What had she been doing while he was locked up?

But he didn't know who else could have posted his bond.

And he couldn't decide whether to hang his head in shame—

Or jump for joy.

SIX ENDLESS HOURS LATER, Vince signed the form inventorying his possessions, then unzipped the pouch and emptied out the contents. After slipping his keys in one pocket, and wallet in another, he slid the watchband around his wrist and fastened it as he walked down the hall.

And then he saw her.

Out of place in this venue of broken dreams, Chloe looked tired but resolute. Brave. Somehow stronger than when he'd been ripped away from her side.

She made his heart hurt, yet simply seeing her soothed something raw, way down deep.

His footsteps slowed.

The officer behind him spoke up. "She's been here for hours. Took on Barnes in the booking area, according to the last shift. Demanded that he let you go right then. When that failed, she pulled some trump card to get you moved to your own cell."

Vince couldn't decide how to feel. Embarrassment that he needed her to bail him out…chagrin because he should be protecting her, not the other way around. But within him something warmed. Admiration stirred.

She'd stood up for him. The boy who'd been shuffled around or ignored since the age of four felt a comfort he'd never expected to find. A tigress lived within that delicate body, the same courageous woman who opened her heart to those women at the shelter, who endured whatever they dished out.

He wanted her so badly he could chew his way through razor wire.

He might be down, but damned if she hadn't just handed him a rope. What would that support cost her? She'd set foot squarely into this situation beside him. Now the stakes were higher than ever—he needed to clear this mess up for more than just himself. Had to be certain Chloe didn't pay the price.

Soft brown eyes gazed across the room at him, bruised shadows underscoring her exhaustion. He wanted to go to her, to pull her into his arms. To squeeze her until he could make himself believe she was real. Breathe in the scent of her hair until his lungs were free of jailhouse despair.

But Vince was a realist. There could be no happy ending for them. Sooner or later, the gap between them would prove impossible to span. He might want nothing more than to spirit her away to someplace where they had all the time in the world and only each other, but that was a fantasy. In the real world, he was a danger to her.

So just as she took her first step toward him—

He turned his back. "Get her out of here," Vince said to Mike, standing nearby. "And keep her away." Feeling as though his chest had been ripped open and everything important was spilling out, he forced himself to leave her behind.

But he heard Chloe's faint cry of pain, quickly muffled.

That's it, love, he thought, steeling himself not to turn around. *Start forgetting me.*

And save yourself.

MIKE HAD WANTED to stay, but she'd played on Vince's need for his help, desperate for the refuge of her home, to be alone where she could think. Blindly, she made her way through the house, hoping it would soothe her as always before.

But it wasn't working. The strain between her and her parents…the soaring emotion of her night with Vince… Don's contempt…Roger's scorn—all of that she could have handled.

Until Vince had walked away, when she longed so badly to hold him.

To be held.

Just then, the phone rang. Chloe darted across the kitchen, snatching the receiver, breathless. Maybe he was only trying to keep things private between them back there. "Vince?"

"Who?"

Chloe frowned. "Who is this?"

"Chloe, it's Ivy."

"Oh." Chloe clutched the phone, seeking poise that had abandoned her utterly. "How—how are you?"

"What is it? Are you all right?"

"Yes, I'm—" The concern in Ivy's tone undid her. Chloe swallowed past a boulder lodged in her throat. "No. I mean, I'm not hurt or anything, I'm just—" Her voice broke.

"I can be there in three hours."

Chloe sank against the counter. "You would do that?"

"Of course." Ivy's voice demonstrated honest surprise. "You're my sister. I love you."

Just like that, barely knowing her, Ivy would drop everything to be with her.

"Do you want to tell me what's going on?"

"Oh, Ivy…" She was so exhausted she couldn't think where to start.

"Never mind. It doesn't matter. I don't have to hear if you'd rather I didn't."

"It's not that I don't want to tell you," Chloe said. "I'm just so…tired."

"Then crawl into bed and get some rest," Ivy responded in a distinctly maternal tone. "You just sit tight, sweetie. I'm on my way."

"Ivy, you don't have to—"

"Of course I do. I love you, Chloe. We all do. Now, you get some rest."

Chloe tried to think what she should say to this kind, generous woman who acted as though this was simply routine, that she should drop everything to be with a woman she hadn't seen in more than twenty years.

But the wallpaper across from her wavered, and bone-deep fatigue dragged at her. "All right, I will. And Ivy—" She squeezed her eyes shut. "Thank you. But tomorrow's soon enough. And if things change and you can't afford the time—"

"I told you I'd come, and I meant it." Ivy chuckled, and the sound of it warmed a little of the despair that had chilled Chloe's heart since she'd awakened with men pounding on Vince's front door. "Now, get in that bed, young lady."

Chloe pressed trembling fingers to her lips. "Okay. Goodbye, Ivy."

"Sweet dreams, little sister."

Chloe held on to the phone for a long time after Ivy was gone, trying to clasp her sister's warmth to her like a blanket against the frozen ache inside her.

Bed. She needed sleep.

Where would Vince sleep tonight?

She shouldn't care. Tomorrow she had to return to the office, had to face Roger and Don and everyone who would be aware that she'd gambled everything on a man who had walked away from her without a backward glance.

Inside her bedroom, Chloe began to shake. Her knees threatened to collapse. Dredging up strength, she moved like an automaton toward her bathroom. She closed that door, too, seeking more barriers between herself and whatever lay in wait.

That night with Vince, she'd felt whole. Known a oneness with him that she'd never experienced in her life.

Now Vince had turned his back on her, leaving her empty and cold. So cold.

She struggled to cling to that one second when he'd first spotted her. The rush of joy she'd seen in his eyes.

Roger and Don couldn't be right. He was only trying to protect her, wasn't he?

But she needed him so much. She'd endured and

risked everything, counting on that moment when he'd sweep her up and share the joy of his release.

Instead, he'd left without a word.

Chloe slid to the floor, curling up the way a sea creature seeks refuge in its shell. But her shell had vanished with the awakening she'd found in Vince's arms, and without it, she was vulnerable and naked. Revealed as a fool.

Doubts swept over her faith.

She'd put herself on the line for Vince, and he'd rejected her in front of everyone, exposing her to the harsh glare of everyone's pity.

I've got to get back to work, Doc. Once before he'd only wanted to use her. And now?

What hold does he have on you? Has he blinded you so much that you can't discern who he is? Instinct curled Chloe into a tight ball on the cold tile floor. Desperately, she nurtured the tiny flame of hope.

But that hope flickered in the too-thin air of loneliness.

And a devastated Chloe wept.

CHAPTER FIFTEEN

SHE AWOKE into darkness, realizing she still lay on the floor of the bathroom. Stiff muscles protested as she sat up. Her head ached from crying so much, and her throat hurt. She grasped the vanity to lift herself to standing and reached for the light switch.

A floorboard creaked. Chloe froze, listening for footsteps. When nothing else happened, she clasped the doorknob and turned it, opening the door to her bedroom with exquisite care.

Don't be foolish. No one's here. She'd locked the doors behind Mike.

Another board protested someone's weight. The knob on the door to the hallway began to turn.

Heart racing, Chloe crossed the floor to her bedside phone, removed the portable receiver and returned to the bathroom. Quickly, she punched in the numbers for 911, terrified that whoever it was out there would hear the beeps.

"Nine-one-one operator," she heard a voice on the other end of the line say.

"Someone's in my house," Chloe whispered.

"I'm sorry, I can't hear you. Please speak up—"

The door flew open, knocking the phone from Chloe's grasp just as a hand clamped over her mouth.

Chloe tried to fight, but he was too strong. Her elbow connected with his stomach, and he grunted, then a sickening, sweet odor clogged her nose.

"I'm sorry—he has to be stopped" was the last thing she heard.

VINCE COULDN'T FIND Tino anywhere, and Leticia and Tino Junior were gone. He needed answers about Balderas, and he needed them now. He didn't trust the investigators not to be in Newcombe's pocket. Someone inside the department was the common denominator in all this, and no one seemed more likely than Newcombe.

He slammed a fist on the steering wheel.

His cell phone rang. "Yeah?"

"Vince, it's Akers."

"What the hell do you want? To rat me out again?"

"Up yours, Coronado. I'm trying to do you a favor. It's about your girlfriend."

"What?"

"The doc. I just heard it on the scanner. Nine-one-one dispatched patrol to her address when a woman said someone was in her house. She didn't answer after that, but there were sounds of a struggle. The unit searched the place, but she's gone."

Vince's stomach took a greasy slide into fear. "I'm headed over there now."

"They won't let you in, but I'll keep you posted."

"Why are you helping me, Akers?"

Akers swore. "Forget it. Doc was good to me, and I thought you might care. Maybe I was wrong—"

Vince was silent for a moment. "No. You weren't wrong. I'll be there in ten." He disconnected and hit the gas. Dear God. Who had her?

And what would they do to her now? Hang on, Chloe, he thought, wishing like hell he hadn't abandoned her at the jail. If he'd gone to her, she'd be with him—and safe.

He'd tried to shield her, thinking distance would be her armor. That she was only in danger if she was near him.

Now she was gone, and—

His phone rang again. "What?"

"Vince, it's Tino. He's got your woman."

"Who? Moreno?"

"Yeah. He wants a meet."

"When? Where?"

"Alone. You don't bring no one or he'll kill her."

Vince struggled to keep his head. "All right. Where?"

"Remember the old warehouse off Comal we used to sleep in sometimes?"

"Yeah, I remember. When?"

"One hour. And he's serious, *carnal*. No cops. Come unarmed and don't tell a soul."

"I understand. Where will you be?"

"I don't know if he'll let me inside, but I'll be in the area."

"Doing what? Aiming a gun at my head?"

"Vince, he's threatened Leticia and Tino Junior. I

got to walk a fine line." His voice turned sad. "I know you tried to help, *carnal,* but me, I ain't gonna get free of this, ever."

Once Vince might have argued, but now all he could think about was Chloe. "She'd better not be hurt when I see her. You tell him that, Tino. He harms one hair on her head, and there won't be a place on earth for him to hide."

"Just be there, bro. I'll do what I can." Then Tino was gone.

Vince tried to shut his mind down cold, because logic and careful planning were his only weapons to save Chloe now. Even if he was prepared to risk contravening Moreno's condition of silence, he wasn't sure whom to trust. Someone inside the force was connected to all this, and he couldn't be sure how deep the corruption went.

The last sight he'd had of Chloe shimmered before him, her face pale with exhaustion and worry, her eyes filled with welcome.

And he'd turned his back on her, on all she'd done for him.

Now he might never have the chance to make it right.

His phone rang again. A glance at the display made his jaw clench as he answered. "Mike, what the hell happened?"

"I wish I knew. Christ, man, I'm sorry."

"You were supposed to be with her."

"She wanted to be alone. She begged me, Vince. So I made sure all the doors and windows were locked, and I had a unit patrolling the area and checking in with me."

"Then what went down?"

"I don't know." Mike's voice was thick with remorse. "And I need some answers from you, buddy. This isn't something Newcombe would do. What aren't you telling me?"

"Nothing—" Vince raked fingers through his hair, wishing he could bring Mike in on it.

"Bullshit. Does this have something to do with Moreno? The guy they said you killed, he was from Los Carnales. I thought you'd dropped that."

"I have to make a stop now, Mike. I'll get back to you."

"Vince, wait—"

Vince punched the End button and threw the phone on the seat.

The phone rang again. Mike. Vince ignored him.

Instead, he made one call himself, to Sally. Playing on past association, which he'd sworn never to do again, he arranged a quick meet at her place to secure a weapon. They might frisk him, and if so, he'd deal with it. He wouldn't go in with a weapon visible, but he wanted the odds as even as he could get.

Then, lies told to distract Sally, pistol strapped to his ankle to augment the knife in his pocket, Vince headed east.

Praying that no matter what went down, he could still save Chloe.

AFTER A CAREFUL casing of the block surrounding the warehouse, Vince stepped inside. The heat was stifling, the air choked with dust spiraling in the dim light. Overhead, a turbine creaked, making a futile effort to vent the staleness, the smell of decades of men and machines… and now dust and mice and despair.

Deep shadows shrouded much of the interior. The small windows high up on one side were caked with layers of grime, letting in only weak bars of sunshine. Waiting outside on the ancient, cracked asphalt would be cooler than suffocating in here.

Nerves jangling, his thoughts clicked and whirled as he tried to ignore how naked he felt without a weapon in hand. If he failed Chloe, there was no one in reserve.

Something behind him crackled. Vince started to turn—

The blow came fast, jagged pain piercing like shrapnel into his head. Vince staggered but quickly recovered, lashing out with a powerful kick. A grunt told him he'd connected.

He was trying to spot his assailant, when he heard a clearly feminine sob.

"Stop or I'll kill her." A familiar voice.

"Tino?" Vince blinked past the swirling dust. "Is that you? What the hell—"

Then his vision cleared, and Vince faltered.

Tino held Chloe tightly, the barrel of his pistol jammed into her side. Her eyes were huge and round and terrified.

And suddenly Vince knew. "You've been playing me, you son of a—"

"I'm sorry, man. I tried to tell you it was crazy to

go after Moreno. None of this had to happen—but you didn't let things drop."

Metal-cold fear tainted his tongue, vying with incandescent rage.

Only a cool head would save her. He jerked on the reins of his temper and shoved down paralyzing fear. "Tell me why you betrayed me." He held his friend's gaze. If he looked too long at Chloe's eyes, he'd lose the control he desperately needed.

Then another voice came from the darkness. "Your friend has more important loyalties than a futile quest to avenge the death of a man who did not understand the meaning of the word."

Vince's fingers clenched into fists. "Moreno."

The man he'd been dogging for months stepped into the light, inclining his head in acknowledgment. "Detective." He glanced toward Tino. "Also, your friend is ambitious. To rise in the organization, he offered to trade upon your past relationship to remove you as a problem." His expression hardened. "Of course, he also promised that the solution would be permanent, and up to now he has failed."

"Too bad." Vince shrugged with indifference he wished he could feel.

"Your quest has cost you. Regrettably it will now cost your lady. Was it worth the price?"

"She's innocent. Let her go."

"You're far too intelligent to believe that can happen. So tell me—was Carlos worth it?"

"He saved my life," Vince said. He glanced at Tino with contempt. "Tried to save yours, too." Vince moved a step to the right, shifting the angle between him and Tino to take Chloe out of Vince's line of fire.

"Quixotic fools, both of you," Moreno scoffed. "Carlos turned his back on family for his ideals."

Vince frowned. "Family?"

"You didn't know he and I were cousins? Carlito thought he was better than the rest of us. Too good and pure to be stained by the family business." He waved a hand. "I let him go and good riddance."

Vince shifted his weight, slowly edging another step closer to Tino. One more and he would be in shadows that might give him cover to draw his weapon.

Eyes staring into the past, Moreno continued. "For years we kept a truce. He stayed out of our way, and we left him alone." Dark eyes flashed. "He was the one who broke the agreement." He shook his head. "But none of that matters now."

Vince needed to buy time. Tino was nervous, he could tell. The hand with the pistol wavered now and then. Tino's eyes darted around.

"So why did he break it?" Vince asked.

"He'd discovered my source in your department."

"Who was it?"

"I will not mention names, only that it was someone whose taste for gambling outstripped his skill."

Vince wanted to ask more, but he had to force Tino to let her go somehow. To focus on him.

"So Carlos turned on you. Some people just don't understand loyalty, do they?" Vince sneered, his eyes locked on Tino. "You save someone's life, give them a chance and they stab you in the back."

Tino's gaze flickered. "You always thought you were better. You walked away from me, *carnal*. All you cared about was pleasing some cop." He practically spat the word. "You and me, we were supposed to be family, but you left me hangin'."

At another time, Vince would consider that angle, hearing, for just one second, a hurt young boy in Tino's tone. In the end, he *had* latched on to Carlos like a lifeline, a boy exhausted from the strain of keeping both Tino and himself alive.

But only Chloe could matter now. She was truly innocent, and Tino had made his choices. Vince moved another step. "So you walked into his arms—" he nodded toward Moreno "—to show Carlos and me that you didn't need us." Slowly, he shook his head, making his pity clear, knowing Tino would hate that most. "Never understanding that you were merely a pawn in a game between Carlos and your new master."

"That's not true." Tino shot Moreno a glance. "I earned my way into Los Carnales."

While Tino's attention was splintered, Vince caught Chloe's gaze and mouthed *Faint*. She frowned, then her eyes went wide and she gave a tiny nod.

Vince immediately shifted his focus to Moreno. "You going to tell him the truth? I mean, sure you need punks at the lower echelons to pull two-bit burglaries and run numbers or drugs, but those guys are a dime a dozen." Out of the corner of his eye, he saw Tino's agitation increasing. "But there was a special satisfaction, wasn't there, in luring someone Carlos wanted to save?"

Before Moreno could answer, Vince shrugged. "Too bad this punk decided to play you, too."

Moreno frowned.

Vince feigned surprise. "You didn't know Tino asked me for help to go into Witness Protection?"

"That's not true—" Tino shouted, eyes darting desperately. "He's lying, *jefe*. I was only—"

Now, Vince mouthed to Chloe.

She collapsed. Tino lost his grip.

"Run," Vince yelled at her, charging Tino, grabbing for his weapon as he slammed into Tino's chest. The pistol skittered across the packed-earth floor. Vince rolled and went for the ankle holster. He came up to a crouch with the gun in his hand, sighting it on Moreno.

"Stop right there, Vince," said a new voice off to his left.

Tino was doubled over, retching and gasping for breath. Vince kept his aim on Moreno but readied himself to fire at Tino if needed. He scanned the shadows for the source of the voice.

A man stepped from the darkness near the door where Chloe had halted.

"Akers." Vince frowned. "What are you—"

Then he saw Akers aim at Chloe.

And it all clicked. "You. You're the inside source in the department. I thought Newcombe was the one after me."

"He is. I just gave him a little help."

"But Gloria—I saw him with her—"

"I threatened her son if she didn't recant. He took the bait, he and Barnes."

"Let Chloe go, Akers. She has nothing to do with you. You told me you liked her."

Akers shrugged. "I do like her. Put down that weapon, and I'll let her leave."

But Vince didn't believe him. He watched Akers while directing his comments to Moreno, making his tone casual. "You get around, Moreno—I'll give you that." He edged a step to the side so that Akers would have trouble keeping both him and Chloe in sight. In his peripheral vision, he checked for Tino. Still on the floor, doubled up. "But your standards have hit an all-time low with him."

Akers reacted to the jab, taking his eyes off Chloe for a second. Vince prayed she'd run.

Instead, she darted toward Tino's weapon.

Akers swiveled toward her motion.

"No, Chloe," Vince shouted. He got off two quick rounds, knocking Akers backward.

Just as a bullet slammed into his own chest.

Thrown off balance, Vince tried to ignore the hammer blow of pain, whirling toward Moreno and squeezing his trigger.

Moreno had drawn a weapon from beneath his jacket. He fired at Chloe.

"No," Vince shouted. His arm wouldn't respond. His knees crumpled before he could see if she—

"Police—freeze—"

Moreno fired again. Shots rang out, and he fell.

Finally, Vince spotted Chloe on the ground, and

agony ripped through him. He staggered to his knees to go to her.

Tino got to his feet.

"Police, I said. Stop right there—"

Tino ignored them, aiming straight at Vince.

Shots slammed into Tino. He dropped like a stone.

"Vince—" All of a sudden Chloe was up and running toward him.

"Get down, Chloe. Don't—" He tried to lift his weapon to protect her.

A new voice intervened. "Stay there, Chloe."

Newcombe. What the hell? Vince's vision wavered.

"He's hurt. Can't you see that, Don?" Chloe sank to her knees beside him.

Vince gathered one last bit of strength, pulling her into his body and rolling to protect her even as she struggled. "Stay down," he gasped. "What are you doing here, Newcombe?"

"I had a tail on you the minute you left the courthouse. Ditch your weapon, Coronado. Chloe, get away from him."

Vince's weapon slipped from nerveless fingers. He stared into the face that was all the future he wanted. "What the hell were you thinking?" he asked her. "Why didn't you run?"

Her smile was a little wobbly. "I couldn't leave you."

"Chloe," Newcombe said.

"Get him some help. He's hurt."

"It's not that bad," Vince said. He tried to rise. His legs had a different idea. Darkness edged in.

"Vince," she cried out. "Don, he needs someone now—"

"He'll get his turn. First I want some answers."

"This man is a hero, not a criminal." Chloe glared. She pulled off her jacket, balled it up and pressed it into Vince's shoulder. "I'll give you answers after he's tended to. And don't you even think about arresting him again."

Vince would have smiled if it hadn't hurt so damn bad.

The ambulance siren grew louder.

"Tino?" Vince managed to say.

Newcombe stood over him and shook his head.

Memories of a nine-year-old boy with terrified eyes wavered in front of Vince. "Why—" he whispered.

"Don't talk, Vince." He could hear the sobs in Chloe's voice.

"Chloe, I—" He had so much to say to her, but his thoughts kept drifting.

As the light faded, he felt the press of her lips. He tried to reach for her, but his hand wouldn't move.

CHAPTER SIXTEEN

CHLOE PACED the CCU waiting room, wishing someone would shut off the TV blaring some stupid comedy. It was meant to help pass the time, she knew, but all it did was make her edgier.

Mike prowled the other side of the room, cell phone to his ear. He'd been on the thing almost nonstop since he'd brought Chloe here.

Her parents had come, needing to assure themselves that she was all right. After they'd hugged and fretted, her mother had even cried over her. Finally, however, Chloe had observed her father's exhaustion and urged them to go home. That he hadn't argued more forcefully told her much about his condition.

One more worry for later, but tonight Vince commanded all her attention. Chloe tried not to glance at the clock again. She'd blatantly lied to the EMTs, telling them that she was Vince's fiancée. He had no family; she would not leave him.

She prayed he'd regain consciousness. There'd been so much blood…

Mike disconnected and looked at her. "How you hangin' in there, Doc?"

"Okay." She attempted a smile, but it fell miserably short. "How are you?"

"Better than Newcombe—he asked about you, by the way."

"Will he leave Vince alone now, you think?"

Mike shook his head with a wry chuckle. "He's less than thrilled to be eating crow again. And truth to tell, Vince still has some things to answer for, such as lying about Tino and pursuing an investigation he'd been told to drop."

"They can't possibly expect to prosecute him for that. He was right all along. I have a mind to—

"Whoa, Doc. Chill. Everyone recognizes what Vince has pulled off. Moreno's dead and Akers is singing like a bird. Los Carnales is hurting right now, and Vince is the reason. Doesn't mean, though, that Sarge isn't going to read him the riot act once he's better."

"Will he be, Mike?" Chloe's fears gnawed at her.

"Sure he will. Takes more than a bullet to bring him down. Vince is tough."

She wanted to believe him. Wished she could know where she and Vince stood. He had to get well. She realized now just how he'd tried to protect her by turning from her, that her faith had been justified all along.

She yearned for a chance to tell him what he meant—

The door to the waiting room opened. Chloe looked up, hoping it would be news of Vince.

A woman stood there, small and blond, her blue eyes wide. "Chloe?"

"Yes?" Chloe blinked. "Who—" Then it hit her. "Ivy? Oh, my word, I forgot all about—"

Then she had no more time to ask questions. The woman rushed to her, throwing her arms around Chloe, hugging her and weeping. "We were terrified when we arrived and the police were at your house. Linc tracked you through your parents' houseman. Thank God you're all right." Ivy pulled back suddenly. "You're not hurt, are you? They didn't lie?"

Chloe found a smile somewhere. "I'm fine, but Vince—"

"What happened? He's the man you were so worried about?"

Briefly, with Mike's help, Chloe explained the night's events.

"To think we could have lost you without—" She hugged Chloe again.

Chloe soaked in the comfort. "I'm okay. But I'm so afraid for Vince."

"We'll never be able to thank him enough, will we, Caroline?"

"No, we won't."

Chloe glanced up. Another blonde stood just inside the room, this one not small and curvy but medium height and lean. Contrasted with Ivy's honey-gold waves cascading down her back, Caroline's pale hair was barely shoulder length and clipped in a neat pageboy. Her eyes were green.

"You're so beautiful." Ivy pulled back, cupping her hands on Chloe's cheeks. "And you're all grown up.

Caroline, come here—our baby sister is taller than either of us."

"I have brown eyes," Chloe murmured in a daze. "Where did I get them?"

"Our mother," Caroline answered. "You have her eyes." But still she stood apart.

"Oh, come here, Caroline," Ivy said. "Stop being cautious. I want to hug both my sisters."

"You want to hug the whole world," Caroline said. But she smiled at Chloe and approached.

Chloe craved the closeness, but innate reserve lingered, something she apparently shared with this new sister. Incredible to have someone else in the world like her.

Ivy didn't wait for them. Tears spilling from her eyes, Ivy swept them both into an embrace.

Caroline remained stiff, sorrow in her eyes. "I'm sorry," she said. "I was the eldest. I shouldn't have let them—"

Within Chloe something powerful stirred. These two women were her sisters. *Sisters*. "You're here now," she managed to say.

Caroline blinked against gathering moisture and nodded, sliding her arm around Chloe and squeezing her hard. "We are. And we're not leaving."

Chloe bowed her head, overcome. For a long moment, she forgot everything in the mighty current of their love.

Then she heard footsteps and a baby's gurgling laugh.

She looked up to see two men, both striking and tall.

One of them could have been an Aztec god, his long black hair tied back at the nape, his eyes an astonishing silver blue. The second man, dark haired as well, resembled more the men with whom she'd grown up, easy with money and privilege. In his arms was a beautiful blond cherub.

"Hello, Chloe. I'm Linc."

Before she could answer, the baby leaped from Linc's arms into hers with startling swiftness. She grasped the child and cuddled her. "Oh, aren't you a love?" she crooned.

"She could be you as a baby," Ivy said.

Chloe drew back to see. "Really?"

"Our aunt Prudie has pictures. I'll show you."

"We have an aunt?" Chloe goggled.

"Great-aunt, really," Caroline said. "On…Daddy's side." In her face, Chloe could see that there was still pain in the memory of the man who'd abandoned them.

"I have so much to learn—" A thought struck her. "Did we have a dog named Charlie? A black one?"

Ivy and Caroline traded glances. "You remember him?" Ivy asked.

"Barely—oh, I have so many questions."

"There will be time for all of them," said the man who'd remained silent. "I'm Diego Montalvo." He took Chloe's hand. At the contact, warmth flowed through her. And calmed her.

"Hello," she began. "I—"

"Dr. St. Claire?" said a voice from behind them.

Chloe's heart seized.

Diego moved aside. Amelia was gently removed from her arms. Chloe faced the aide, heart pounding. "Yes?"

"Detective Coronado's nurse sent me to find you. He's waking up."

"Oh—" Chloe glanced around her at the concerned faces. "I'm sorry—I have to— Please—would you stay awhile?"

Nestled against Linc's side, openly crying, Ivy spoke first. "You couldn't blast us out of here with dynamite."

Linc laughed. "Believe her, Chloe. This woman could give lessons on being stubborn."

Chloe bit her lip. "Vince says I could, too." Her heart swelled. "I can't believe you're all here." She swept her gaze over them.

"Go on," Diego urged. "We'll be waiting."

Chloe hurried to follow the nurse. *Vince. Oh, Vince, you have to wake up. I want you to meet my family.*

LIGHT SEARED his eyeballs, and Vince groaned.

He inhaled, then hissed with pain. What—

"Vince?"

"Unh—" He tried to speak, but his throat caught. "Dry," he croaked.

"Thank God you're awake. Here, let me—" A chip of ice touched his lips, and he accepted it greedily, sucking in blessed moisture.

A hand stroked his forehead, cool and comforting.

He heard a sob and turned his head toward it, grimacing with the movement. He opened his eyes again.

And there she was. "Chloe? What happened—where—"

"Easy—you're in the hospital. You're—" Her voice cracked. Her lips attempted a smile, but her eyes were dark with worry. "You're going to be fine. They kept saying you would, but you didn't wake up, and I was so—" One slender hand covered her lips. Tears spilled over her lashes. "Oh, Vince—" She bent to him, pressing her face into his throat, her head resting on his unhurt shoulder.

Vince tightened his fingers in her hair, loose and tumbling as he'd seen it only once, the night they'd made love. "Are you all right?" If he lived a thousand years, he'd never forget the sight of her, eyes wide with terror, a gun jammed into her tender flesh by the man he should never have trusted.

"I'm fine, but you—oh, Vince, I was terrified for you."

"*You* were terrified—" Closing his eyes couldn't dispel the images. "When you ran toward Tino's weapon instead of outside, I thought Akers would—"

"I couldn't leave. You were outnumbered."

He cleared his throat. "You picked a hell of a time to become reckless, Doc. I've never been so damn scared in my life." He lifted his head and pain exploded. He fell back against the pillow.

After a long pause, he found the breath to continue. "I don't know whether to yell at you or kiss you."

"I know which one I'd choose." Her tone aspired to sass, but the wobble in her voice belied the attempt. "I'm through taking the safe way out."

"You took so many chances for me." He inhaled and winced. Forget deep breaths. "Barnes…Newcombe. You posted my bail. Why?"

Her eyes rounded. "You can't guess?"

He knew what he wished for, but the facts of their lives hadn't changed. He shook his head.

Chloe's first instinct was to back away. To place a careful distance between them, letting civility substitute for messy emotion as she'd done all her life.

Then she thought about what she'd learned of Vince's past, how it had given him no reason to place faith in love, and understood that it was up to her to be bold. He would never ask her to gamble on him.

She would have to be the brave one this time. Risk her heart. Be the first to acknowledge what was between them.

"I could say it was because I believed in your innocence, which I did. I could say it was because I admire you, which I do. I could say that I wanted to prove Roger and Don and my parents wrong—" She clasped his big hand with one of hers, lifting the other to stroke his dark eyebrow with her thumb. "But all of those would be cop-outs. The truth is that I love you. Just that simple."

"But—"

She squeezed his hand, shaking her head. "I thought I would lose you, Vince. I'm not listening to any *buts*. You've made it very clear how many barriers you see between who you are and who I am, and I grant you that they won't magically disappear, no matter how much I want that."

She paused, fighting nerves, then plunged ahead.

"What I need to know is if you care enough about me to tackle those barriers, the two of us together. No story-book endings, no magic wand. I'm not the same woman you met, and I don't want to go back, but I can't tell you where I'll wind up."

Then she smiled. "They're out there, Vince—my sisters. Waiting for me." Abruptly, she sobered. "But I have a past to confront while still finding a way to heal things with my parents.

"And you...you've suffered a betrayal and lost a friend. You don't trust love. You've never had a family. Yours is a dangerous job that frightens me." She worried at her lip. "Taken altogether, we've got a lot of strikes against us."

Vince said nothing, but he never removed his gaze from hers.

"Knowing you...it's changed me. I don't have any right to ask you to wait for me to find out who I'm becoming, but—" She looked away, then back, steel-ing herself. "That's what I'm asking. I want you to stop throwing up obstacles based on things that don't matter and give us a chance. Will you?"

"Chloe—" His voice was ragged, his eyes raw. "I can't—"

She closed her eyes against the heartache and pulled at her hand.

He didn't release it.

But she had to understand her risks. "I could be lousy at love, don't you see that? And I'll never make a lot of money—"

"I don't need your money," she interrupted. "I have

enough for both of us, and anyway, I know how little it means as a substitute for love."

"I might be a terrible parent."

Hope stirred. "You want children, Vince?" When he didn't answer, she forced herself to press on. "We've both seen the results of bad parenting. Maybe we'd try harder than most to do it right."

When she looked at him like that, as if she actually believed it was possible, he couldn't seem to clamp down on the hope threatening to choke him. "What about love, Doc? You so sure you're ready to gamble that I'm any good at it?"

"What are you most scared about, Vince? That I'll say no—" In her eyes was the gleam of the woman who'd challenged him at darts and hit four bull's-eyes in a row. The woman who'd stood up to the entire law-enforcement establishment on his behalf. "Or that I'll say yes?"

"Don't you have one ounce of self-preservation?" he challenged. But she'd lost her chance to run. He'd never let her go now. He tugged at her hand to bring her close. "I'm too weak to get on my knees to propose, so maybe you could just pretend that I did and—"

He sobered as he saw her eyes filling. "God, Chloe—" he said in a ragged whisper. "More than I ever wanted anything in my life," he murmured, "I want you to say yes." He grabbed her with his one good arm and held on tight.

Chloe buried her face against his shoulder, hearing the beat of his strong, valiant heart, and knew that here, finally, she'd found the center of her family. The great passion, the love she'd waited for all her life.

She filled her lungs with the first peaceful breath she'd had in days. Years. Joy bubbled up from deep inside her.

"I want to share my families, Vince, both of them. To meld all of us into something new." She rose, smiling at him, seeing all his walls down at last.

"Ready or not, tough guy...I'm saying yes."

CHAPTER SEVENTEEN

Two months later

CHLOE AWOKE into the purple-gray shadows that presaged dawn, blinking at the ceiling of the room where she'd concocted girlhood dreams.

And smiled. Her wedding day. One hand rose past the covers to rest where butterflies danced.

"Sweet dreams, Doc?" The mattress sank beneath his weight.

She jolted. "What are you doing here? Don't you know it's bad luck?"

Vince lobbed that hellion's grin at her, dimple winking. "Superstitious? Tut-tut." He clucked his tongue. "A Ph.D. and still slave to an old wives' tale."

"Vince, I just don't want to risk—"

He rolled his eyes. "Don't go getting careful on me now. You put your career—hell, put your *life* on the line for me, but some superstition has you running scared?" He shook his head, that blue gaze sparking. "It's about a hundred hours until I get you alone—and naked. I had to see you again." His smile flashed, and she was toast.

"I've had some second thoughts about waiting," she said, watching his reaction.

His eyes widened, then blazed. He swooped down to capture her mouth—

And instead leaped to his feet, shaking his head. "Stop that." He started pacing. "Sweet mercy…the longest two months of my life, and you're tempting me to blow it in the homestretch."

She laughed and sat up, shaking her hair. "I have bed head, no makeup and I need to brush my teeth—how can you be tempted?"

Vince stopped and stared at her. "You're serious."

What she saw in his face rejuvenated her jitters. She nodded.

He scrubbed one hand down his face. "I've gotta get out of here," he muttered. "You're killing me."

"How did you get inside, anyway?"

"Bathroom window."

She goggled. "You climbed to the second floor and made it in that tiny bathroom window?"

"I told you I was desperate." His expression was thoroughly unrepentant.

"And if my father had caught you?"

Vince shrugged. "Linc said he'd take care of him."

"Linc? He knows you're here?"

"He was up with Amelia, saw me out the window." He chuckled. "Gave me a thumbs-up."

Chloe burst into helpless laughter. "Will you ever stop surprising me?"

With shocking swiftness, he scooped her off the bed and covered her mouth with his. After a long and thoroughly carnal kiss, he pressed her face into his shoulder and exhaled loudly. "I sure hope not."

Then, just as quickly, he placed her back on the bed and pulled the bedspread over her, trapping her arms beneath it. "Now, stop working your wiles on me, Dr. Vixen. Don't you know it's bad luck to see the bride the day of the wedding?"

He grinned, claimed one more scorching kiss and strode to the door.

"Wait," she managed to say, still trying to recover. "The window?"

He lifted one shoulder. "I'll take my chances."

"Vince—"

He turned. "Changed your mind yet about marrying me?" In his eyes she saw the real reason he'd risked coming here.

She put all her love in her smile. "Not a chance, Detective. You're stuck with me."

His eyes flared hot as molten steel. "Not stuck," he said. "Luckier than I'll ever deserve." He faced the door again.

"Vince—"

"Yeah?"

"You're not the only one who's lucky, you know."

She saw his shoulders settle. Hand gripping the knob, he looked back at her. "Fair warning—the next time I get you in my arms, Doc, no one's making it out alive."

She blew him a kiss, absurdly happy. "I'm counting on it."

Vince groaned and banged his head on the door, then swung it open. "Mr. St. Claire," he shouted. "You'd better come quick—there's a man in your daughter's room."

Chloe was still laughing long after he vanished.

TOO MANY HOURS LATER, Chloe stood before the cheval mirror as her mother adjusted her veil one last time. "You make a beautiful bride, darling." Dolores St. Claire's eyes filled. "Oh, dear—"

"Here you go—" As always, Ivy was prepared for anything, handing over a tissue and patting Dolores's shoulder. "Our girl is gorgeous, isn't she? She's going to knock 'em dead descending that incredible staircase in this gown."

Chloe shot Ivy a grateful glance. Ivy had wanted to give her the wedding in Palo Verde, but she'd been sympathetic to Chloe's desire to heal the breach over her parents' disclosure. Chloe had sought compromise by having not the huge society wedding her mother had always planned but a more intimate one here in the house where she'd grown up.

Someone knocked on the door just as a pale Caroline slipped in from the bathroom. Chloe frowned in concern.

"Mrs. St. Claire?" Diego. "It's time for me to escort you."

"Come in, Diego," Chloe said.

He closed the door behind him, breathtaking in a tux. His gaze went immediately to Caroline. Crossing the room in long strides, he clasped her waist, murmuring in her ear. Caroline blushed.

"Oh, my word," Ivy gasped. "She's pregnant." To Caroline, she said, "How long have you known?"

Caroline looked up, shaking her head. "Do you believe it? Diego realized before I did."

His smile could have lit up the world. "Did the tea help?"

She nodded and leaned against him. "Bless Mama Lalita and her herbs," she said, fondly remembering Diego's grandmother.

"Are you sure you shouldn't be lying down?" Chloe asked.

"Don't encourage him," Caroline said. "You'd think all the rules were suspended because it's his baby, as if he hadn't cared for dozens of mothers who worked until the last minute before he delivered their children."

Color washed across Diego's cheeks, but he remained unrepentant. "The rules *are* suspended for you, *querida*."

A decidedly inelegant snort issued from Caroline. "Go take Mrs. St. Claire downstairs." Then she said softly, "I'm fine, I swear it."

Before he left, Diego held her close, and Caroline softened against him. He kissed her, then turned, offering his arm to Chloe's mother. "Chloe is very beautiful, but the mother of the bride may outshine the star of the show."

"Speaking of stars, is Zane really downstairs, attending *my* wedding?" Chloe asked.

"Do you mean my bratty little brother?" Diego asked. "Of course. You're family."

Chloe grinned. "From an only child with no extended family, all of a sudden I have relatives galore."

Her mother's eyes met hers, an apology in them. "Oh, darling—"

"It's okay, Mother." She clasped her mother's free hand. "We're all together now, and that's what matters."

Her mother squeezed her hand and left with Diego.

As soon as the door closed, Ivy squealed and rushed Caroline. "Oh, honey, I'm so happy for you. A baby cousin for Amelia—" She clapped her hands. "We're going to throw a celebration in Palo Verde. We have our sister back and now a new Malone baby is on the way. I can't wait to see Aunt Prudie's face—oh, Caroline, it's all coming back together, isn't it? After so many years—" She wiped at her eyes.

Caroline met Chloe's gaze, and they shared a moment of understanding. Neither would ever be as free with her emotions as Ivy, but each of them had come to count on having Ivy's unfettered love in her life.

Caroline's own eyes turned suspiciously bright. "It is wonderful. I'm grateful that this child will be surrounded by such love." With that, Caroline pulled both her sisters into a rare hug.

After a few moments, Ivy sniffed. "We're going to crush Chloe's beautiful gown."

"It's only a dress," Chloe said. Then, to lighten the mood, she continued, "Vince says it's a shame to go to so much trouble for a gown he can't wait to tear off anyway."

Caroline laughed and Ivy fanned her cheeks. "I still

can't believe you're making him wait until after the wedding. That's an awful lot of man out there, straining at the bit." She grinned. "I thought I'd die laughing when he woke your father up this morning after climbing the roof. That's a desperate man, honey."

Chloe couldn't help blushing. "I'm feeling a little desperate myself." Memories of their one night together had cost Chloe countless hours of sleep. In the first days after the shooting, Vince's wounds had kept him weak enough to stem his hunger, but soon he'd stalked her every move like a caged panther, those electric-blue eyes crackling with the desire to know again the wholeness they'd found together. A quick, simple wedding had been essential to them both. "It seemed right when we agreed to it, but—"

"¡Qué padre! is the phrase a friend of mine used for Diego," Caroline said, laughing. "What a man!"

"Oh, yes," Chloe sighed.

The three of them burst into giggles that would have fit the girls they'd had so little time to be together.

A knock sounded on the door. "Chloe?" John St. Claire's voice. "Are you ready, sweetheart?"

"I am, Daddy," she responded. "Come on in."

"I'd better go find the flower girl," Ivy said, clasping Chloe in a brief but heartfelt hug.

"Last I knew, she was practicing walking between Linc and Mr. St. Claire, chattering away," Caroline said. "Linc acts as though he understands every word." Surprising Chloe with a quick kiss to her cheek, she paused. "We'll see you downstairs. I love you, little sister."

They both left, and Chloe took her father's arm. He

was noticeably weaker, but he stood ramrod straight. "How are you?"

"As fine as a father can be when some other man is stealing his princess." Then he smiled. "I'm holding my own. And now that we've found a donor, I'll be better soon."

"I'll be back from the honeymoon in time, and if you need me—"

He patted the hand she'd placed on his arm. "You don't think about any of that today." His gaze turned solemn. "He's a good man, Chloe. I'm sorry I didn't see it soon enough."

She stood on tiptoe and kissed his cheek, then gently wiped away the lipstick. "No more regrets, Daddy. This is a new beginning for all of us."

"You know that I love you?"

"I do."

"Then let's make your grand entrance and put that poor man out of his misery."

With that, they descended the staircase. Chloe saw arrayed before her the varied members of her new clan: tiny Great-Aunt Prudie, wiping her eyes with a handkerchief from her beau, Carl; Diego's mother, sister, grandmother and whole family of big, handsome men—including one superstar who winked at her.

Caroline had reached the front of the massive parlor before Ivy made it down the white carpet, slowed by holding Amelia's hand. The toddler took each rose petal and first brought it near her mouth, then glanced up at her mother with a mischievous grin. When a smiling Ivy shook her head gently, Amelia dropped the crumpled petal and grabbed a new one, looking hopeful, as if this time Ivy would change her mind.

Quiet chuckles sounded as Linc watched his wife and daughter from where he and an amused Diego ranged as groomsmen, with Mike Flynn as best man. On the other side, Wanda stood beside Caroline, starstruck gaze locked on Zane.

At last she saw Vince, straight and tall and gorgeous. His eyes tender and hot. Most important…not haunted.

That devil's grin flared, the one dimple winking welcome, his expression promising so much that she shivered.

He would never be safe, probably not often easy. He would keep her off balance every day of their lives.

Chloe smiled back, no longer the woman of careful, measured steps. Vince had lured her to dance on the cliff's edge and somehow she'd found the courage to take a terrifying leap.

Learning, as familiar ground vanished, that she could soar.

And that the welcoming arms of love would be waiting.

* * * * *

Fall in Love with...

MEN
in UNIFORM

MUBPA10

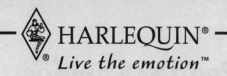

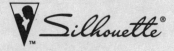

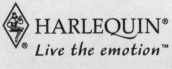